THE
HUNTED

THE HUNTED

GABRIEL BERGMOSER

faber

First published in the UK in 2020
by Faber & Faber Ltd
Bloomsbury House
74–77 Great Russell Street
London WC1B 3DA

First published in Australia in 2020
by HarperCollinsPublishers Australia Pty Limited
harpercollins.com.au

Printed and bound by CPI Group (UK), Croydon CR0 4YY

A CIP record for this book
is available from the British Library

ISBN 978-0-571-35866-3

MIX
Paper from
responsible sources
FSC® C020471
FSC
www.fsc.org

2 4 6 8 10 9 7 5 3 1

PROLOGUE

The sun beat down on the highway as the lone car drove.

Behind the wheel, the girl kept her eyes forwards. The clear blue sky, the burning glare, the distant horizon. She didn't look over her shoulder, or in the rear-view mirror.

She drove fast, coming right up to the edge of the limit. The landscape, dry, arid and expansive, raced past on either side. She saw it out of the corner of her eye, but she ignored it, just as she did the pain in her leg and the pounding of her heart. She drove as the sun set and sank, until the pale blue of the sky became splashed with blood again and the land around her appeared like it was on fire.

It was only then that she looked in the rear-view mirror.

CHAPTER ONE

Now

Frank was woken by gunshots and was halfway to the door before he realised it had been a dream. He closed his eyes, swallowed, and in the darkness moved back to his bed. He sat down and kept his breathing steady until the shaking stopped.

The same dream. The one that was so vivid and real because it wasn't a dream, not really. A memory of trees and dead eyes in the dark, laughter and gunshots ringing in his ears, the taste of copper blood.

He ran a hand through his thinning hair, stood and walked out into the hall. He put his ear to Allie's door for a moment, but there was no sound. He hadn't yelled out, then. Feeling slightly better, he stepped into the bathroom and switched on the light.

He wasn't sure whether it was comforting that he looked nothing like the man who had lived that dream. Standing in front of the cracked mirror in his boxer shorts, he didn't cut much of an impressive figure anymore. The gentle swell of his post-fifty gut was threatening to stop being gentle pretty soon and his haggard face, sunken eyes and grey hair made him look a full ten years older than he was.

He brushed his teeth quickly, then returned to his room and dressed in the dark. He didn't need electricity to find things that were always in the same place. He tucked a flannelette shirt into his jeans and did up his boots. Wishing the flashes of that dream weren't still circling in his head, he walked back down the hall.

In the kitchen he opened the cupboard and took out the cereal he'd brought over from the roadhouse for Allie. He placed it on the bench, then retrieved a bowl and a spoon. He arranged them in front of the seat he thought she used, then, suspecting it looked too regimented, shifted them slightly. He glanced at the fridge. He was never sure whether he should put milk out or not. He didn't know how late Allie slept in and the days were hot at this time of year. It would be different had he felt he could just ask her, but the way Allie kept to herself suggested she wouldn't appreciate the intrusion. Just as, he thought with a wry smile, he knew he wouldn't have. No wonder Nick was having trouble with her; his son had always disliked the things that weren't said.

The call had come just over a week ago. Frank was sitting in front of the TV, debating whether he should get up and fix the bent antenna to try to steady the image, when the phone rang. It took him a second to be sure of what he was hearing. Even telemarketers didn't know how to reach him.

He'd answered with a twinge of long-forgotten fear. That hadn't changed when he'd heard the voice on the other end:

serious and mature. It sounded like somebody official. It was only when the voice faltered saying Frank's name that realisation hit.

'Nick,' Frank said.

His son cleared his throat. 'Yeah. How, um, how have you been?'

Frank glanced around the kitchen. His son couldn't see it, but that didn't stop him wondering why he hadn't tidied the place, or at least hung a picture. 'Fine.'

Silence.

'You?'

'Busy, with end-of-year reports and everything. Emily's the same, but she's doing well.'

Frank hadn't asked after his daughter-in-law, but to be fair it wasn't as though she'd be asking after him.

The silence returned. It struck Frank how much he yearned to know what to say. A side effect of lengthy solitude was a tendency to forget how small talk worked.

'Listen.' Nick's voice dropped a little lower, the way it always did when he wanted to sound confident. 'I actually called to ask you a favour. Things are a little flat out at the moment, and Allie – well, I mean, she's fourteen, you know? The terrible teens or whatever you call them.'

Frank didn't know what you called them.

'I think she ... well, I mean it's probably just growing pains or whatever, but she's been acting up at school. She got into a fight and ... and it's just that there's only so much Emily and I can do with things being the way they are. Even if we had all the time in the world, I kind of feel like it wouldn't help. You know what it's like when you're that age – your parents are public enemy number one.' Nick's voice was getting higher, faster. Whatever he wanted to ask, he was scared to do it. 'So look, we've been spitballing ideas and we wondered if, well, if the best thing for it wouldn't be a change of scenery. For Allie to … to get away from everything and, you know, maybe get some perspective.'

Frank's grip tightened around the phone. A new, crawling fear was moving through his gut, something he was altogether unequipped to deal with.

'And I mean, Emily's parents live overseas and … and you're out there by yourself, so, like, well, maybe it'll be good for you?'

'What will be?'

'If you … if she came and stayed with you for a while.'

Frank leaned against the bench. His mind moved fast into overdrive, racing through excuses. What the fuck was he supposed to do with a surly teen skulking around the place? He could barely look after himself; he wouldn't have the first clue of how to talk to her and the house … The kitchen suddenly looked a lot worse than basic. The mould creeping behind the sink, the cobwebs in the corner, the way the fridge sat at a slightly uneven angle; it all seemed obvious and insurmountable, a handful of the million wrong things in his life that he really did not want reported back to his son.

'Nick, look—'

'You'd be doing us a favour, Dad. A really big one.'

He could hear it in Nick's voice: the plea he was trying so hard to bury beneath nonchalance. The last time his son had spoken to him that way, they'd still lived in the same house and Frank had been too drunk to do anything more than crawl into bed and pretend it wasn't happening.

'Alright,' he said. 'Alright, when were you thinking?'

After that, it had all happened fast, faster than Frank was used to or ready for. And now, here they were.

He stopped briefly on the porch, as he did every morning. His weatherboard house was small and on the wrong side of modest. But he wasn't trying to impress anyone. Stretching out in front of him, past the outline of a curving dirt driveway that the gloom hid too well, all he could see was the gently swaying long brown grass, spanning the distance between where he stood and the dark, barely visible shape of the rear of the roadhouse, the invisible highway just past it, and the vast sky beyond, alive with the first glow of dawn. He took a deep breath. The air was already hot. All he could smell was earth. Sometimes, after rain or if there had been a bushfire nearby, it was different. Sometimes the air smelt alive and fresh or full of warning. Most of the time, it was just earth. On the horizon the fingers of creeping red sunrise were starting to grow. He didn't bother to jump on the quad bike or get in the car. He liked his morning walk and besides, the day would be considered busy if anyone stopped in before noon.

It was just under a kilometre from his home to the roadhouse, a kilometre of dry grass and hard dirt rising and falling in erratic hills and surprise ditches. Frank knew it well enough by now; the sea of grass might hide the contours of the land, but years of the same daily walk eradicated the unpredictable. When he'd bought the place almost a decade ago, the previous owner had told him that the house was intended to be the start of a farm, before the land had proved too rough and stubborn to tame. That anecdote didn't seem a great selling point, but Frank quite liked it. The grass grew fast and the ground beneath it resisted being smoothed or shaped into anything other than what it was. Good luck planting anything that didn't already grow of its own accord. The roadhouse and the house blended into the surrounds, the lay of the land camouflaging them to the unfamiliar eye. Especially at this time of morning, stepping out the front you might as well have been looking at a never-ending expanse of grass in every direction, one that welcomed snakes and just about nothing else. One of Allie's few questions to him had been whether he had ever been bitten, but Frank had long since learned how to watch out for them.

Allie sat on her narrow bed, against the wall. She'd heard Frank's heavy footsteps moving around the house. Here and there he'd paused, but she'd stayed put. It wasn't until she heard the front door close that she moved off the bed, and even then, she waited for a few more moments before she walked out into the hall.

She didn't like her room. As much as Frank had tried to clean it up, to make it look presentable with wilting flowers jammed into a vase and a pile of dog-eared old books on the bedside table, nothing could override the dusty smell of disuse that filled the whole house. The place was a middle-of-nowhere dump and the fact that her parents thought it would be good for her just showed how little they understood anything.

She didn't like thinking stuff like that. She had honestly planned to be nice to Frank, to try to get on with him – even if just to piss her mum off more than anything else. But, damn, he made it hard, rarely saying more than two words at a time, spending all day over at the roadhouse, slumping in front of the TV at the end of it to watch some staticky old show that she was pretty sure even he didn't like.

'Listen, if it's really bad, you can call us,' her mother had said, with the same fake happy tone she used every time she insisted things between her and Dad were fine. 'But I expect you to be a grown-up about this, okay? It's a great lesson – sometimes we need to get out of our comfort zones.'

Funnily enough, Allie knew she hadn't thought it was a great lesson a few days earlier when she'd overheard her parents loudly arguing about the very idea of her coming here. But that was her mother. Everything could be reshaped into a bullshit learning experience.

Allie went to the small kitchen – it wasn't much more than a bench and sink, with an old oven, a groaning fridge that was slightly too big for the space, and a table with two chairs. Frank only seemed to own a handful of plates and cups, and a few bits of unmatching cutlery. She looked at the cereal and the bowl, perfectly arranged, like every morning. Usually she just put them away. She didn't like cereal, but she felt ungrateful telling Frank that. She pulled the chair out and sat. That horrible, pit-like feeling in her stomach was back. It was hard to avoid it when you were stuck out here alone for hours, surrounded by flimsy walls that might as well have been as thick and tall as a prison's. It was the creeping feeling that it didn't matter what she did, somebody else would always control the outcome. She tried to stand up to Hannah Bond, she was suspended. She tried to keep her head down, she was sent here to Frank's silences and cereal.

As much as it had scared her at first, Allie didn't even mind the fact that most days she was woken early by a yell coming from his room. It made her feel like he might actually be alive.

Owning a roadhouse hadn't been high on the list of life goals when Frank was a kid. But then there wasn't much high on that list, and as years passed and options dwindled, he'd found himself entertaining a half-baked fantasy of solitude and routine. He'd bought the roadhouse for a pittance, along with the house, the whole catastrophe spanning no more than a couple of acres. He'd let himself settle into the quiet and hoped that, in time, it would rub off on him.

The roadhouse sat on a stretch of highway, the petrol pumps set back a good hundred metres from the bitumen. The nearest towns were hours away in either direction; Frank's livelihood relied on the roadhouse being the only place you could stop for food or fuel in one of the more desolate parts of what counted as civilised Australia. Too grassy to be a desert, too ugly to mean anything to a tourist, too dry to be farming lands. For kilometres in any direction, the most exciting things you could expect to see were a handful of run-down old barns, the odd creaking rusted windmill and maybe a few remnants of farming equipment dumped with the understanding that no-one was likely to notice or kick up much of a fuss. Nobody came out this way unless they had a bloody good reason. Most were just passing through, and would forget about this patch of earth and the gruff man who served them by the time they pulled back onto the highway, heading somewhere worth going.

The sun was up a little higher by the time Frank crossed the concrete stretch behind the roadhouse. He unlocked the back entry door, letting himself into the drab but neat storeroom. He didn't bother to turn on the lights as he walked through the narrow adjoining hall to the kitchen. He switched on the overhead light and brought the deep-fryer to life. The kitchen had a slightly unpleasant greasy smell to it, which Frank guessed wasn't ideal but punters desperate enough to eat here didn't seem to mind. He kept the place clean enough to pass muster, but otherwise didn't do a lot more than deep-fry frozen food. It was a hard thing to mess up.

Extending from the kitchen, a cramped dining area, tiled and occupied by three tables, made up the room, which looked out large glass front windows to the unprepossessing vista of his two pumps, the highway and the grass beyond. To the right of the dining room was a plasterboard wall punctuated by a large glass sliding door that opened onto the main shop, a door Frank habitually left open. The shop was no more than a large room, really, home to three shelves holding snacks, car supplies and a few out-of-date magazines and with a rickety screen door facing the pumps. There was a counter and cash register at the room's rear – sitting there, Frank could keep an eye on the pumps through the glass front, and slip through the internal door behind him to get to the storeroom, or round to the kitchen via the hall. Frank did his best to keep the place in half-decent nick, but he was under no illusions: nobody expected a middle-of-nowhere roadhouse like this to be especially inspiring. A service station only had to provide service, so that was what he did.

It was the thought that had sprung, almost defensively, when Allie had first arrived, pulling up in Nick's four-wheel-drive out the front. Frank had been doing a half-arsed stocktake of the shelves when he saw them. He didn't recognise the vehicle, but his stomach dropped all the same.

He put down his notebook and tried to look pleased as they walked in together, Nick with an expression that he was pretty sure reflected his own, Allie trailing behind him, a skinny thing in an oversized hoodie and tight-stretched jeans even though it was already over thirty degrees. She didn't spare a glance for Frank, her eyes instead moving around the roadhouse, taking everything in with a look of increasing despair. It was enough to make Frank want to mumble an excuse and hurry out to the storeroom, locking himself in there until Nick decided that maybe the best option was to take his daughter home and write this off as a stupid mistake.

Instead Frank shook Allie's hand while she didn't make eye contact and mumbled something he was sure Nick had told her to say. Then she took out her phone and found a seat in the dining area, from which she didn't move until Nick was gone and Frank offered to show her the house. The look on her face as she walked through the front screen door was almost enough for Frank to call Nick back then and there. But he hadn't. He had put on a brave face and so begun the largely silent stalemate they were living through now. Nick had said two weeks, which didn't feel much different to a decade from where Frank was standing.

By the time the sun was up, the roadhouse was fully operational. He restocked the shelves, checked the pumps and finally settled behind the counter to read his book. Occasionally he'd look up if he caught a glimpse of movement in the periphery, but the few vehicles that passed didn't stop. They must have filled up back at Coogan. He went back to his book.

He was almost surprised when, in the late afternoon, he heard the van pull up. After a few seconds a young couple came through the front door. The guy was tall and thin – a bit gangly, with a tangle of blond hair and wide, nervous eyes. He wore a black T-shirt and faded jeans. The girl – short, slim and attractive, with brown hair and a relaxed stance – wore a baggy hemp shirt, Thai fisherman pants and sandals. The van wasn't painted with rainbow swirls, but he figured they'd fix that oversight at the next town.

'Doesn't work,' the girl said. Her accent was English.

Frank lowered the book. He didn't reply.

'The pump,' the girl said. 'Can you take a look?'

The guy was perusing the shelves. The girl was waiting, hands on hips and an expectant, impatient look on her face.

Frank stood. Hands in his pockets, he walked past them, taking his time. The guy didn't look at him once. The girl watched Frank move for the front entrance. He opened the screen door and stepped out into the heat. The sun was high and the sky was the kind of bright blue that would be pretty if the heat didn't make you feel like you were in a sauna that couldn't be escaped.

As he'd expected, the handle of the pump's nozzle was a little stiff. Frank gave it a good squeeze. Petrol spurted. He looked back through the front windows of the roadhouse. The hippies were a little closer to the counter now. Frank replaced the nozzle and cast an eye over their car. There was a half-empty bottle of wine on the passenger seat. He ignored the twinge in his chest as he headed back inside.

'It's fine,' he said, walking through.

The guy jumped. He was a metre or so from the counter now.

'You sure?' the girl said. It was hard to tell if she was putting on the confusion or not.

'A bit stiff is all,' Frank said, passing the shelves and returning to his spot behind the counter. 'Anything else I can help you with?' He resisted the urge to look pointedly at the cash register. No need to invite or imply trouble if it wasn't going to happen.

The girl gave her partner a withering look. 'Go work those muscles, babe.'

The guy shook his head and loped back outside. Frank kept his attention on the girl.

'Anything else I can help with?' he repeated.

The girl bit her lip. Her voice lowered slightly. 'Can I get a pack of smokes, please? Menthols, cheapest brand.'

Frank turned and slid open the cabinet behind him. He ran his hand over the plain packets, checking the handwritten prices as he did.

'Sorry.' The girl's voice had taken on a note of urgency. 'Do you mind hurrying?'

Frank didn't speed up. He found what looked to be the cheapest brand, took it from the cabinet and dropped it on the counter just as the boyfriend re-entered.

'As requested,' Frank said.

'I thought you quit.' There was a note of accusation to the guy's voice.

'Yeah, um, I lied.' the girl mumbled as she handed over some cash. 'Sorry, Charlie. I'm a terrible person and all that.'

Charlie didn't laugh. 'They're bad for you.'

'I know, but I am cutting down, babe. This'll be my last pack, I promise.' She nodded to Frank. 'You smoke, right? You get it?'

'Nope,' Frank said. 'It's bad for you. Anything else?'

'Food would be good, actually,' Charlie said. 'Del?'

Together they moved over into the dining area. Frank hoped they weren't bloody fussy – nothing sourced from a freezer would fit that bill – but he went through the internal door behind the counter and crossed the hall into the kitchen.

'Is any of it vegetarian?' the girl – Del? – called over to him.

'You could try the veggie pie, but I can't guarantee it.'

Her mouth twitched in what, left alone, could have turned into a laugh. 'I'll risk it.'

As instructed, Frank zapped one vegetarian and one beef pie. 'Been in Australia long?' he asked, as he delivered the plates to their table.

'Six months,' Charlie said.

'Two years,' Delilah added. 'Practically a local.' Charlie rolled his eyes. 'I'm Delilah, by the way, and this is Charlie. And you … ?'

'Frank,' he said as he settled into a nearby table. 'Dunno what brings you out this way. It's not like there's much to see.'

'I wish I could say we had some deep and meaningful reason,' Delilah said. 'But I think Charlie took a wrong turn. Still, it's cool to explore a bit. See the kinds of places people miss.'

'Take it from a bloke living in the kind of place people miss,' Frank said, 'there's better stuff to see.'

'We've seen it,' Charlie said. 'The Harbour Bridge, the Opera House, Flinders Street Station, the Great Barrier Reef—'

'Daintree, Nullarbor, Uluru,' Delilah said. 'We've ticked all the tourist boxes.'

'Well, you've seen more of the good stuff than me,' Frank said. 'Dunno why you're sticking around.'

A creak from behind him. He glanced over his shoulder to see Allie standing in the doorway behind the counter. Her black hair hung down over her delicate, dark-skinned face. Her brown eyes narrowed as she looked back and forth between him and the couple.

Absurdly, a sudden rush of self-conscious panic hit Frank. The last thing he wanted was strangers' eyes on him as he tried to be grandfather to somebody who had no interest in him. It wasn't that he gave a shit what Charlie and Delilah thought; more that he would be happier with them not witnessing the inevitable awkwardness. 'My granddaughter,' he said, hoping he sounded appropriately warm. 'Allie. You here for something to eat, love?'

Allie said nothing. It could be hard to tell whether her silences meant yes or no, but given she had come over from the house, he was inclined to assume this one was a yes. He quickly excused himself and headed into the kitchen. Allie joined him, looking with obvious distaste at what was on offer.

'I can make you something?' Frank suggested.

'What are you reading?'

Frank was confused.

'The book,' she said. 'On the counter.'

'Oh,' Frank said. '*Jaws*. Not as good as the movie, but without a DVD player ...' He'd meant to make a joke out of that, but wasn't sure where to take it.

Allie tugged at her sleeve. 'I didn't know you liked to read. I was going to get you a book but Mum ... Anyway, that's why I got the binoculars.'

Frank blinked, surprised. Not by Allie's mother's advice – he could just imagine her smug chuckle at the suggestion of a book – but that Allie had thought to buy him a gift. He'd figured the binoculars were something Nick had made her bring.

'Well, for next time,' Frank said. 'Not that you have to get me anything.' He almost said something about her visiting being enough, but caught himself, not wanting to sound clunky or forced.

'I'll take a burger,' Allie said. 'No pickles.'

It didn't take Frank long to fry up a frozen meat pattie and toast a bun. He added some limp lettuce and watery tomato, and squeezed on a blob of BBQ sauce. He dished the lot up, and Allie carried the plate to the dining area, taking a seat as far away from Charlie and Delilah as possible. She kept her eyes down as she ate. Frank didn't check to see if the English backpackers had been watching them. He didn't want to know.

He had just turned his attention back to the kitchen, figuring he might as well have something himself, when he heard it. A shriek of tyres out the front. He looked up as an old station wagon came to a halt near the pumps. It had stopped at an odd angle. The bonnet had just missed the bowser and was now facing the roadhouse.

Frank waited for the car to correct itself. It didn't.

He walked through the dining area, past the staring Delilah and Charlie. He opened the front screen door, stepped out and put his hands on his hips, waiting.

Seeing the car clearly now, he felt a prickle of unease. It wasn't just old; it was battered. And …

The driver's door opened. Somebody stumbled out.

She might have been young, not much older than Allie. But it was hard to tell. Stark against the afternoon sky, she didn't look human. She was coated all over in what he recognised as dried mud and blood. She staggered away from the car. Veered towards him. Her dark eyes, striking in the filth that covered her face and matted her hair, were locked on his.

She opened her mouth as if to speak. She swayed on the spot. And then she fell hard onto the concrete.

CHAPTER TWO

Then

At first, Simon had enjoyed the long highways, passing expansive paddocks populated by grazing cows and tangled kilometres of arid bush. Mountains lurked in the background, rocky formations jutted jagged from the otherwise flat landscape, and small towns of plain brown buildings arranged around war memorials came and went within minutes of each other. Above it all stretched an endless blue sky and the burning sun tracking slow across it. Every now and then a cloud appeared – the small, fluffy, lazy kind that broke up the blue rather than threatening rain. It was all so beautiful and contrasting: the colour of the sky, the dryness of the land, the sense that this was *Australia*, the country of tough extremes that had never truly been tamed. He had taken it all in with a satisfied sense of appreciation.

After the first day he had listened to music and audiobooks, then, concerned he was diluting the experience, turned them off and tried to appreciate the landscape again. The problem was that after hours and hours in a hot station wagon with a faulty air conditioner it was hard to feel especially appreciative of anything. Part of him started to worry he had somehow ended up on a circular road, as what he could swear was the same paddock with the same cow passed for what had to be the sixth time. Without company, there was no real distraction from how boring the trip was getting. In the mirror, he looked rough: unshaven, with bags under his eyes and a sheen of sweat on his face. Part of him didn't mind that: it made him feel more authentic than just an honours student going off on some bullshit trip to find himself. He had tried to explain to his friends back home that this was something more, but that hadn't stopped the jokes. Nor had it stopped the uncomfortable feeling that maybe the jokes were justified. Looking for experience was a beautiful idea when you were lying on a couch reading Kerouac in your share house; less so when your determination to just follow the road only meant ending up on more road. And when driving was the extent of what you were doing, even the most generous petrol budget started to look naïve. Probably something he should have thought of before setting off on a road trip with more road than worthwhile places to stop.

What he needed was somewhere to stay for a few days, to spend a bit of time, relax, and see the kinds of things that weren't forthcoming back in Melbourne. Somewhere authentic; not like the few promising little hamlets he'd stopped at only to discover them filled with city people like himself, all looking for an escape but essentially just transplanting their everyday lives a few degrees west. Saving all that money to 'go see Australia' felt pretty stupid when the only experiences on offer were small-town versions of the already familiar. He pulled over and consulted his map, an old one he'd picked up at a second-hand shop in Brunswick a few weeks back. He studied it, but it was hard to tell how long this kind of land went on for, and where he might find what he was looking for. If he was reading it right, there should be a town about one hundred kilometres along.

After driving through a satisfying sunset that turned the entire sky into an inferno of blazing pink and orange, he found a roadside strip of shops and houses which, according to a 'Welcome to Cotham' sign, constituted a town. He pulled his car over not far from a brightly lit bluestone pub which stood alone on a block of land hemmed in by narrow side streets that had no discernible destination. Simon stepped out onto the road. There was still the barest light of day keeping the sky closer to a velvety blue than black, and he allowed himself a few moments to watch the darkness deepen and the stars come to life. It was hard to be cynical about that.

Making sure his car was locked, he headed into the pub. It was almost empty, but a sign said there was going to be a band that night. That boded well. He greeted the elderly, confused-looking bartender as he took a seat at the bar and ordered a beer, taking it all in. Part of him had expected it to be grimier than this, but the place was well maintained, if old fashioned; carved out of stone, with mahogany booths and a pool table near an empty fireplace. Country music played and the walls were adorned with pictures of men Simon assumed were famous footballers. With a sinking feeling, he realised the pub would not have been out of place in a suburb in Melbourne. But he had to wonder how it could survive in the middle of nowhere. Maybe truckers frequented it. Maybe it was a money-laundering front. Maybe it was a secret biker clubhouse. Maybe he shouldn't ask the bartender any of this.

By the time he finished his first beer a few more people had wandered in, mostly middle-aged men who shot him curious looks, and about halfway through his second, the band took to the stage. They suited the clientele: all grey beards and flannelette shirts, and they muttered something unenthusiastic before launching into their set.

It struck him as they started to play that he had been hoping for something unexpected from them, some glimpse of the genuine, but no – they were a Celtic band, playing fiddles with impossible speed while a drum kept time and a flute lilted under it. They sounded good, but that was more the pity. They sounded like they belonged to another country. He finished off his second beer and had just ordered a third when the girl walked in.

She caught his eye immediately. Medium height and lean, she had shoulder-length black hair and wide dark eyes to match. Her face was fine-featured, but the set of her jaw and the way her eyes scanned the room gave her a hard edge. She was dressed plainly: shirt, jeans and a large, worn black leather jacket, despite the lingering heat. A small backpack was slung over her shoulder, the strap grasped tight in her right hand. She was extremely pretty and entirely out of place.

A few of the older blokes seemed to have noticed her and, for a panicked couple of seconds, Simon worried he was going to have to step in and be chivalrous, but nobody bothered her as she walked over to the bar and sat on the stool next to him. She asked for a straight vodka and did not look at him as she knocked it back and ordered another.

It occurred to him that he was a bit tipsy. That was pathetic; two pints shouldn't have had that effect, although dehydration and little more than a muesli bar to eat that day probably hadn't helped. He sipped at his beer and tried not to look at the girl as the few patrons clapped politely and the band started another song.

'You like Irish music?' he asked.

She didn't look at him. 'It's Scottish.'

'Right. Yeah. So it is.'

She drank. He did the same.

'Sorry,' he said. 'You probably want to be left alone.'

'What makes you think that?'

'I don't know. A vibe?'

'I had no idea I was giving off a vibe.'

'Only a little.'

'But enough to say I want to be left alone?'

'Better safe than sorry.'

She ordered another drink. 'Can't argue with that. Although, vibes aside, why would I come to a pub if I wanted to be left alone? I could just be drinking at home.'

'You could,' he said, sipping at his beer. Maybe it was the booze or maybe he was just feeling bold. 'So, why aren't you? If we can assume I've read the vibe right, that is.' He gave a goofy smile.

She met his gaze now and those eyes made him want to both turn away and look at her forever. 'I don't have a home to drink in,' she said. 'And I don't fancy drinking on the street. So, here I am.'

'You're homeless?'

'Yep.' Her expression did not change.

'But …' He could feel his face growing hot. 'But you don't … you don't look homeless.'

'Oh, well, I guess I'm lying then.'

'Where do you sleep?'

She shrugged. 'Motels, mainly. Sometimes I rough it.'

'How many motels are in this town?'

'One, maybe. Can't be sure. I've never been here before.'

'You're a hitchhiker?'

'I prefer to call myself nomadic.'

The answer seemed laughable. Simon didn't pretend to be especially worldly, but he knew enough to know that a girl like her shouldn't be on her own on the road, thumbing down total strangers for a ride. It wasn't safe. There were dodgy men out there. Maybe, a vague thought occurred to him, she *was* lying or exaggerating, and he ought to be cautious. But, looking at her, the only thing he felt was a growing intrigue tinged with a hint of something else, something close to excitement.

'What about you?' she said. 'City kid?'

'Why would you think that?'

'You look like one.'

'What does a city kid look like?'

'If I had to guess? You or me.'

She wasn't wrong. He finished off his beer and raised his hand for another. It took him a moment to notice she was still watching him.

'What?' he said stupidly.

'I'm wondering if you're going to introduce yourself.'

'I ...' The hot flush worsened. Shit, he was out of practice. 'I'm Simon. You?'

'Maggie.'

'Short for Margaret?'

'Long for Maggie.' She finished her drink. 'Game of pool?'

A couple of wiry, singlet-wearing guys with cigarettes behind their ears were finishing off a round. Maggie placed a two-dollar coin on the rim of the table without acknowledging them or the obvious looks they gave her as she joined Simon, who had found a side table to wait at. He had bought them another round but was conscious that his budget wouldn't stretch to many more. Calculating the costs in his head was giving him a gnawing sense of guilty anxiety, but Maggie's smile as she drank went a long way towards banishing that thought.

Lining up the cue to break, he half-wished he hadn't agreed to the game. Pool was a universal language Simon had never been fluent in, especially when he was drunk, which realistically was the only time he would ever play. But he tried to look casual and relaxed while focusing on hitting the triangle of balls as hard as possible to create that satisfying cracking noise he associated with somebody being good at the game. The break wasn't great, but Maggie said nothing about it as she followed it up by easily sinking a ball. As she went to take her shot, Simon caught the briefest glimpse of a small, circular scar below her collarbone, like a cigarette burn. Her next shot missed, and Simon took advantage of where the white had ended up to, with more concentration than he cared to admit to, sink a ball. His next shot, predictably, missed wildly.

'Off my game,' he said by way of gallant admission.

Maggie grinned and sank another ball, then another. 'Yeah, me too.'

Simon laughed. They played in silence for a while, mostly missing, occasionally sinking. He was so intent on not embarrassing himself that it took a while to notice Maggie was observing him with an expression not far off quizzical.

'What's up?' he said.

'Well, I've told you *my* story …'

'No, you haven't.'

'I've told you enough. What's yours? You on the run?'

He snorted. 'Do I look like I'm on the run?'

'You look like you're drowning your sorrows.'

'I'm not drowning anything.' A miss. He stepped back as Maggie surveyed the table. 'I'm looking for something.'

'What?'

He paused. He knew, even if the knowledge was fuzzy, that he could overshare when he was drunk. Be too sincere and end up feeling like a dickhead the next day. But then, this girl was talking to him and he'd probably never see her again and he was by himself in the middle of nowhere and what the hell.

'Australia,' he said.

He braced himself for the scoff, but it didn't come.

'Okay, you've got my curiosity,' she said. 'How does that work? I'm pretty sure it's easy to find something you're standing on.'

'That's not … Okay, I need more booze for this.' He reached for his wallet then paused. Ten dollars for each pint and spirit, one for each of them, another few rounds …

'I'll get them,' Maggie said, with no sign that she'd noticed his hesitation. 'And how's this: I'll get the round after as well *if* …' She raised a finger. 'And only if the explanation is a good one.'

'Deal,' Simon said.

Maggie swung her backpack down and unzipped it, turning away from Simon as she did. She reached in and as she did, he thought he saw—

He blinked. The bag was closed and back over Maggie's shoulder as she walked to the bar. Simon leaned on the cue, eyes on her back. That distant prod of vague warning had returned.

There would be an explanation. There had to be. Nobody just walked around with a bag of what looked to be mostly hundred-dollar notes stuffed in tightly. For a start, it was stupidly dangerous and this girl seemed far from stupid.

The warning was louder, more insistent now. He glanced at the exit. He'd been here longer than he meant to be, and he wanted to make good time tomorrow. He placed the cue against the table.

Then Maggie was back, handing him a beer.

He tried not to look at the backpack. He took a sip and met her eyes. He was approaching a level of drunkenness that his friends always teased him about – he would become overly passionate about what he was talking about, and *who* he was talking to – but that didn't change the fact that this girl was sexy, and he liked her. A lot.

'Have you ever been overseas?' he asked.

She shook her head.

'So, a few years ago I went to London, with friends,' he said. 'And when I was a teenager to New York. Family holiday.'

'Rich family.'

Simon was unsure what to say to that, so he pushed on. 'Anyway, what struck me was how, I don't know, how similar they were to Melbourne. I mean, yeah, you have the big tourist destinations and whatever, but honestly? Most streets you walk down, there isn't much difference.'

'Maybe you just need to travel more.'

'Maybe,' Simon said. 'But that's not the point. It made me think: I've lived in Melbourne my whole life. But Melbourne isn't really Australia, is it?'

'It is, though.'

'No, it's ...' Simon gestured clumsily, trying to find the words as Maggie took her next shot, then her next. 'It's just a *city*. I like Melbourne, but, I mean, how can I call myself Australian if I haven't *seen* Australia? If all my experiences are confined to one place that isn't much different from a million others?' He knew he was getting louder, but he didn't care. He was on a roll. 'Everything you hear about in the songs and poems ... you know, boundless plains, jolly swagmen and billabongs, ryebuck shearers. I don't even know if that stuff *exists*, but how can I know if I don't look, right?'

Maggie was concentrating on the table. He reached out to grab her arm, to draw her attention back before she laughed him blushing out of the bar.

It was just a flash, so fleeting he almost didn't notice. Her knuckles, suddenly white around the cue, her eyes cold and hard on him, a tautness in the muscles of her forearm. For a mad moment, Simon thought she might attack him. He backed away and in the second he did she missed her ball, stepped back and gave an embarrassed shrug. 'Right, you've managed to take my mind off the game.' She drank. 'Go on.'

She was relaxed, smiling. He'd imagined it, whatever *it* even was. He drank then lined up his shot. 'Look, it would be awesome to check out Uluru and the outback and stuff, but I want to see more than that. I want to go off the beaten track. Maybe work on a sheep farm. Spend time in an Indigenous community. I don't know. But a city isn't enough. I want to experience this place, and everything it has to offer. I don't know, have you ever read *On The Road*?'

That was a mistake. Maggie rolled her eyes.

'Wait,' Simon raised both hands. 'I know that's what all guys like me bang on about, but don't you think there's something to it? To jumping in a beat-up old car and chasing experience?' He took a shot, but his aim was off and the cue skimmed the white ball, moving it only a few inches.

'I'm pretty sure Jack Kerouac was mainly chasing his next hit, but okay.' She shot and missed.

'Well, forget the drugs and the booze.' Simon knocked back more beer. 'This is about more than that. Experience, yeah, but the kind of thing you can only get in Australia. *That*'s what I want to find.'

They were down to the black ball now. Absorbed in their conversation, Simon had barely noticed that he was more or less keeping pace with Maggie. He aimed for it and managed a hit that brought it right up to the pocket. He went to say something to Maggie, some dumb joke about him making it easy for her, but she wasn't looking at the ball. Her eyes were on him, one finger tapping the corner of the table.

'You know, you kind of look a bit like him,' Maggie eventually said.

'Like who?' said Simon.

'Jack Kerouac,' she said. 'But you actually smile. Which is good.'

Simon let out a nervous laugh. He felt his face warm.

'Can I come with you? *On the road*?' She made air quotes with her fingers.

He had not expected that. 'Why would you want to come with me?'

'Because I have nothing better to do and seeing Australia seems as good a use of my time as any.'

'Yeah but … but you've just met me. I could be a murderer or something.'

'Yeah … but I don't think you are. It's just your *vibe*.'

He looked back at her and tried to think of a reason he should say no, but then realised that he didn't want to and he was already sick of travelling alone and she really was very beautiful.

'Okay,' he said. 'Okay, fuck it. Why not. Let's go see Australia together.'

She raised her glass and he met it with his own. He tried and failed to hide how thrilled he felt.

She sank the black. 'Just remember. Kerouac died young.'

CHAPTER THREE

Now

Frank had picked the girl up and was walking back through the roadhouse entrance before he even realised what he was doing. She was limp in his arms, her eyelids fluttering. He could see that the source of at least some of the blood was her right leg, deep lacerations obvious through a rag serving as a makeshift bandage.

'What the fuck …' Delilah was on her feet, Charlie trailing behind her. Allie hadn't left her seat; she just stared as Frank laid the girl down on one of the tables.

'Call an ambulance,' Charlie said. 'Now.'

Delilah ran for the counter. Charlie stood across from Frank, looking the girl over. He reached down and touched her injured leg. She stirred, slightly. He examined what he could see of the wound with a grimace.

'Not good?' Frank said, feeling like an idiot as soon as he did.

'I'll need to get it clean to take a look,' Charlie replied. 'But it looks pretty bad … I have no idea how she was driving.'

'You a doctor?'

'Nurse. Del?' Charlie looked over to the counter. 'How you going?'

Delilah was looking down at the phone in her hand, frowning.

'Delilah,' Charlie urged.

'The line's dead.' She looked up at them. 'There's nothing.'

Frank hurried over and snatched the phone from her. He put it to his ear. There was only silence.

'Is that ... Does that happen sometimes?' Delilah asked.

No. 'Yeah. Line must be down or something. Who's got a mobile?'

Delilah looked embarrassed. 'We drained it playing music in the car, and the charger's busted. We were going to replace it in the next town but ... do you have a Samsung charger?'

Frank bit back his frustration. He turned to Allie. She was already on her feet, phone in her hand.

Then—

'No,' the girl on the table croaked. Allie stopped dead.

'Keep still,' Charlie said. 'We're going to call help.'

'No help.'

Frank was taken aback by the force in her voice. The girl's eyes were open, locked on Charlie, wide and desperate. 'No ambulance. No police.'

'You're hurt,' Charlie said. 'Look, you—'

'*No.*' The girl sat half up, her arm shot out. Her hand closed around Charlie's wrist so tightly he yelled out. Frank moved instinctively as the girl rose from the table, breathing heavily, eyes boring into Charlie's. 'No ambulance. No police.'

Her grip loosened. Her eyes lost focus. Charlie caught her as she fell back.

'Stay with me,' Charlie said. 'Come on, stay with me. What's your name?'

Her eyes closed. Charlie put his ear to her mouth, listening. After a moment, he nodded and with Frank's help gently laid her back on the table. 'I need a first-aid kit,' he said.

'There's one over at the house,' Frank replied. 'But shouldn't you—'

'Why don't you have one here?' There was none of the previous softness in Charlie's voice.

'I ... I don't have much need of it here,' Frank said. 'Why aren't we calling triple-0?'

'You heard her,' Charlie said.

'That doesn't mean we should listen. Look at her, she—'

'Whatever happened to her, she seemed pretty sure of herself. She's breathing, she's stable. Let me have a look over her and then decide what the best thing to do is.'

He sounded certain, and that might as well have been a warning bell. Frank stepped in close. He grabbed Charlie by the arm. Instinctively, the younger man went to pull away, but Frank didn't let go. 'Have you been drinking?'

'Excuse me?' Charlie said.

'There's a half-empty bottle of wine on the front seat of your van,' Frank said.

Charlie's eyes darted away, but Frank saw the familiar flash of anger and shame.

'We call an ambulance,' Frank said.

'For fuck's *sake*,' Delilah stepped between them, shoving Frank away from Charlie. 'He was *driving*. He had a swig, sure, but we're not fucking idiots. We're on holiday; *I* was drinking.'

'Look at her,' Frank said. 'She needs serious care.'

'Which Charlie can give.' Delilah's voice was cold, cutting. 'He's a nurse. He has saved lives. What the fuck have you ever done?'

The silence was heavy and sudden, the falling blade of a guillotine. Frank was all too aware of Allie's eyes on him. He stepped back, away from Delilah's glare.

'Now,' Delilah said, voice deliberately calm. 'Can you bring the first-aid kit here?'

Frank shook his head. 'Here all I've got is tables for her to lie on. We'll take her to the house. It's directly behind us; you get there via a road around the corner. There are couches, a bed, all of that. You can see to her properly. Just give me five minutes to shut everything down and—'

'We need to go now,' Charlie said.

Frank looked between them. He could feel the situation careening away from him. Unbidden, through all the chaos that was his thoughts, an old, paranoid suspicion was taking hold: *What if this is a trick, what if they planned it, what if—*

'I'll stay,' Allie said.

They all turned to look at her.

Allie's eyes were darting, nervous, but her voice was firm. 'I know how to work the register and everything – I've seen you do it. You take them over, I'll keep watch.'

Frank opened his mouth to speak. He wasn't sure what to say. Wasn't sure how to say it.

'We have to go,' Charlie said.

'Okay,' Frank said. 'Okay. I'll be back in a few minutes. Just ...' He didn't want to tell her to be careful. She wouldn't need to be. He tried to catch Allie's eye, tried to communicate whatever half-baked reassurance he couldn't say out loud. She wasn't looking at him.

Frank picked the unconscious girl up. She didn't move, but the slight rise and fall of her chest was at least a little reassuring. She was light, almost unnaturally so. 'We'll take her car,' Frank said. 'Get it clear of the pumps.'

Charlie and Delilah hurried after him as he walked to the station wagon. Charlie opened the back door and Frank directed him to get in first and slide all the way across, before, as gently as he could, Frank lifted the girl in, so that her head rested on Charlie's lap, her body diagonal on the back seat. Delilah had already moved into the front passenger seat as Frank shut the door and opened the driver-side door. He paused. He looked back at the road. Still empty. The sky above the tarmac wavered slightly in the late afternoon heat. Frank listened, but there was no approaching vehicle, nothing but the wind in the sea of grass, gentle and lazy. He got into the car. The leather of the steering wheel was scalding, the seat not much better. The heat alone could have been enough to make someone pass out.

Delilah was looking over a small backpack that had apparently occupied the seat before her. She went to open it.

'Don't,' Frank said.

Delilah looked at him, eyebrow raised. 'Why not?'

'Would you like someone going through your stuff?'

Delilah shrugged and set the bag down. As Frank adjusted the seat back a little, his heels touched something. He paused, glancing down. It was an old leather jacket, but the uncomfortable twinge in his chest was one of recognition.

He turned the key, which was still in the ignition, and put the car into gear. 'How's she doing?' he asked Charlie as he pulled away from the roadhouse with a wave in the direction of where Allie stood behind the counter.

'The same,' Charlie said. 'She's breathing, but that doesn't mean much until I can get her cleaned up and take a better look.'

If he had been on the quad bike, Frank would have crossed the land behind the roadhouse, but trying that in a car was risky, and rough enough for him to not want to risk it with an injured girl in the back seat. The proper turn-off to his house was about two hundred metres down from the roadhouse, a narrow break in the grass to the left. The dirt road was uneven and a thick cloud of dust billowed up behind them as they went, but it was better than getting stuck in a ditch. Frank ignored Delilah tersely asking if he could be careful. This was as good as it got out here.

After a couple of minutes, Charlie spoke again: 'What do you think happened to her?'

Frank didn't reply. It was the question that had to have been on all their minds from the moment she collapsed out the front of the roadhouse. The few ideas he did have were either ridiculous or terrifying, or both. He glanced in the rear-view mirror, looking at the girl's prone, filthy form. *Who are you?*

The driveway which wound off to Frank's house was easy to miss unless you knew it was there. It snaked its way through the grass, past rocks and piles of wood Frank had neglected to get rid of after abandoning poorly developed expansion plans years ago. Bringing strangers here gave Frank a stab of shame that he resented; it wasn't anyone's business what kind of place he lived in. But he kept his eyes forwards and didn't look at either Charlie or Delilah as they approached the squat shape of his house rising from the grass. He pulled the car to a halt outside, got out, and helped Charlie lift the girl from the back seat. This time the young nurse carried her. Delilah stayed at his side, as if scared he'd drop her.

'The door won't be locked,' Frank said. 'Straight through and immediately to the right – that's the living room. I'll be there in a sec.'

Delilah looked at him with obvious curiosity, but Charlie was already moving and she hurried after him. Frank stayed put until they were through the front door, then returned his attention to the car. His eyes moved along the side. Neither Charlie nor Delilah had said anything about the blood. Maybe they didn't recognise it: it was dried out, so it was dark, almost dark enough to be mud. Maybe they were pointedly ignoring it. Frank couldn't blame them. He reached out to touch it but stopped short. He got back in the driver's seat, watched through the windscreen for a second, then, when neither Charlie nor Delilah came out to find him, he shifted forwards and picked up the hard, heavy object under the leather jacket. He uncovered it quickly; there was no point in delaying the inevitable. Still, maybe part of him was looking for an innocent explanation.

What he found was a shotgun.

Allie hated the roadhouse. Everything about it felt musty and worn out, as if the sadness that filled Frank's home had somehow spread across the grass. She'd noticed it the first moment her dad had brought her here, trying to sound encouraging and going on about how she could help run the place, as if that was such an exciting opportunity.

If she was being honest, stuff like that was what made her the angriest. Being sent to stay here was boring, sure, but it would have been alright if her parents could have at least been honest about it. Instead, they suddenly started acting like it would be great for Allie to spend time with a man they had no photos of around the house, about whom they had told her nothing even when she asked. She wondered how her dad had explained the situation to Frank. Probably that she was acting up, just because she'd stood up to Hannah Bond when she had blabbed about how all the other mums knew Allie's mum was having an affair. Maybe Allie shouldn't have hit her. Without Hannah, she wouldn't have known.

Stuck out here, all she could do was think. Before, the situation with her parents had clouded her thoughts. Now, it was the girl who'd just arrived and what must have happened to her. She hadn't even looked human, lying there on the table. More like something from a movie, a creature that crawled out of a swamp, all matted hair and blood. She shuddered. There on her own, the small roadhouse felt claustrophobic.

The silence was the worst part; why didn't Frank ever have music playing? It would brighten the place up a bit, at least. Then there'd be something to focus on apart from the smell and the heat and the never-ending road outside. Even when her grandfather was here, she felt alone. Isolated and far from the safety of the city.

Stupid thought. She pushed it away. She shouldn't complain. Not after seeing what someone who was really in trouble looked like.

She had just reached into her pocket to take out her phone when she heard the screen door swing open. She looked up, surprised. There'd been no sound of a car.

A man stood in the entry, hands on his hips and eyes scanning the room. He was tall and thin. His skin was weathered and leathery. He wore a filthy suit jacket over a plain singlet tucked into his jeans. The fact that his grey hair was receding hadn't made him think twice about growing it long.

His eyes landed on Allie and he grinned. There was nothing *wrong* with the grin, not that she could put her finger on anyway, but it made her want to back away. As he approached her, she had to force her feet to stay where they were.

'Afternoon, love.' He spoke with a relaxed drawl. 'How you doin'?'

She shrugged, hoped that would be enough.

He stopped about a metre from the counter. He raised an eyebrow. 'You here alone?'

'My … my grandad's out the back,' she forced herself to say.

'He must trust you a lot,' the man said. 'Letting you be the big boss.'

Allie didn't reply. The man started walking again. He reached the counter and placed both hands flat on it. Allie couldn't help herself. She took a step back.

If the man noticed, he didn't let on. His grin grew. 'Name's Reg.'

Allie's mouth felt very dry. 'Would you like some fuel, Reg?' Her eyes darted to the glass front. There was no car parked out there.

'Just wanted to ask a couple of questions. That alright?'

Allie didn't know what to say, so she said nothing.

Reg leaned forwards slightly. The grin faded. 'You didn't happen to see a girl pass through here, did ya?'

CHAPTER FOUR

Then

Simon woke to a splitting headache and momentary confusion about where he was. He tried to sit up only for pain to shoot through his temples. He lay back with a grimace. More gingerly this time, he sat himself up. He was in what seemed to be a small, musty motel room. It took him a minute to realise he wasn't alone.

The fragments returned. More drinks at the pub, many more, then a stumble to the motel down the road. Shit, had he paid for it? He didn't think so. He hoped not. He rubbed his eyes. Too many things to think about. He checked the bedside clock. Nearly midday. Shit.

Moving carefully, he slid out of bed, glancing back at Maggie, still under the covers. Trying to concentrate made his head hurt. They hadn't had sex. He was a little disappointed, but by the time they'd got back to the motel he'd been too drunk to do anything other than pass out. But more concerningly, he had told her she could come with him. This strange girl who had walked into a bar in the middle of

41

nowhere, who had claimed to be homeless and yet, he now remembered, had paid for the motel. How the hell did any of that work?

The cash.

The night was coming back in fits and starts, the order all wrong. The pool game, Maggie buying the drinks, a flash of seeing the money stuffed in her backpack.

He moved over to the door and, as slowly and quietly as he could, opened it. The day was sweltering. The clear blue sky seemed to flicker and shift above him, a probable combination of heat and hangover. The stretch of shops that had seemed quaint in the evening now looked garish and glaring, turned almost into floodlights by sun reflected in windows and off the metal of the parked cars. He already had a bad hangover sweat and this wasn't helping. His stomach was churning and he knew he should eat, but the very thought of food made nausea rise. He covered his eyes with his hand and tried to order his thoughts.

Who was she? Aside from beautiful and funny and—

No. That line of thinking wasn't going to help. He had to try to be clearheaded here. The night before he had been drunk and lonely; a warning sign like the bag of money was all too easy to ignore. Today, things looked different. Or at least, they were supposed to.

The fact was this: no normal person hitchhiked through the middle of nowhere carrying a bag of cash. All it took was the wrong person seeing it and you would be in serious danger. The only explanation that made any sense was if that potential danger paled in comparison to something else, something that made what Maggie was doing the safest choice. The problem was, it was very hard to work out what that something could be.

Simon rested his head back against the sun-warmed bricks of the motel, shielding his eyes from the brightness with one arm. Without wanting to, he was hearing what his parents would say. That he should be polite but firm, be honest about his concerns and say it was nothing personal but that he didn't want any part of whatever trouble she was involved in. And she had to be in some kind of trouble, surely. The flash of wariness or whatever it had been when he first reached for her last night told him enough, or would have if he hadn't been several pints in.

He took his hand away and, squinting against the light, looked up the road towards where his car sat. He could quietly slip back inside, gather up his stuff and be gone in ten minutes. She didn't have his number; he doubted she even had a phone. She had more than enough money; he wouldn't be screwing her over. He could put her out of his mind and be gone. He might feel bad for a day or two, but that would be it. Maggie would be a slightly weird memory, a vague 'what if' that he would exaggerate later for the sake of a better story.

And yet.

What kind of story would he have if he came back empty-handed, figuratively speaking? *Hey guys, I drove across the country alone and it was pretty hot and boring but at least I saw a lot of paddocks.* Maybe Maggie was trouble but looking at her he found it very hard to believe that she was a threat. Strange, maybe, but strange didn't mean bad.

The door opened. Maggie stepped out. 'Hey.'

'Hey.'

For a moment neither of them said anything.

'Did you ... did you still want to come?' he asked.

'I wasn't that drunk.'

Simon managed to stop himself from punching the air. Given his concerns, this instinctive reaction was a surprise, but it really had been a long time without company.

They took turns to shower before gathering up their things and heading out into the early afternoon heat. There was a milk bar down the road where Simon did his best to keep down a slightly stale sandwich while Maggie, sitting across from him in silence, seemed to be managing a great impression of someone not hungover.

Stomach roiling, Simon led Maggie to the car. As she stepped into the station wagon, Maggie picked up Simon's map from the passenger seat. She unfolded it with a raised eyebrow. 'Very authentic.'

He couldn't tell if that was supposed to be mocking or not. 'I wasn't sure if I'd have reception. Call it a plan-B map.'

'Whatever you say, Kerouac.'

With the engine running, it felt like a furnace inside but thankfully the air conditioner eventually kicked in for once and soon the temperature had dropped to somewhere in the vicinity of comfortable.

They drove in silence. Out the window, the landscape was much the same as it had been before the town. Paddocks, brown grass, tufts of trees and occasionally the almost translucent blue shape of a distant mountain. Somehow,

Simon felt almost embarrassed by this. The lack of variety had been okay when it was just him, but he felt weirdly responsible for the fact that their trip hadn't got off to a more interesting start. Maggie reached over him and retrieved the map from his door pocket. She opened it out and looked it over for a few minutes, before re-folding it and stuffing it in the glovebox. Eventually Simon put the radio on, but out here the best they got was crackling country tunes interspersed with tired old voices complaining about the weather or the state of the country. Sometimes he would glance sideways at Maggie, who had not turned away from her window. He could make out her reflection: thoughtful and maybe a little sad. Sometimes, however, he imagined he noticed a change. A hint of alertness, eyes focused on something. Those instances passed too quickly for Simon to know what to make of them.

They stopped to get a drink at a run-down takeaway shop and sat outside beneath a faded umbrella. He couldn't seem to think of anything to say, but then Maggie didn't seem especially talkative. He supposed that was okay. He didn't mind silence. He just hoped that she didn't think he was boring.

Finally, as the afternoon went on and the heat slowly softened, he figured he had to speak.

'Do you know where you're going?' he said. 'Considering the hitchhiking and all?'

She didn't reply straight away. Her eyes remained on the window. 'Nowhere, really,' she said. 'Maybe north. Somewhere tropical. I don't know.' She turned to look at him. 'What about you? Do you have an idea of where you're going to find this country?'

He blushed involuntarily. Telling her his idea might have been what convinced her to join him, but he wished he hadn't been so honest. When she said it aloud, it sounded dumb.

'I don't,' he said. 'I just figured it wasn't in Melbourne.'

'I suppose not. It's a pretty awful city.'

He was a little taken aback by that. He didn't love Melbourne, but it was no worse than any other city. As far as they went, it seemed like one of the better ones.

'Any reason for feeling that way?' he said.

'Yes,' she replied, but didn't add anything else.

They kept driving until another sunset became another evening then another night. Aware that Maggie might not have quite grasped what the sleeping arrangements would be, he admitted that he only had one swag and tried not to make it come out the wrong way.

'If we find another motel, I'll pay for it,' she said. 'If not, no worries. It's warm enough to sleep under the stars.'

The morning's doubts threatened to rise again. *Had he made a mistake?*

It soon became clear that there was no town and no motels in the area, just wide grassy fields to either side, stretching boundless under the brilliant starry sky.

'What about there?' Maggie said, pointing to the centre of one of the fields.

'Why there?'

'It's as good a place as any.'

He still felt strange turning off the road onto the grass, the old car protesting against the unfamiliar ground below it with warning creaks at every bump. He supposed there were no signs telling him it was illegal, but it seemed a little odd, parking so far off the road with only half-dead grass and occasional trees in every direction.

Maggie set about digging a hole in the ground to light a small fire, which Simon was pretty sure *was* illegal, but he was a little too fascinated by the ease with which she did it to care. Some dead leaves, carefully arranged twigs, the surrounds cleared of grass. Maybe he should have said something about the potential bushfire hazard, but hunger won out and, besides, Maggie seemed to know what she was doing. It took her only minutes to get the fire started. They set up a pot over the small blaze and cooked some instant noodles. He had only one packet left, which made him want to kick himself. He hadn't planned to have anyone else along and Maggie was aware of the fact, but still, he didn't like having to tell her there was barely enough food for them both. He'd intended to restock his supplies before getting back on the road that morning, but in his hangover fog he hadn't thought of it.

'You should have mentioned earlier,' Maggie said. 'Could have tried to catch some rabbits.'

Simon waited for a wink or a grin. It didn't come.

She nudged the pot with a stick, turning it over the fire.

'You know how to hunt rabbits?'

'More or less,' Maggie said. 'I had a foster dad at one stage who was right into camping. He used to take all of us out on these weekend trips. Getting in touch with nature or whatever. Hunting, skinning, all the rest. We used guns occasionally, but he taught us how to get by without them.

Set traps, keep an eye out from the trees. "Ready, not rigid," he'd make us repeat.'

'Skinning?' Simon said, still caught on that detail. 'As in skinning rabbits.'

'If you eat meat, someone somewhere skins it. Weird thing to get squeamish about.'

'Still,' Simon said. 'It seems ... I don't know ... wrong, making kids do it.'

'It was all about bonding over shared hardships.' That brought on the grin. 'Not that it did much of that.'

'When you say "all of us", you mean ...' Was it somehow inappropriate to ask? 'All the foster kids?'

Maggie nodded. 'There were about seven of us.'

'And you all ...' He felt stupid but he didn't know what else to ask. This territory felt tender and dangerous. 'And you all liked camping?'

'I did,' Maggie's eyes stayed on the fire.

'You said ...' Simon tried to find the words. 'I mean, tell me if it's none of my business, but you said "at one stage". Does that mean there were other, you know, um, foster homes?'

Maggie didn't reply.

It was late. The sky was a blanket of stars in the darkness, clearer here than he had ever seen. He dug some beers from the cooler in the boot and together they sat on the bonnet, slurping noodles, drinking lukewarm beer and watching the sky without a word. Here in this huge field beneath the stars he felt smaller than he ever had before, although not in a way that scared him.

He looked at Maggie, whose eyes were on the stars, and asked her the question that had been bouncing around his head all afternoon.

'Why did you leave Melbourne?'

She neither looked at him nor replied straight away. She took a sip of her beer and lay back against the windscreen. 'Sometimes you just have to leave.'

'Any reason for that?'

'I just said the reason.'

'You vaguely implied a reason.'

'Vaguely implying a reason should strongly imply that I don't want to talk about it.' She turned her head and looked at him. 'I've spent my whole life feeling trapped and scared. And finally I made a choice that would get me out of that. It came at a cost, and that cost means I can't go home. So I'm going to keep travelling.'

'Until you find a new home?'

'I hated the last ones,' she said. 'Why would I want another?'

That made some sense, he supposed, but it seemed a sad way to live.

'And you don't think that's a problem?' he said. When she didn't reply, he wondered if he had overstepped.

'You wouldn't either, if you knew the alternative,' she said eventually.

CHAPTER FIVE

Now

Frank walked into the living room. The girl had been laid on the threadbare couch, and Charlie was hunched over her leg with a bucket of water, a blood-soaked sponge, some antiseptic and the open first-aid kit. Delilah, arms crossed, stood over him.

'How are we going?' Frank asked.

'Come see for yourself,' Charlie said, head down.

Clean of mud, her leg somehow looked even worse. Several deep gashes lined her calf, the skin around them purple and swollen, the tears in her skin ragged, uneven.

'Was she bitten by something?' Frank asked.

Charlie shook his head. 'Maybe. It's hard to tell.'

Frank kept his expression impassive. 'Anything I can do to help?'

'Not right now,' Charlie said. 'I want to finish cleaning the wounds first, see if we can get her to drink something, then work out if there's any major infection. It doesn't *look* septic, but still.' He paused, fixated on her leg, brow furrowed. 'If it's

50

bad, we might have to call an ambulance after all. Otherwise I'll do my best to stitch her up. I've seen it done a thousand times. My guess? She passed out mainly from dehydration and exhaustion, although the blood loss didn't help. These wounds are at least a day old.'

'So she's running from something,' Delilah said.

Allie hoped her expression gave nothing away. She wasn't sure if she should be honest or not, but something about this man, about the way he looked at her, made her shake her head. 'No ... no girl.'

'You sure about that, love?' Reg asked. 'Grandpa didn't ask you to keep it a secret?'

'No,' she said. That, at least, was true.

'It's just ...' Reg looked around, then shifted a little closer, as if telling a secret. Allie could smell stale booze and cigarette smoke on his breath. 'I kind of need to talk to her. It's pretty important. If you *did* see her, you're not doing anyone any favours by keeping it to yourself.'

'I didn't see her,' Allie said.

'Maybe Grandpa did then,' Reg said. 'Mind if I nip out back and have a word with him?'

Allie just stood there.

Reg winked. 'Grandpa's not out back, is he?'

Frank leaned against the wall, watching as Charlie worked.

Delilah switched her gaze between them. 'This is crazy. Can't we just call someone?'

'I thought you said I knew what I was doing?' Charlie said, threading a needle without looking at Delilah.

Frank said nothing.

'This is bad, though,' Delilah said. 'Really bad. If someone is after her and we're in the middle of it … Charlie, it's not about what you can or can't do. It's that we don't know the first thing about this girl and how this happened.'

'We know that she didn't want us to call anyone. That's all we can work with.' Charlie was focusing on the wound now, the needle held in a steady grip.

'You're stitching her up with a fucking *sewing kit*,' Delilah snapped. 'What part of this seems responsible to you?'

'The part where this girl clearly thinks calling anyone is a bad idea. She practically begged us.'

'So what?' Delilah's voice was rising. 'What kind of person doesn't want an ambulance to help? It's obvious she didn't know what she was saying.'

'How'd you figure that?'

'Well …' Delilah gestured at the girl. 'I mean, look at her. She's completely out of it. If she's dehydrated and has lost blood, she won't be thinking straight. She could have been hallucinating or something.'

Charlie looked at her. 'Hallucinating not wanting an ambulance or police? Pretty specific, Del.'

Delilah shook her head. 'This is ridiculous. We shouldn't be dealing with this.'

Frank crossed his arms. If he was being honest, he agreed with Delilah. He should have made them call triple-0 the second the girl collapsed out the front. It was years since he had had any run-ins with the police, but the old instincts were still there. His prior record might be enough for them to decide to search the place, and he wasn't especially willing to take his chances with how they'd react to a fake gun licence. A stupid, selfish thought. In any case, with an ambulance, with police, came complications. And Frank didn't want complications. He just wanted this kid to patch the girl up and then hopefully the lot of them would get out of here and leave him be. He closed his eyes and pinched the bridge of his nose. He exhaled. 'Charlie knows what he's doing. If she gets worse or it seems too much, we make the call. Fair?'

He opened his eyes. Charlie shot him a grateful look, Delilah shifted on the spot, but didn't argue.

'Who do you think she is?' she asked.

'Someone in trouble.' It was as close to the truth as Frank was willing to get.

'But *how*?' Delilah pressed. 'I mean, you've got to be curious.'

'That's not the word I would use.'

'Then what?'

Frank didn't reply. Charlie took a deep breath, placed the tip of the needle at the end of the first gash, and pushed. Involuntarily, Frank flinched. The girl didn't move.

'He *is* out the back,' Allie said, hearing the tremor in her voice and hating it.

'Give him a yell, then,' Reg said.

Allie just looked at him.

Reg bared his teeth in something well past a smile. 'Don't stress, love. You don't need to lie to me. I'm not a bad guy.' He turned and headed for the shelves. With a shaking hand, Allie took her phone out of her pocket.

She stopped. Frank had only given her his home number. She didn't even know if he *had* a mobile. And the lines were down. Her heart was speeding up by the second. *Why were the lines down?*

'Doesn't look like the business is thriving.' Reg turned.

Instinctively, Allie shoved her phone beneath the counter. There was a louder clatter than she'd intended.

Reg watched her. There was a hateful amusement in his expression, something not dissimilar to Hannah Bond and her taunts. But far worse. He took a packet of chips from one of the shelves. 'Doesn't look like Grandpa can afford much trouble.' He opened the packet. Reached in and took out a handful of chips, half of which he stuffed into his mouth with a loud crunch, the remainder peppering the floor. His eyes stayed on Allie as he chewed.

Allie said nothing.

'Whaddya reckon?' Reg swallowed the mouthful and went for another. 'Can Grandpa afford trouble?'

'I … I don't know.'

Reg's eyes were wide, as if telling a cruel joke. 'Well, you better figure it out quick smart. Because, love. That girl *is* trouble. More than trouble. She's dangerous.'

In the kitchen, Frank rinsed the sponge and refilled the bucket with hot water. Charlie's orders, and fine by him. His stitching up the girl's leg, her sleeping through what had to have been an agonising procedure, was not putting him at any more ease. A sense of water closing over his head, of a situation he couldn't control slowly dragging him down, was constricting his chest, making him feel out of breath and on edge. Once the bucket was full, he turned off the tap. It kept dripping.

'The phone here is dead, too,' Delilah's voice, from behind him.

Frank didn't reply. It didn't make any sense.

'Where's the nearest hospital?'

Frank tightened the tap. 'Define nearest?'

The drip kept going.

'You don't have a mobile,' Delilah said. It wasn't a question.

'I do,' Frank said. 'But it stopped working about a year ago.'

'And you didn't get a new one?'

Frank gave the tap a hard, violent wrench. The dripping stopped. Allie should have been back by now. He picked up the bucket, turned and pushed past Delilah, crossed the hall and strode back into the living room. He needed to get back to the roadhouse, as much as he didn't want to leave these people alone in his home. Delilah would have to come with him, as insurance.

Behind him, he heard the dripping start again.

'Now look, this ain't your problem or your grandpa's, and I don't mean to change that.' Reg tossed the packet of chips hard to the ground. They scattered everywhere. 'But you gotta understand the situation. This sheila … she's a bad egg, love. Done the kind of stuff I don't want to repeat around a nice girl like you, y'know?'

'So call the police,' Allie said.

Reg had reached the counter again. He placed his hands on it. 'Wish it was that simple, love. But the cops … nah, the cops never do what they need to around these parts. They'd take one look at her pretty face and decide they had to go easy. But that's the thing. Some people don't deserve easy. You understand that, right, love?'

Allie said nothing.

Reg cocked his head to the side slightly, examining her. 'This probably all seems pretty scary to you, eh?'

Allie said nothing.

'That's why you need to trust me.' Reg came further forwards. He was almost all the way across the counter. 'Because Reggie ain't lying to you, love. Reggie's trying to help you. Trying to save you from being the next person this bitch hurts. You don't want to get hurt, do you, love?'

'No,' Allie whispered.

'No. 'Course not. Pretty face like yours.' Reg's grin grew. 'I'm not gonna hurt ya. I'd never damage a pretty face like that.'

'I think …' Allie swallowed. Her fists clenched. 'I think you should go.'

Reg's grin didn't falter. 'Looks like I made a bit of a mess on the ground there. Reckon you should clean it up before Grandpa gets back?'

Allie could feel the tears coming and she hated it.

'Won't look good for business, chips all over the floor like that. Bit of advice: you wanna keep a place like this presentable. Otherwise people might start to ask questions about the kind of bloke who doesn't keep his livelihood in order. Might start to get suspicious.'

'I think you should go,' Allie said again. Her voice was high, unsteady.

'Bit rude, darlin'. I'm just trying to help.' Reg winked. 'Tell you what. You clean up, I'll supervise. Make sure you do it right.'

Allie stayed put.

'Go on now,' he said.

His hands on the counter looked bony but strong. His fingernails were chipped; one had a dark red mark in the middle. Allie's heart was getting louder, each beat unbalancing her a fraction more.

Reg's hand went up, fast. Allie flew back as Reg slammed the counter, the sound enormous in the close quarters of the roadhouse.

His smile was gone. '*Now*, love. While I wait for Grandpa.'

Slowly, certain that her legs were about to give way, she knelt and, trembling, found the dustpan. She moved around the counter and started to sweep up the chips. She could feel Reg's eyes on her, hear his breathing. She swept up the last of the mess and stood. She made herself face him. 'I haven't seen any girl. Neither has Grandad.'

'But that's the thing,' Reg said. 'I reckon you're telling me a bit of a porky there. I reckon you *have* seen this girl.'

'I haven't.' Her voice was almost a squeak. She sounded desperate to convince him. She sounded like a liar.

'Then where the fuck is Grandpa?'

The internal door behind the counter opened. Frank, jaw set, stepped out. His eyes were on Reg. Allie had to stop herself from running to him. She hadn't noticed before how tall he was, how he filled the doorway. There was no hunch to his shoulders now, no worn sadness to his face. He didn't look away from Reg.

'G'day, mate.' Reg stepped back. 'Name's Reg. Was just asking your granddaughter where you were.'

'Out the back,' Frank said without moving. 'You mind telling me what the fuck you want?'

Reg raised his hands. 'Whoa, chill out there, mate. Just want to ask a couple of questions.'

'Ask me outside.'

'Lead the way,' Reg said, with a flourish.

For a moment, Frank just stood there. He looked at Allie. Then walked past the counter, past her and to the front screen door.

Allie didn't move. Reg looked at her. Mouthed something. *Trouble.*

Frank opened the screen door for Reg, turning briefly back to Allie as the other man stepped out. 'Head back home. Now.'

Allie waited until both men were outside and the screen door had swung closed. Then she moved around the counter and reached for where she'd put her phone.

It was gone.

She looked up and through the glass to where Frank was talking to Reg.

She dashed through the storeroom and hurried out the back entrance. Delilah was standing in the storeroom and tried to say something, but Allie ignored her and pushed past. Outside, the sky had dulled to a washed-out blue, the few clouds brushed with dark pink. The weather had changed, a cool edge had entered the summer air. A gust of wind, short and sharp, made Allie shiver. She wanted to be away from here. She found Frank's rusty old bike, propped up against the back of the building where she had left it. She didn't bother with her helmet. She jumped on and started cycling as hard as she could back to the house.

Frank stopped in front of the roadhouse entry and crossed his arms again. Reg walked ahead, eyes scanning the empty road, then turned back to him. 'I'll level with you.'

Frank did not reply.

'I'm looking for a girl,' Reg said. 'I know she went this way. I know she can't have had much fuel. There's about a ninety percent chance she stopped here. And, believe me, you'd know her if you saw her. She woulda been in a right state.'

Frank said nothing.

Reg looked him up and down. His mouth twitched. 'You ever find yourself in a situation where the law wasn't quite enough? Where somebody had done something so fucking shit that you knew no prison was gonna give that bastard what they deserved?' He waited for a reply that didn't come, then nodded. 'Yeah. Yeah, I reckon you did. I'm not gonna bullshit you, mate. That's what's going on here. This girl is a piece of fucking work. But that doesn't concern you. No reason you can't just keep on with your life. If she's here—'

'She's not here,' Frank said. 'I haven't seen her.'

Even as he said the words, doubt prodded hard. He owed this girl nothing. She could very well be as dangerous as Reg was claiming and, if so, he was putting everyone at risk by letting her into his house. It wouldn't be the first time he had stood up for the wrong person and suffered the consequences. And even if she wasn't a threat, then he could well be inviting a whole different kind of disaster.

But he didn't say anything more. He just stood there and waited for Reg's reply.

Reg seemed to be searching his face. Then he shrugged. 'Alright. Didn't mean to scare you. Just a complicated situation, y'know? Gotta make sure it's handled right.' He turned to the road. His head tilted as he looked over the concrete.

Frank saw it in the same instant that Reg did.

The other man pointed at the spot where the girl's car had stopped. 'That's not blood, is it?'

Dark droplets from the girl's wounded leg had dried on the concrete.

'I cut myself,' Frank said. 'Cleaning the pumps.'

'They look pretty grubby to me.' Reg turned back to Frank. Looked him over. 'And I don't see any Band-Aids.'

'It was a couple of days ago.'

'Right.' Reg looked down the road. He sniffed the air. 'Fair enough, then.' He put his hands in his pockets and nodded to Frank. There was no mirth on his face anymore. 'Best of luck, mate.'

He started walking. Frank watched as he left the roadhouse behind and kept going, heading east.

Frank looked at the sky. It was changing to a light purple. In the distance, sunset flames streaked the horizon. Evening was almost here. He looked back towards Reg.

He had vanished.

CHAPTER SIX

Then

The day played out in silent heat as the car tracked along the highway. They passed a couple of roadhouses and stopped once, but hardly said a word. Simon took the chance to check his map, but there wasn't much ahead. The fact that he had no idea where he was going had never felt so obvious.

When, as afternoon neared evening, Maggie spoke, Simon was ready for the worst.

'I was thinking,' she began, and Simon braced himself for her asking to be dropped off, 'that maybe we need to head off the beaten track.'

'What do you mean?'

'Well, right now we're on a highway that sooner or later will just take us to another big town, or a city. But I saw on the map there's a turn-off soon. Why don't we take it and see where we end up?'

'Lost, probably,' Simon said. 'Besides, I already have no idea where we're heading. I don't want to make that worse.'

'West,' she pointed at the sun. 'Didn't you say you wanted to see something genuine? Do you think you're gonna find that in the places this highway leads to? Why not shake things up?'

He was sure there were reasons not to, and good ones too, but at that moment none seemed to occur to him. He looked back at her. Thought about the night before, about lying awake in the swag while she slept in the car at her own insistence, about the buzz of uneasy excitement that made him wonder if the sleeping arrangements would change in the nights to come. If there were nights to come. Up ahead, Simon saw a sign that marked the turn-off, sun bleached to the point of illegibility, and slowed. He tried to think of an excuse, but had none that didn't sound pathetic. He wasn't even fully sure himself why he didn't want to take it. So he nodded and turned the wheel.

The new road was narrow and in pretty bad condition, all crevices and potholes. The scrubby grass on either side soon gave way to bent, knobbly old trees, at first just a few, but then thickening the further they went, hemming them in on either side and obscuring the remaining sunlight. After looking at the map again, Maggie said there might be a dirt road coming up. Simon muttered something non-committal, privately hoping that there would be no road and they could turn back, but a few minutes later he saw what amounted to little more than a wide dirt path pulling off the road and into the trees. He put the blinker on, though he didn't know who for, and berated himself for being so cautious, so *citified*, as he made the turn.

The shift was instantaneous. The background of wind and birdsong vanished into the silence as soon as they took the path. The ride became rougher. The track was littered with rocks and the car was quickly covered in dust – at times, it was almost as if it were trying to throw them both out, jumping hard as it went over bumps and thick eruptions of spinifex in a road on the verge of being reclaimed by nature. The trees, at first a pleasant backdrop, started to feel more oppressive the deeper they went, branches stretching over them like fingers about to close tight, the knotted roots buried in bushes, leaves hanging so low in places that they scraped the roof of the car. In some places the road vanished altogether, taken over by the dry, twisting furrow of what once might have been a riverbed. The further they went, the heavier the canopy got. The light fractured, feeble beams barely illuminating the broken curl of the dirt road. Decaying branches almost blocked their path in places. One old tree was bent so low Simon wasn't sure if the car would fit underneath it.

'Maybe we should head back,' Simon said. 'I don't think this goes anywhere.'

'There's still a road.' Maggie's eyes remained forwards. 'If there's a road, there's a destination.'

'Road' seemed a bit rich for what the track had turned into, but Simon said nothing. It eventually peeled off in a few different directions, so Simon took one, then another, occasionally glancing at Maggie as if for guidance. But her eyes were fixed on the window, scanning the trees as if looking for something. It seemed like she was paying more attention to their surrounds now than she had been before. Or was he imagining that?

The snatches of sunlight above them started to dim, what was left filtering ghostly through the distorting leaves. A glance out the window revealed that at some point the dirt road had given way to just dirt. He wanted to turn back but wasn't sure they could find their way and he didn't want to seem scared, so he just kept driving – until they heard the first gunshot.

It took him a moment to register what it was; the last time he'd heard one in real life was at a shooting range he'd been to for a mate's eighteenth. He had figured that would be the only time. But there it was, again and again. Within seconds his palms were sweaty and his heart was racing. He slammed the brakes. He knew he had to reverse, but his body wasn't responding. His hands on the wheel might as well have been stone.

Maggie sat up straighter, eyes locked on the bush ahead.

There were no more shots. Simon managed to breathe. His grip loosened. 'Okay,' he said. 'I think we've gone far enough. Let's—'

Maggie raised a hand.

Ahead, a shudder in the bushes, then another vehicle emerged from the hunching trees.

It was a battered old ute, white paint scratched away in patches, the first signs of rust creeping up the steel of the side panels. There was a heavy bull bar on the front and huge headlights above the cab, lights that were off but looked bulkier than any he'd ever seen. Two unshaven young men stood in the tray, both holding shotguns. There were snarls and barks coming from the back. Instinctively, Simon pushed himself back in his seat, as if he could disappear into it. He couldn't see the dog, but hearing was enough. He was shaking. He raised his foot to slam the accelerator and reverse.

Maggie grabbed his arm. 'Wait.'

The ute stopped. The driver's door opened. The man who got out looked not much older than Simon. He was tall and broad shouldered with thick hair, brown and wavy. He was good-looking in a rough, sun-tanned kind of way, but his worn flannelette shirt and torn jeans didn't do him any favours.

The other two jumped off the tray, flanking the driver like loyal pets. One of them, hair long and greasy under a faded backwards cap, wore a stained singlet and reflective sunglasses. The third man stood closest to the barking dog. He was short and stocky, hair cropped close, eyes unblinking and locked on Simon's car.

'G'day,' the driver called out. 'What's going on here?'

'We should go,' Simon said.

Maggie opened the door and stepped out. 'Hi.'

The tall man's smile grew as he took her in. 'Hi yourself. Hope we didn't scare you.'

'Was that you shooting?' Maggie said.

'Huntin' pigs. Didn't think we'd see anyone else. Not many 'round these parts.'

'What are these parts?' Maggie asked.

'We're from a little town, back that way.' He pointed with his thumb over his shoulder. 'Pretty remote, y'know? Don't get a heap of visitors or nothing. So maybe we can be a bit reckless with the hunt.'

'A lot of wild pigs around here?' Maggie said.

'More than you'd think,' the stocky man said.

The man in the sunglasses hadn't spoken. His smirk was fixed on Maggie. The dog was still barking.

'You're a while from the road,' the driver said. 'It's getting dark. You sneakin' off somewhere for a bit of fun?'

Maggie's laugh was easy, relaxed. 'We're just travelling together. I'm Maggie, Simon's the driver. We're basically backpacking. Did you say there was a town near here?'

Simon looked out at Maggie. What the hell was she doing?

'Home, yeah,' the driver said.

'Is there a motel there? I slept in the car last night and I wouldn't mind a bed.'

'Can't help with the motel, but can help with the bed. Me old man owns a couple of empty houses. Lets guests sleep there when they want. You'd be more than welcome. Haven't had anyone new around for a while. Plus there's a bit of a do on tonight. Whole town's gettin' together for a barbie – plenty of beers, plenty of snags. Had a hell of a hunt yesterday and figured we earned ourselves a decent sesh. Feel like joinin'?'

Maggie bent down and spoke through the open passenger door to Simon. 'Better than any other option, right?'

Simon disagreed. Strongly. But Maggie was looking at him expectantly and he supposed experiences like this were part of it. He really didn't want to look scared in front of her.

The leader introduced himself to Maggie as Steve, the man in the sunglasses as Kayden and the stocky one as Matty.

Maybe it seemed rude or stand-offish, Simon not getting out of the car, but he couldn't seem to bring himself to. Still, as Maggie got back into the car and directed him to follow them, he tried to act normal.

'Lucky, right?' Maggie said. 'I wasn't keen for another night in the car.'

The ute in front pulled around. Simon tried to look calm. *It would be so easy to turn around and drive away.*

'You okay?' Maggie said.

'Sure.' Simon pressed the accelerator.

He couldn't help but feel claustrophobic as the darkness grew deeper, creeping around them like shadows strung between the too-close gums.

'What's up with you?' Maggie asked.

Simon tried to peer past the ute. Still no sign of civilisation. 'I'm just not sure about these guys.'

'Never met hunters before?'

'No, actually.' Maggie was shaking her head in an almost pitying way, a way that made Simon feel prickly and defensive. 'What?'

'You're so sheltered. They're just country blokes.'

'I know that.'

'Being hunters doesn't make them, like, dangerous or anything.'

'I think that's actually the opposite of true.'

'Are you scared?'

'I'm not scared, I just … Where are they taking us? Where is this town?'

'Up ahead, they said.'

'Where?'

'Would you relax? I'd have thought you would want a bed for the night.'

'That's if they're taking us to beds and not to ...'

'To what?'

Simon didn't reply.

'You know,' Maggie said, 'for someone who wants an idea of what the real, rough Australia looks like, you're remarkably judgemental.'

He looked at her, the slight smirk on her lips making him feel as embarrassed as he did annoyed. 'Why do you say that?'

'It's just, right now you seem a lot like a sheltered middle-class kid suspicious of anyone a little rough around the edges.'

'I'm suspicious of people with guns. So shoot me.'

'You never know, they might.'

Simon flinched. Maggie laughed. He let himself breathe.

Up ahead the trees cleared and, to his relief, they saw lights.

Calling it a town might have been an exaggeration. To Simon, it looked more like a larger than usual farm, a cluttered complex of house-like structures arranged around a single dirt street with the occasional ramshackle shop. There was only a vague order to the town layout; some buildings sat close to the road, others at odd angles and further back, as if they had just been dropped there with no intention of making them fit. Many of the structures were closer to sheds than anything else, constructed with a mishmash of corrugated iron, brick and wood jammed together as if by a child playing with a mix of old blocks and broken Lego. Windows were coated in dust, some with rough portholes rubbed out of the grime, and doors hung from rusted hinges. Overgrown grass sprouted from uneven foundations and milk crates were scattered around liberally. The place looked like it was built to be temporary – like the seeds of what would become a shanty town – but nobody had ever bothered to either finish the job or shut it down. Here and there parts of the roads and paths were paved, but never much more than a few patchy metres of lumpy concrete that would probably be more damaging to tyres than the dirt and the dust. Vehicles sat outside some of the houses: old utes, dented vans and dusty jeeps, most with rusted bull bars fixed to the front.

Simon couldn't see any people, but he could *feel* them and that was the worst part. The windows were dark, like the empty eyes of an animal skull left too long in the undergrowth, but Simon could have sworn they were being watched from every one of them – fingers parting old curtains, unblinking eyes steadily following the path of their car. Beside him, there had been a slight shift in the way Maggie sat; she'd adopted a rigid alertness and focus that Simon sincerely hoped was apprehension.

The ute ahead came to a halt and the three guys got out. Simon stayed put as Maggie followed suit. It took him a few seconds to grit his teeth, open the door and step into the warm night. The air smelt of smoke, dust and a hint of something else, something pungent that made Simon's stomach turn.

'Well, lookee who decided to join us,' Steve said, crossing his arms as he leaned against the back of the ute. 'Got bored of your car did you, mate?'

Simon tried to look relaxed. In the tray, the dog hadn't stopped barking. It was a huge thing, would have come up to Simon's waist. Black with narrow, squinty dark eyes and saliva dripping from uneven teeth under a curled lip.

Kayden saw Simon's expression. 'Don't stress, mate. We only let Blue off the chain when there are pigs around. You see any?' He was chewing what Simon hoped was gum and didn't see the need to close his mouth while doing it. His teeth were crooked and yellow, exposed enough to make Simon's skin crawl.

'Don't fuck with 'im, Kayd,' Steve said. 'Poor bloke's a bit spooked as it is.'

Blue seemed to be fixated on Simon. The dog's eyes rolled as it pulled at the chain.

'He likes you, mate,' Kayden said.

'This is where youse can stay.' Steve jerked his head at the nearest house; a plain weatherboard building. 'Couple of bedrooms, not that you'll need both.' He winked. 'Plenty of room, you're welcome to stay as long as you like.'

Simon forced himself to mumble a thank you in Steve's direction.

'He speaks,' Steve said. 'Was startin' to wonder if you were a mute, mate.' He walked over to the peeling wooden front door and pulled it open with grubby hands. 'Come check out the digs.'

Simon trailed after Maggie. The house had a strong smell of mould, but otherwise it was neat enough, if pretty basic. The bedrooms were small with narrow metal camp beds and the living room had no TV nor much furniture – just a couple of sagging unmatched armchairs facing a featureless wall.

'It ain't fancy, but it'll do you,' Steve said, as they returned to the open front door.

'We can't thank you enough,' Maggie said.

'No need,' Steve replied. 'Share and share alike. Now, how about we get some bevvies in us?'

Outside, Kayden hadn't moved. He watched the house, eyes trained on Maggie as they followed Steve out. Matty was back with Blue, muttering something to the now silent dog. Simon could hear a rise of voices coming from down the road: whoops and catcalls, barks of rough laughter.

'This way,' Steve said. 'We're missing all the fun.'

He led them away from the house towards the sound, where the town opened up into a large, brown field, pockmarked with ashtrays and half-full bottles without labels. In the distance the bush closed around it in a dark mass of trees, but the field was already filling with people who looked cut from the same cloth as Steve and his mates. Shorts and singlets, pot bellies and leathery-skinned limbs, stubbies in callused hands and cigarettes dangling from chapped lips. As they gathered around a rising bonfire in the centre, several cars were pulling up, pounding loud music coming from them creating a chaotic, wince-inducing symphony. Not that anyone seemed to mind: people hooted and embraced, passing drinks around and setting up folding camp chairs close to the fire even though the night was already warm. Simon could smell cooking meat, strong and overpowering.

'Oi, Dad!' Steve yelled.

A towering man in faded jeans and a torn singlet turned at Steve's call. He looked like a boxer gone to seed, a man whose punches could still kill you despite being more padded than they used to be. His thinning hair was brushed back and his ruddy face was unshaven. He took in Maggie and Simon without expression.

'They're taking the spare house for a couple of nights.'

'Just tonight,' Simon said, trying to sound calm.

'Got plans, have you, mate?' Steve's father replied.

'No,' Maggie said. 'We just don't want to outstay our welcome.'

Simon felt a surge of relief at that. It was the closest thing he had heard to sanity from her in the last hour.

'Rubbish,' the older man replied. 'You stay as long as you need. Won't have you going back to the big city talking shit about our hospitality. The name's Kev, by the way.'

'Beers?' Steve said.

An older woman had approached, a couple of cans in hand. She gave one each to Simon and Maggie then stepped back, expectant eyes on them. Simon thought she looked like a vulture, with her thin, bony face and saggy neck.

Maggie, whose eyes were locked on the woman, opened her can.

'You're a gem, Rhonda,' Kev said. 'I tell ya, if I wasn't a married man—'

'You'd have to get your own bloody beers.' She bared her teeth then turned and headed for a clump of women looking over from a distance. Simon felt a strange prickle on the back of his neck at the sight. He looked down at his unopened drink.

'It won't bite you,' Kev said.

'City kid probably isn't used to a country brew,' Steve said. 'Don't be too rough on him.'

Red faced, Simon cracked his beer, looked Steve in the eye and drank.

'Would you look at that. Damned if I'm not impressed.'

'There're a few eskies around, so help yourself,' Kev said. 'Snags being cooked over the fire. Get yourselves a feed, get comfy. We'll see you 'round.'

He turned and walked off. Steve and his cronies followed, although Kayden looked back at Maggie for a beat too long. They joined a group of girls. One of them, thin and waifish with a curtain of blonde hair covering her face, also seemed preoccupied by Maggie. Steve had flung an arm around her, but she didn't look away.

'You cannot tell me you are comfortable with all this,' Simon muttered, glancing down at the beer again. He didn't recognise the brand.

'I can and I am,' Maggie said. Before Simon could reply, she'd walked towards the crowd.

He stood there, holding the beer and feeling like an idiot as he watched after her. He wondered where he would be now if he had decided to slip away from the motel the day before. Further down the highway, still a little bored but with no idea that this town even existed.

He had already lost Maggie in the mass of people. They were silhouettes in the now towering bonfire light, dark and writhing against growing flames. The burned-meat smell was overwhelming now, and off-putting. He took a sip of the beer. He didn't like the taste at all. It was acrid and horrible, like all beer had tasted when he'd first started to drink. He wished he hadn't taken that turn-off. He glanced back to where his car was parked.

'Come on, mate.' A voice from behind made him jump. 'You just got here.'

It was Matty, a blackened sausage in his hand and – Simon realised with a tightening feeling in his stomach – Blue beside him, off the chain, thick slobber dripping from his open mouth.

Matty must have seen the fear in Simon's eyes. He looked at Blue and whistled. The dog froze. His stubby, rounded ears twitched.

'It's a command,' Matty said, as he looked at the dog fondly. 'Means "get ready".'

Simon knew he was shaking and he hated it. He had never thought himself so easily scared. But then, he had never been in a place like this before.

'Sit,' Matty said.

Blue did.

The knife was a bright flash in the firelight. Simon recoiled, but all Matty did was cut some of the sausage away. Blue's nose twitched.

'Stay,' Matty said.

Blue was still.

Matty threw the piece of sausage in the air. It spun down, passed the dog's nose, then Matty clapped, Blue lunged, Simon stumbled back and the sausage was gone.

'Good boy.' Matty looked at Simon. His face was blank. 'Does as he's told.'

With a whistle, Matty strode away, the dog padding after him.

Simon lifted the beer to drink, but it didn't reach his mouth. His arm had gone weak. Instinct made him want to run for the car. He didn't. He set off to find Maggie.

He saw her from a distance, on the other side of the fire now, in a throng of younger people, including Steve, the blonde girl and Kayden. Maggie was nodding along to whatever they were saying, swigging from her can. Steve was talking animatedly. The blonde girl's face was impossible to make out through her hair, but he could see that Kayden's eyes were locked on Maggie. His grin was the same as in the bush. There was hunger to it, hunger that turned Simon's stomach.

With a quick check to make sure no-one was looking, Simon dumped his half-full beer in the dirt. Then, shoulders hunched, he moved around the fire to Maggie's group. Being near her felt somehow safer than the alternative.

He stuck close to Maggie after that, for what it was worth. She barely seemed to notice he was there. She barely seemed to notice other things either – like Kayden's eyes on her, or the way Kev's smirk grew whenever he passed her, which was too often for Simon to assume it was coincidence. However – and it sickened Simon to admit it, even to himself – there was some minor relief in their attention being on Maggie rather than him. Unnoticed was the best way to be when it came to these people.

Then suddenly Steve was clapping him on the back, forcing another can into his sweaty hand. 'You don't have a drink, mate! That's not on.'

Without meaning to, Simon glanced at Maggie. She was looking at him with a neutral expression that could have been either mildly interested or amused. He didn't want to know which.

'You've got some catchin' up to do,' Steve said. 'What's this, your second? You're bein' too shy, Simon – just grab 'em straight from the esky, mate. Smash that back first, we know you can.'

A squeeze of the shoulder, just a little too hard.

It had been a shift as sudden as it was absolute; all eyes were on Simon now.

'This bloke,' Steve announced to the group, 'is a dead-set legend. You know what I saw 'im do before?'

Simon's face was hot.

Steve's voice dropped to a dramatic whisper. 'I saw 'im *scull a beer*. Almost a whole beer.'

The laughter was rough, raucous and too loud. Simon wanted to shrink away into nothing.

'Hey, let's not be a pack of pricks.' Steve raised both hands. 'This bloke, he's more than meets the eye. Managed to bag one hell of a sheila.' He gestured to Maggie. 'And she doesn't strike me as the type to go in for a pity root.'

Maggie said nothing. The blonde girl looked at her.

'Just as well,' Steve said to Simon. 'Kayden had eyes on little Maggie here. You might've had a fight on your hands. But you're tougher than you look, so you'll be alright, hey?'

Kayden was watching Simon now, smiling as he chewed.

Simon shrugged.

'How's that for modesty,' Steve said. 'More drinks?'

The night wore on. Simon felt lost and untethered. Maggie was hardly paying him any attention; she kept slipping out of his sight, leaving him alone in a swirl of whispers, quickly averted eyes, and snatches of harsh cackles. He didn't know how long they'd been there. He didn't want to check his phone in case that provoked them somehow. He also didn't want to remind himself that he had no reception out here. The gathering was getting louder as the fire built and built. There were drunken yells, frequent snaps of cans being opened and always the eyes: keen, piercing and focused, even with the drink.

More beers were thrust into his hands. He didn't want to drink, but he didn't see a choice. His thoughts grew duller. The jagged fear, conversely, worsened, like something unnaturally heavy in his gut.

He found a crate and sat as close to the fire as he dared, staring into the flames. By now, he had given up attempting to tail Maggie. From what he could tell, she was having a great time. An ugly, paranoid part of his brain suggested she had lured him here deliberately, as some kind of attempt to humiliate him. At that stage it made about as much sense as anything else. He drank more. He wanted to get the hell out, but doubted he could drive now even if he wanted to.

'Trent's still out there?' The voice, deep and slow, belonged to Kev. The big man was talking to Steve and someone else Simon didn't recognise, a thin and craggy-faced man with a grubby suit jacket over his singlet and straggly grey hair.

'Dog with a bone, Uncle Trent.' Steve swigged from a beer. 'Told him to let the big pig go. We already got a couple of bullets in the fucker; it wasn't goin' far.'

'Don't underestimate,' Kev said easily. He swayed on the spot, hands on his stomach as he looked into the flames. 'Fear is like petrol. Bad for you, but fuck it makes you go.'

'Bullets are like bullets,' Steve said flatly. 'They kill you no matter how fast you are.'

'Trent might take shit too seriously,' the thin man said. 'But if he stops a big pig rotting in the river and flowing back to us, I'm inclined to let him do his thing.'

'You couldn't find the pig,' Kev said to Steve. 'Maybe Trent will.'

'I found something better.' There was a note of anger to Steve's voice. 'Because I know when a cause is lost.'

Something icy was cutting through the tipsy haze. Simon stood. He had to find Maggie.

'You're the boyfriend.'

The blonde girl was sitting cross-legged on an overturned oil drum nearby. Her tangled hair and the low firelight made it hard to see her face. She was holding a bottle of rum, which she swigged from. Her hair parted slightly and Simon caught sight of wide blue eyes locked on his.

'Simon,' he said, trying to sound steady.

'Simon.' The word was elongated, as if she was trying it out. 'You're the talk of the town, mate.'

Simon shuffled on the spot and glanced around, looking for Maggie.

'That sheila of yours is a bit more popular, though,' the girl said. 'Pretty new thing for all the blokes to drool over.' She sniffed. 'If I were you, I'd be over there making sure they know what's what.'

'She's not my ...' Simon cleared his throat. 'We're not actually together.'

'Nah?' The girl angled the bottle at him. 'Then she's the one, maybe, who needs to know what's what. Kayden, Matty, the others, sure. She can work her way through all of them. But if she touches Steve, different story.'

The heat was becoming oppressive now, the fire turning the warmth of the night up to sweltering. Simon felt stuffy and uncomfortable. He couldn't seem to think straight and this girl wasn't helping. 'She's not ... Look, she wouldn't be interested in them, so—'

'Why not?' the girl asked. 'Not good enough for her, eh? You the better option, are you?'

'No,' Simon said. 'No, I just ...' He didn't know what to say. Out of the corner of his eye, he saw Maggie talking to one of the older women, and made to head for her, mumbling something apologetic.

'Do much running, back in the city?' the girl called after him.

Simon looked back at her. 'Why?'

She shrugged. 'Just curious. You fast?'

Simon couldn't speak. He turned and hurried towards the house. As he did, he was sure he could hear the girl laughing to herself.

CHAPTER SEVEN

Now

Frank moved fast. He went through the kitchen quickly, turning off the deep-fryer and the rest. He put the cash from the day in the safe and hit the lights.

'What the hell is going on?' Delilah demanded as he passed her in the storeroom.

He ignored her as he looked out the back. His bicycle was gone; the only vehicle was the quad bike he'd used to race over. Charlie and Delilah's van was parked out the front, but they could get that later. It was the least of his worries. He shut the back door, mind racing. His eyes moved to the top shelf of the storeroom.

'Frank.' There was a scared note in Delilah's voice now.

He wasn't sure what to tell her. He had insisted she come with him, due to a maybe misguided mistrust of the two backpackers in his house. Now, fairly certain they were harmless, it just seemed like another annoying complication.

'Hopefully nothing.' He reached up to the shelf and felt around until his hand landed on the pistol. He took it down.

Delilah stepped back. 'Why the fuck,' she said, so slowly it was clear she was trying to keep her voice even, 'do you have that?'

Frank looked from the gun to Delilah. 'There was a man. He was looking for her.'

Delilah swallowed and looked at the storeroom door.

'You asked me what I think happened to that girl,' Frank said. 'Join the dots. She turns up, looking the way she does, hurt bad. Then a few minutes later, this guy arrives. And besides …'

'What?' Delilah asked, seeing the look on his face.

'I know guys like that,' Frank said. 'Knew, anyway. We have to be careful.'

'There's careful, then there's pulling a gun.'

Frank couldn't think of what to say. The look in Reg's eye, that leer, the way he held himself – it was the same way they'd all been, out in the bush, guns in hand, downing beer and rum and the other stuff, whooping and cheering every time they saw movement in the night and fired. Deer, mostly. Those brown eyes, dying in the dark, were in his head again.

Frank crossed the room and moved the tins on the opposite shelf until he found the one he wanted. He opened it and took out the ammo. He loaded the gun, the movements mechanical and near automatic even after all these years. He hefted the gun and was surprised by how natural it felt to have it back in his hand.

'You're being paranoid,' Delilah said. 'You know that, right?'

They both heard the creak of the screen door out front opening.

Allie reached the house, threw her bike down and ran onto the porch. She felt like she was about to throw up. She didn't like that man. Not the way he spoke or looked. She didn't like that she had left her grandad with him or the fact that it was going to be dark soon. She just needed to get into her room, lock the door and not leave until it was morning. She could get her phone then. She must have pushed it back further than she'd thought, past the boxes and cobwebs. Maybe.

The moment she was through the front door, she remembered. In the living room, the girl was still on the couch, a little cleaner, especially her now bandaged leg. She was still asleep.

The girl is trouble.

Charlie held the girl's wrist, apparently taking her pulse. He looked up and started on seeing Allie. 'Shit, you scared me. Where are the others?'

Allie said nothing.

'Is Delilah with you?'

Allie shook her head.

Charlie turned to the window. His expression was almost pained. 'I think we made a mistake not calling an ambulance straight away. I've done the best I can. But I can't tell how bad she is, not without proper equipment. I just ... I think we should call one. Now.'

Allie opened her mouth to speak. Nothing came out.

Charlie stood. 'Can I borrow your phone?'

*

Frank's arm twitched as he prepared to raise the gun. He didn't. Instead, he tucked it in the back of his jeans and kept his hand on it as he pushed the internal door open and stepped up behind the counter.

The man who'd come in couldn't have been a bigger contrast to Reg. He was medium height, shoulders slumped and paunchy, a little unshaven but not nearly enough to get rid of the office-bound look he had. Slicked-back hair, double chin and a crumpled yet clearly expensive suit. Frank glanced past him to the car parked out the front. Even from here it looked worth a lot.

'I almost thought there was no-one here,' the man said. 'Lights off and everything. I've filled up; I just want to pay for the fuel and maybe get a bite to eat.'

'We're closed,' Frank said. He didn't take his hand from the gun.

'But the door was open.' The man pointed with his thumb over his shoulder. 'You're still here.'

'We're closed,' Frank said again. 'Get going.'

The man looked confused. 'Buddy, I've got a full tank of your fuel out there. Do you want me to pay or not?'

Frank looked past him again, into the darkening sky. 'It's on me. Now get out of here.'

'Hang on a minute,' the man said. 'This is a bit of a joke. You're the only roadhouse for kilometres. You do realise people need supplies, don't you? It's not late.'

'It's late enough.'

'Look here.' The man shook his head. 'I've been on the road all goddamn day and I just want something to eat and drink. I don't know why that's such a big ask. I'll be quick.'

'Grab some chips or something.' Frank nodded to one of the shelves. 'Then get out. I don't give a shit about the fuel. We're closed.'

The door behind Frank opened. He didn't have to turn to know it was Delilah. The man raised an eyebrow and crossed his arms.

'Oh right,' he said. 'Of course. Typical. You're having fun on the job and that's why you're turning away paying customers.' He shook his head. 'It's a disgrace, buddy. You have a responsibility out here. People can be stuck here without you and—'

'Mate.' Frank looked the man in the eye. 'I'm asking nicely. Please leave.'

'I'm not letting you strand people here because you're fucking horny,' the man said.

'You've got the wrong idea,' Delilah said from beside Frank.

The man snorted. 'Oh yeah, sure thing. I bet that's—'

Frank pointed the gun at the man's face. Delilah gasped. Frank could feel his pulse, resonating through his entire body, just like it used to back on the hunt. His head pounded. 'Get out.'

The man was frozen, staring at the barrel.

Frank held the weapon steady. He softened his voice. 'Please.'

The man didn't move. He didn't look like he could.

'Frank,' Delilah whispered. 'What the hell are you doing?'

'I need you to leave,' Frank said to the man. 'Now. There isn't time.'

'Time for what?' Delilah stepped around, so that she was between Frank and the man, although out of the way of the gun. 'Frank, this is crazy. What do you think is going on here?'

Frank looked at her. She was wide-eyed, terrified. He looked at the man. His expression hadn't changed, but a dark stain had spread across the front of his suit pants.

Frank looked to the window again. Night was falling. Everything stayed quiet. He lowered the gun. He was shaking suddenly.

'Jesus,' he breathed. 'I'm sorry. I thought ... I really thought ...'

A sound in the night. The distant roar of an engine.

Frank's eyes moved to the window. The darkness was receding. He walked forwards, passing both Delilah and the man. His hand tightened around the gun again as he reached the entrance to the roadhouse.

To the right, down the highway, the glare of powerful high beams approached. A wall of light, highlighting the whole road, accompanied by the sound of engines. It wasn't one vehicle but several, ten at least, moving fast, all blurring together in a snarl of diesel thunder.

Frank backed up as the vehicles neared and started peeling away from each other. Some went straight to the front of the roadhouse. Others around the back. Surrounding the place.

Frank turned to the others.

'Out the back.' His voice was low and hoarse. 'Now.'

CHAPTER EIGHT

Then

Simon woke up on the couch, head at a strange angle and a crick in his neck. He briefly wished he had slept in the car. Maybe he would have managed more than an hour.

He got up and stepped outside. It was a warm morning and for a moment the smell of gum leaves and fresh air almost made him relax.

'G'day there.' Wearing the same clothes and the same amused look as yesterday, Steve was leaning against a tree across the road.

Had he been waiting there, watching the house? How long for? 'Hi.' Simon tried to return the smile.

'How'd you sleep? They're not four-poster feather beds, but I reckon they beat a car seat.' Hands in pockets, Steve crossed the road, eyes wandering over Simon's shoulder to look into the house.

'They do. Thanks.'

Steve stopped a few metres from Simon. 'Maggie up?'

'Why?' Simon asked, a little more quickly than he'd intended.

Steve raised his hands. 'Whoa, mate, relax. Just askin'.'

'She's asleep.'

'You sure?'

He nodded.

'So you are fuckin' her.'

Simon gaped at Steve, who still looked as though he was in the middle of telling a hilarious joke. 'What?'

'Well, if you're sure she's asleep, you'd have to have been in her room, right? So unless you're some fuckin' perv—'

'There were no ... no sounds coming from her room,' Simon said, wondering why the hell he was justifying himself to this creep. 'She might be awake. I don't know.'

'But before you said you were sure she was asleep.' Any hint of a smile vanished. 'Which is it?'

Simon shook his head and when he spoke he could hear the waver in his voice. 'I don't know.'

Steve cocked his head to one side, as if examining Simon. 'Best you don't lie to people, mate. Never know who might take it badly.' With a wave, he turned and started walking, yelling out to a couple of others as he headed up the street.

Simon stared after him. It took him a second to realise he was trembling and another to tell himself he was being idiotic. He started to go back inside, then stopped. He rested his head against the door.

What had Steve actually said that was threatening? Last night, in the dark by the fire after driving through the bush, everything about this place had seemed like a huge mistake.

He turned and looked over the street again. He wasn't going to lie to himself that he was comfortable here, but this *was* what he had been looking for, wasn't it? Something different, something genuine. A bearded, stooped man gave Simon a toothless leer as he strolled by. Simon forced himself to wave back. He took a long, deep breath.

Just country blokes.

Putting his hands in his pockets, he stepped down and started to walk up the street, doing his best to look relaxed. He said hello to the couple of people he passed. Maybe he could learn a bit more about this place, be less judgemental and try to make the most of it, even if he didn't really like it. It would be fine. It *was* fine.

He had just about reached the end of the street when he became aware that someone had fallen into step behind him. He looked back and flinched.

The blonde girl from the night before was right there, on his heels. In the light of day, her hair looked matted and greasy, her frame unnaturally skinny.

'Um. Hi.' Simon's voice sounded pinched.

She was uncomfortably close. Simon resisted the sudden, strong urge to shove her away.

'Steve came by the house?' she said.

Simon nodded, unsure of what to say.

'He wanna talk to that bitch?'

The bite on the final word took him aback. 'Um ... no. No, he left. He just asked about her and left.'

'What did she say to him last night?'

'I don't ... nothing. Nothing.'

Closer again, too close. A strand of her hair brushed Simon's cheek. He made himself stay still. She stank of cigarettes and stale alcohol, and something coppery and metallic, something—

'I'll fucking break her, you know.' The girl's voice was soft and calm, almost teasing. 'Get her skinny little neck in my hands. It's not hard. People think you've gotta be strong but, nah, it's about where you put your hands. About putting pressure in the right place and twisting just so. Quick and easy. Then she'll be gone and you'll be alone here.'

Simon jerked back. He couldn't breathe.

The girl hadn't moved.

Simon ran past her. He half-expected her to stop him, braced himself for the lunge and the hands around his neck, but she stayed put. He ran until he was back at the house. He paused at the front door and looked back. The girl was nowhere to be seen.

He charged in and knocked on Maggie's door, then again, louder, when there was no reply. She pulled it open, bleary eyed and wrapped in a blanket.

'What?' she said.

'I want to go.'

She just looked at him.

'We came, we've stayed, we've had the experience. Now can we leave? The people here ...' He lowered his voice, although he wasn't sure why. 'I don't like this place.'

'Are you always this melodramatic?'

'I'm not being—'

'Listen.' She lifted both hands. 'Just today, okay? We spend the day, then leave tonight.'

'I'm not staying here until dark.'

'Simon, what exactly do you think is happening here?'

'It's not about what I think, it's about what I feel.' Maggie raised her eyebrows. 'Why?' he said, feeling a hint of desperation now. 'Why are you *so* keen to stay?' He stared at her and suddenly he felt very, very stupid. 'Who are you?'

'Excuse me?'

'Who are you, really? You're backpacking around the place with lots of cash, picking up random lifts, drinking in dodgy pubs and … and you were the one who told me to take this turn.' Realisation hit and hardened into certainty as her face remained impassive. 'You knew this place was here.'

'No, I didn't.'

'But you suspected.'

She shrugged.

'Why?'

'I had my reasons.'

'I gave you the fucking lift. I have a right to know why you wanted to come here.'

She looked away, brow furrowed. Then she exhaled. Her shoulders, which he hadn't realised were hunched up, dropped.

'I knew there was … something here,' she said. 'I knew because it was around this area my mother was last seen.'

Any response he might have planned seemed to evaporate. Any understanding he thought he had gathered vanished.

'Your mother ...' He swallowed. 'Your mother disappeared in this area and you ... you led us right into the middle of it?'

'Don't be stupid,' she said. 'Mum disappeared almost twenty years ago. I don't think she's here.'

'Then why are you?'

'Because somebody might know something,' she said. 'If there's even a hint of a rumour, then it will have been worth it. And don't look at me like that. You would have done exactly the same thing.'

'I never would have led us into—'

'What?' she said.

Simon's fists clenched. He was breathing heavily but trying to keep his anger in check, trying to will Maggie to understand what they could have walked into, all for the vaguest hope of picking up a long dead trail. An ugly truth dawned on him. She had led him here without being honest with him, which implied she knew he wouldn't like it – so on some level, she had to know this place was bad news. And that made her more than selfish, it made her dangerous.

'Okay.' He tried to keep his voice steady. 'Fine. You want to stay here, be my guest. But I'm leaving.'

'Simon—'

'No,' he said. 'You lied to me. You led me into this shithole and I'm not sticking around just to get manipulated into more idiotic decisions. Good luck finding your mother. I really hope it's worth it.'

Not letting himself look at her for a second longer, he turned and stalked off.

There were more people on the street, who watched with interest as he marched out and got into the front seat of his car. He kept his eyes determinedly ahead; he wasn't trying to impress Maggie anymore and that meant he had no reason to humour these hillbillies. To do anything other than put his foot down now was just wasting time.

Still, he didn't want to show any signs of fear or weakness, so he drove up the street and back towards the bush road at a steady pace. Just a guy going for a drive. Never mind his pounding heart. It would slow when he hit the highway again.

On the track, even at this time of day, the trees made everything almost dark, the path ahead somehow harder to make out than it had been the evening before. Covered as it was in branches, leaves and rocks, it was barely distinguishable from the surrounding land. He tried to remember the way they had come, kept an eye out for tyre tracks in the scuffed dirt, or anything familiar. But he was distracted by thoughts of Maggie. He felt used and stupid, a naïve kid trusting a pretty girl because, well, because he wanted to get laid. In that moment, for all of his earlier conviction, he found it hard to see himself as anything other than a run-of-the-mill university graduate trying to give a road trip more gravitas than it deserved. What a wanker he'd been.

Maybe his best course of action was to go back to the city. Or to just accept reality and spend the rest of his trip getting drunk and chatting up girls he met in backpacker bars. At least then he wouldn't be wasting time pretending there was more to this – more to him – than there was. He laughed bitterly. *The real Australia.* What a stupid fucking idea. As if he had any idea what that would even look like.

Something moved ahead of him and, realising he hadn't been paying attention, he hit the brakes. It took him a second to register it wasn't an animal or a falling tree.

Hands behind his back, framed by the overhang of weighed-down gums and the shadows they cast, Steve stood in front of the car, a broad beam on his face.

Simon stared at him. He went to reverse, glancing in the rear-view mirror just in time to see a ute pull up behind him. The doors opened and Matty and Kayden stepped out on either side. His stomach lurched. They were holding rifles.

Drive, a tiny voice in his head was saying. *Drive forwards now.* But he was frozen in his seat.

The driver-side door was wrenched open and rough hands pulled him free from the car. He hit the ground hard, staring up at Kayden, who looked just the same as he had the night before, eyes obscured by the mirrored glasses.

'Leaving so soon, mate?' Matty said. 'Blue liked you. He'll be heartbroken.'

It was then that Simon heard the dog, barking wildly from the tray.

'What a man.' Steve had walked around to join the others. His hands were no longer behind his back. He was holding a cricket bat. 'Guess there really wasn't more than met the eye. It'd be a shame if it wasn't so straight-up shit. Leavin' your sheila behind and everythin'. Pretty little thing all by herself, surrounded by strangers. That's average, mate. We could be anybody.'

Kayden chuckled.

'Good shit, Kayd,' Steve said. 'I reckon you'll get Maggie all to yourself after this. Fuck, I'd have a crack myself, but you know what Kate's like.' He drew a finger across his neck. 'Guess I'll just have to be jealous. Gotta say, she looks like a good fuck. Like a feisty one. You'll have to tell me all about it.'

Kayden chuckled again.

Matty whistled. Blue's barking stopped. There was a thud as the dog jumped from the tray.

'You hungry, boy?' Matty called.

'Get up,' Steve said. 'You can at least do that.'

'What are you going to do to me?' Simon couldn't stand. He was shaking all over. 'P-please,' he said. 'Please just let me go, I won't tell anyone, I swear—'

'Tell anyone what?' Steve said. 'We haven't done shit. Yet.'

CHAPTER NINE

Now

Warren Jenkins was late. Really late. He wasn't looking forward to the excuses he would have to make to shut the missus up. The bottle of wine on his passenger seat might do the trick. Five bucks from the bottle-o. Hopefully by the time he got there, they'd all be too drunk to notice what a cheapskate he'd been. It wasn't like these dinner parties were anything other than an excuse to get pissed anyway.

He checked the clock. He'd be at least an hour late and Diane could be a bitch when she was drunk. He stepped a little harder on the accelerator. The speedometer crept sightly past the limit.

He swore under his breath. Something was blocking the road up ahead. He squinted: two cars, nose to nose, cutting off the highway. Utes, by the look of it, years past their prime. If someone was playing silly buggers, then he had no time for it. But …

The two blokes leaning against the vehicles wore police uniforms.

Warren slowed as his heart picked up slightly. He tried to remember how many beers he'd had. It wasn't like this was a busy highway, and any dickhead could drive in a straight line. Booking him would be criminal. But still.

One of the cops was walking forwards. He looked about the same age as Warren himself, probably in his forties. He was scrawny and his face almost skeletal. He raised a hand.

Warren swallowed and stopped the car. He pressed the button to lower the window.

'Just, um, trying to get home,' he said, hoping he sounded relaxed and confident.

'Road's closed, mate,' the cop said.

'That's …' Warren bit his tongue. He had been about to say bullshit, which it was. There was no other way back home. But if they weren't going to breathalyse him, he didn't need to give them a reason.

'Why?' he said.

'Servo blew up,' the cop said.

Behind him, the other one lit a cigarette.

'Yeah, it's pretty fucked,' the cop went on. 'Noxious fumes and shit everywhere. Bushfire hazard. Too risky tonight.'

Warren glanced at their cars. He'd never known cops to drive utes.

'You'd best turn around, mate,' the man went on.

'Home's that way, though.' Warren pointed past them.

'Not tonight, it ain't,' the cop said. 'Turn around.'

Warren met his eyes. The cop smiled slightly. It came off almost like a silent challenge. Warren took in his uniform. There was a dark stain on the right sleeve.

Warren tried to look genial. 'Sure thing, officers.'

Warren knew when something was off. A churning in the gut, a slight smell of wrongness in the air, a feeling that the world around him was a little off kilter. Whatever was going on here, he was willing to bet it wasn't what he'd been told, just as he was willing to bet the two men weren't cops. But more than anything, Warren Jenkins knew when it was time to turn tail, run as fast as you could and forget what you had seen.

Frank ducked behind the counter and fell into a crouch as the door to the hall slammed shut behind Delilah and the businessman, who were heading for the storeroom. He lifted the gun, feeling the comforting weight in his hand. Wishing it was more comforting. *Not enough. Not nearly enough.*

He peered over the counter, then shifted back down again. The light from the cars was blinding; they'd positioned them around the pumps, facing inwards, making it impossible to see. At least four cars out the front. At least.

He heard the door behind him open slightly. Delilah, evidently bent low, was looking at him through the gap.

'Who the hell are they?' Her voice was high and scared.

Frank shook his head. But he had an idea. An idea that suggested he should have just told the bastard what he wanted to know. He thought of Allie, back at the house.

He closed his eyes. Pushed away the icy fear creeping through him. Crushed it down and put it in a box, just like he'd been taught the first time he'd been taken out on the hunt.

He had to be calm. Level-headed. And he had to make sure that, whoever these people were, they had no idea he lived in a house less than a kilometre behind him.

'It's about her, isn't it?' Delilah said.

Frank nodded.

'Why?'

'Don't know,' Frank said. 'Doesn't change our situation.'

'We should have called the police,' Delilah said. 'As soon as she turned up.'

It struck him then. 'The guy in the suit. His phone.'

Delilah didn't need to be told twice. The door clicked shut. Frank listened, waiting for the telltale sound of the screen door.

Delilah found the man huddled in the storeroom, balled up in the corner, hugging his legs hard to his chest. He had clearly been crying.

Unbidden, a memory hit her. A man just like this one – fancy suit, puffy jowls, double chin – who was so confident, so sure of himself as he sat behind his desk and lectured Delilah about service, about just smiling and nodding and taking the bullshit while remembering that the customer was always right. And it was as she'd stood there smiling and nodding and remembering that her boss was always right that it occurred to her, quietly, that she hated him, that she had been striving for years to follow the rules and work up to that same position and for what? So that in middle age she could make somebody else put up with the bullshit while she sat back and counted her money? So that she could be the one with the smirk and the suit and the jowls? No amount of money was worth becoming that. She'd quit within a week and booked her ticket to Australia. Because it had seemed, at the time, so very far away from everything she wanted to escape.

Reality snapped back and she crossed the room to the man, bent down next to him. She reached out and put her hand on his knee. He yelped and she pulled back.

'Just me,' she said.

He stared at her, breathing heavily.

'Delilah,' she said. 'My name is Delilah. You?'

He went to speak but no sound came out. His eyes remained locked on hers.

'Hey.' She touched his knee again. He flinched but she didn't back off. 'What's your name?'

'Greg.'

'Right. Greg, listen. We're in trouble. I don't know what sort, but it isn't good. I need your phone.'

He just kept staring. She tried to ignore the surge of hot fury she felt at his vapid expression.

'Greg,' she said, a little firmer. 'If we can get the police out here, we might be okay.'

He shook his head. 'It … it's in my car.'

Shit. It would have almost been funny if jagged spikes of terror weren't threatening every second to turn her into a quivering wreck.

Of all the bad luck in the world. She knew she should get out there and tell Frank, knew she should be trying to think of a backup option, but the sheer cruelty of the whole thing had floored her, left her almost unable to move. Things like this just didn't happen. Not to people like her.

Greg wiped his eyes with the back of his hand. He reached into his pocket and took out a flask. He unscrewed it and took a swig. Bleary eyed, he looked back at the door. 'I think I might have fucked up.'

Frank had felt this way before. Like he was dangling from a string above a sea of knives. He wanted to look up, to check if the string would hold, but any movement could shift the weight and snap it. So he was frozen. Waiting for Delilah to come out and say she'd phoned the police. Waiting for the attack. Waiting for anything.

He half-considered crawling back into the storeroom himself, but then there'd be no way of knowing what those bastards were doing out there. He knew some were behind the roadhouse and the back entry was as accessible as the front, but he figured he'd have heard something if they were already inside. It wasn't much to hang hope on. Just another fraying string.

Moving very slowly, he shifted forwards onto his knees, then up until he was peering just over the counter. Too-bright light still filled the roadhouse but now, framed against the glare, he could see a stark silhouette. Very close to the screen door. He lifted the pistol.

Maybe he could find a way to get to the house, without alerting them to Allie's presence, then pick up the unconscious girl and bring her to them. If they wanted to get rid of witnesses, well, he could fight, and he could give

Allie a chance to get clear. And maybe the unconscious girl on his couch did deserve it. Maybe handing her over wasn't the wrong thing to do. Maybe it was the only sane choice. He lowered the pistol.

'G'day,' a deep voice came from the figure. 'Mind if I come in?'

Their sightlines were a lot better than his. Chances were they would open fire the moment he aimed the gun. If they were armed. It was a deadly chance to take.

The voice again, mocking. 'Righto. A bit put-out. Fair's fair. Let me introduce myself. I'm Trent, and I'm hoping that you're the kind of bloke who'll listen to reason, because there's really only one outcome here that we're all gonna be happy with. You're gonna give us that girl.'

The mockery was gone. The voice was hard. Certain.

'Maybe you don't believe us yet. Let me give you some food for thought. This is Australia, mate. Boundless plains to share and all that. We help out our own, but when they spit in our face, they ain't our own anymore. Then, they become something else. Reg told us all about you. Bloke like you, out here alone … I'd bet good money that you've seen some bad shit. Maybe even done some yourself. And that's why you're gonna play nice and give us the girl. Because to not do that is to spit in our faces and become that something else you sure as shit don't wanna be. You or your granddaughter. You're one of us. The girl ain't. So go on and choose just what kind of bloke you wanna be.'

Anger seared through cold fear. Frank moved fast. He pointed the gun just over the man's shoulder and fired. The shot filled the space and rang in his ears. Cracks splintered out from the bullet hole in the window. The figure didn't move. Frank ducked behind the counter again.

'Alright.' There was amusement in the voice. 'Point taken. I'll assume you can hear me then.'

Frank said nothing. He thought he could hear laughter from outside.

'You wanna be chivalrous. I get that. Thing is, mate, there's shit that's more important than chivalry. Staying alive, for one. Fairness, for another. That girl wronged us. And I ain't lying when I say we did absolutely nothing to her.' There was no amusement in his voice anymore. 'Now we've got your kid's phone and I don't have to tell you that the one on the counter there is useless, given that we've cut the lines. No-one's coming to help. You got no choice but to play ball here, mate. I know you got no reason to trust us. But if you're a smart man, you won't test me when I say that if you don't hand the girl over in the next half-hour, we'll burn this place to the ground. And when you run out screaming, that's when the real fun will begin.'

The gun in Frank's hand seemed especially pathetic now.

'Your move, mate.'

Frank looked over the counter. The silhouette was gone, back behind the safety of the lights. He sat back down on the floor, leaning against the inside of the counter, trying to think.

The internal door cracked open. Pale and sweating, Delilah crawled out and sat next to him. For several seconds neither of them spoke.

'You shot at them?' she asked.

'They had to know I was armed,' Frank said. 'Otherwise nothing is stopping them from just bursting in here. The glass is thick; I knew it would hold.'

Delilah stared at him. Her face was bone white. 'You … you know what you just did, right? You accepted their … their fucking *challenge*. We could have …' She swallowed. 'Fuck this. Fuck this, Frank. Charlie and I have nothing to do with whatever bullshit is going on here. We just stopped for some goddamn fuel and, and now we're …' Her breathing was fast, wild, nearly hyperventilating. 'We're going to die. Oh god, we're going to fucking die.'

'No, we're not,' Frank said, despite not believing it. 'It all depends on how we play things. Did you call the cops?'

Delilah's voice was tinged with hysteria. 'His phone is in his fucking car.'

'Of course it is.' Frank rested his head against the inside of the counter.

'How are you so calm?'

Frank didn't reply. He didn't know how to tell her that he was the furthest thing from calm.

Delilah looked sick. 'Okay. Listen.' She took Frank's hand. Her sweaty grip was strong. 'It's not just the girl in danger now. We're all in this. Pretty soon Charlie's going to wonder where we are and come looking for me. And Allie will come with him, because I seriously doubt she wants to wait there alone. None of us asked for this. None of us want to be involved. The girl, she did something, right? Those people wouldn't be here if she wasn't bad news.'

'They wouldn't be here if they weren't, either.'

'I think it doesn't much matter who they are. What matters is what they're going to do and they were pretty clear on that. And if they get in here and find that we don't have the girl—'

'They'll do whatever they can to persuade us to talk. I know.'

'Then you know what we have to do.' Her grip tightened.

Frank pulled his hand away. 'We have what they want. That gives us leverage. You really want to risk losing that leverage?'

'I don't want to risk what they might do if we don't hand her over,' Delilah said.

CHAPTER TEN

Then

Maggie couldn't dwell on what had happened. Simon had been a means to an end and while she wasn't proud of herself, she had got to where she needed to be. The question now was what she was going to do next.

Ignoring his concerns had felt wrong, like putting on a shirt backwards. It wasn't that she necessarily thought this place was dangerous, but it wasn't exactly comforting either. She had pretended to accept their drinks last night, chatted and poured some out every chance she got, while Simon hung around looking broody and paranoid and essentially distracting her from what she was here for. He was still distracting her, even now he was gone.

None of it was his fault. But he was clear now. That brought on at least a mild sense of relief. She would be an angry story he told people in bars for the rest of his trip; if he was lucky, it would get him a few sympathy beers from the kind of free-spirited, careless girls he was probably better off with.

The bitter pang of something like jealousy surprised her. Those girls, giggling and flirting and smiling, girls who would see Simon as smart and sweet, girls worrying about uni and their jobs and nothing else. She hated those girls – not for thinking the way they did, but for the fact that she couldn't be one of them. Even if she tried. And she *had* tried, with Simon in the pub. Whatever her objective, she had tried in that moment to let her guard down, just a little. And maybe she had even let herself believe, for a while, that she could. Maybe she had imagined the road trip continuing after they found nothing at this town, Simon none the wiser to her intent, the two of them drinking and having fun and forgetting.

Simon could do all of that now that he was away from her. But it didn't change the fact that she had broken a promise to herself, to never again ignore someone when they said they were scared.

It had been hard, smiling and playing dumb in the face of his wide eyes and desperate attempts to keep his voice steady. It had been hard because in him she had seen Ted, small and skinny even for eleven, telling Maggie what he couldn't tell anyone else because knowing where she had come from, she might understand.

'He doesn't *hurt* you, though,' Maggie had said to Ted, thirteen and self-assured, thirteen and certain she knew better because she had seen worse.

Shoulders hunched, cross-legged on the floor of his room, Ted had shaken his head. 'Not like that. But it's … it's the way he talks. The way he tells me I have to toughen up. The way he tells me if I don't do the things he wants, the stuff he thinks is, is *funny*, I'll never be …' He glanced up at Maggie, ashamed to admit it. 'I'll never be a man.'

'Hamish isn't a man,' Maggie said. 'He's only fifteen.'

Fifteen but looked twenty, all broad shoulders and a cocky smirk, all dialled-up charm whenever he spoke to their foster parents, trustworthiness personified. She had thought he was a harmless irritation at first, a suck-up with fake maturity that made stupid adults swoon. Or if not stupid, then adults like Ben and Debbie, attention spread thin over too many kids.

'He knows I'm scared,' Ted said. 'It's like, it's like he *uses* that because nobody would believe me and …'

Maggie had put a hand on his shoulder. Even now, ten years later, the depth of her condescension made her sick. 'He's an idiot,' she had said. 'But he's harmless. Ignore him and he'll get bored.'

She had been frustrated when the scared look on Ted's face remained. 'You pathetic little kid,' she had wanted to scream, 'you want to know what pain really is? Grow a fucking backbone.' But she hadn't said any of that. She had said something pointless and gone back to her room and punched the wall. By the next morning she had put the whole conversation out of her head.

Now, she made herself remember it every day.

On the couch in the living room of Kev's spare house, she stared into space and tried to concentrate. What she needed to do was sift through everything that had happened last night, examine every detail and work out if there was anything worth following up or if this town was just another dead end. It was harder than it should have been, pushing Simon away, banishing thoughts of the trip she had wanted to be a part of more than she'd expected. But just because it was hard didn't stop it being necessary. She thought about the faces and whispers, the distinct itch of being watched every step of the way. She had felt it as soon as she stepped out of the car. The only question was whether it had been the curiosity of a town unused to newcomers, or something more.

The intensity and consistency of it led her to believe it was the latter, but that didn't mean she knew what that meant. They had looked at her with too much interest, with suspicion – even, she thought with a thrill of fragile hope, with recognition. She had done her best to memorise the faces of all the women she saw, but none had prompted any buried recollection or stab of forgotten connection. That didn't mean her mother wasn't here and, given what she had gone through to get this far, she wasn't about to leave without being thorough, but a hopeless flat feeling made her suspect that she'd be on the road and directionless again before long.

The only way forward was to have a look around and see what she could dig up. So, after taking a moment to get her innocuous, relaxed smile right, she headed out.

She was surprised to find someone waiting for her: Rhonda, the woman who had given them drinks the night before.

'Thought I'd see if you were up,' she said as Maggie stepped outside. 'Ciggie?'

Maggie accepted a smoke from the proffered packet. She tried to look like she was enjoying herself as she inhaled. Rhonda was eying her closely.

'What you after?' the older woman said.

'What do you mean?'

Rhonda shrugged. 'People don't head into these parts unless they have a good enough reason. If you're looking for something, you might as well spit it out.'

Maggie considered her options, then settled on the truth. The only reason they had to not be honest with her was if they were hiding something. 'I'm looking for a woman,' Maggie said. 'She was in this area about twenty years ago. I doubt she'd still be here, but I'm trying to get a sense of where she might have gone.'

'Someone you know?' Rhonda took another drag.

Maggie nodded.

'Family?'

'My mum.'

Rhonda looked away, eyes narrowed slightly. 'Twenty years is a long time,' she said. 'But I reckon I'd remember. Don't get too many newcomers. My opinion, your mum wouldn't have been here. Ladies from Melbourne got no reason to come here.'

'I did,' Maggie said.

'Yeah, but unless your mum was also looking for someone, why would she? Was she looking for someone?'

'Leaving someone.'

'Running away.' Rhonda snorted. 'Doesn't sound worth finding, if you ask me.'

'Maybe not worth finding,' Maggie dropped her half-smoked cigarette and stepped on it. 'But worth asking why.'

'You ask a question like that, you might get an answer you don't like. Or don't need to hear. My advice? Forget her. Girl gets to a certain age, she doesn't need a mother anymore.'

'I never said I needed her.'

'Even so,' Rhonda crushed her own cigarette. 'Best head home, love. Don't think there's much for you here.' For a moment they looked at each other and when Rhonda spoke again there was a very slight hush to her voice. 'Best leave soon.'

She turned and walked down the street. Maggie waited until she was well away. Then, wishing she didn't have that awful cigarette taste in her mouth, she looked towards the field where the bonfire party had taken place.

She had not only been paying attention to the women. There was an edge of defiance to the thought, as if she wanted to yell it at Simon. She had observed and she had been careful. The small groups, peeling off to mutter to each other while glancing around. The way Kayden had tailed her, all night, materialising out of the dark no matter where she was. Never saying anything. Just watching with that horrible half-smile through the constant chewing. She had played nice. There was no point in making enemies when she hadn't found what she was looking for. But the thought of it made her sick, now.

Kayden, however, had not been the most disconcerting part of the night before. That had come later, when most of the punters had gone to bed, Simon had long since skulked back to the house and Maggie was hoping that the thinning crowd would give her more of a chance to analyse faces and answers. She had been on the far side of the fire, closer to the tree line than the town. She was standing alone, beer can in hand, as she looked over the remaining drinkers and tried to work out what to do now. Her face was set in an automatic pleasant mode and she raised the empty can to her lips without even thinking about it. A charming visitor who could down bevvies with the best of them.

She heard footsteps behind her, light on the dry grass. She took her time turning; relaxed, unfazed.

The man who approached was probably in his mid-thirties. A rifle hung from a strap on his back. He wore a headlamp over close-cut dark hair. His face was thin, his features hard. Even in the relative dark, she could see his cold blue eyes.

He came to a halt about a metre from her. Maggie gave a little wave.

The man said nothing.

'I'm Maggie,' she said. 'I'm staying here tonight.'

The man didn't reply.

Maggie raised her can. His gaze followed it. She put it to her lips.

'Why are you pretending to drink?' His voice was rough but level.

Maggie lowered the can.

The man's head cocked to the side, just slightly. Expectant.

She had heard a name a couple of times: someone who wasn't here, Steve's uncle on his mother's side, based on what she'd put together.

'You're Trent?'

'It's the weight,' he said. 'Of the can. Hard to fake well, if you're not concentrating.'

He started to walk again. Close to Maggie, he paused. His voice, when he spoke, was low. 'It's a good idea to concentrate.'

She hadn't underestimated the people here; or at least she didn't think she had. But Trent was a reminder that as careful as she thought she was being, she had to be vigilant. Her best course of action was to be gone from here as soon as possible. That wasn't paranoia. It was just common sense. She would search the town, as fast as she could, look for any faces she hadn't seen the night before, then slip off into the trees.

Her stomach growled. Before anything else, she needed food.

She hadn't been walking long when she came across a largish demountable building, its open door and cracked windows revealing an interior full of crates and a small card table at the far end. Inside, it smelt of dry dust, which made her want to cough. In the crates were piles of old cans and plastic packets. She decided not to check the use-by dates – the packaging was faded and she didn't recognise any of the brands.

She was surprised when a man emerged from a door she hadn't noticed behind the card table. She had seen him last night: a skinny man wearing a suit jacket, oddly, over a singlet. He was eating something out of a paper bag and stopped upon seeing Maggie. His smile was yellow. 'Well, if it isn't the talk of the bloody town,' he said. 'You after some grub, love?'

'Something to eat, yeah.' Maggie was sick of pretending to be friendly. She did her best anyway.

'Tell you what,' he said. 'Reggie can do you better than this sorry shit. Got some fresh food from the hunt the other day, in the ice chest out back. Gimme a sec.'

He ducked back through the doorway. Maggie glanced around, trying to think of an excuse to stick with the out-of-date cans. But before she could, he was back, holding out a paper-wrapped parcel.

'Beef sandwich, love,' he said. 'Bread's a day old, but there's nothing bad growing on it. Should be tasty enough.' He handed it to her. Maggie took it without pausing. The man didn't look away. His grin stayed wide and unsettling.

'How much do I owe you?'

He chortled. 'Won't hear of it, love. Share and share alike here, eh? It's not like the fucking city. Excuse my French. You've got a pretty face and a pretty smile, and that's payment enough.' The man held out the paper bag. 'Jerky?'

She took a handful. It felt stick-hard. She thanked him, then walked back into the sun. She wolfed down the sandwich – the bread was more than a day old – but once she was a fair way down the road, she dropped the jerky in the dirt.

The town wasn't big and it didn't take long to do a lap of the whole place. There wasn't much more to it than what she had already gathered; it seemed frozen in the sixties, or maybe even further back. Even the houses looked derelict and abandoned. It was hard to see how living here was sustainable or what the people did for money.

Slowing, Maggie approached one of the houses, intending to see what she could through the window. She felt eyes on her. She turned.

The man was tall and thin. He was bald, with a long, haggard face, his eyes sunk deep and wrinkles stark. He sat on the front step of the nearest house, polishing a long rifle

equipped with a scope. It was the most high-tech thing she'd
seen since getting here. Her eyes lingered on it for a moment,
but the man was still watching her. It was hard to tell if there
was anything in his expression: amusement, anger or worse.
He just watched.

'Going hunting?' she asked, because she couldn't think of
what else to say.

'Maybe.' His expression didn't change.

She nodded to the gun. 'Expensive?'

He said nothing. He lifted the weapon so that the barrel
was pointed at the sky. He kept staring at Maggie until she
turned and walked away. She wanted to look back. She didn't.

The slow realisation that she wasn't going to find answers
here was giving perspective to Simon's fears. She had never
liked being stared at. In the past year, especially, it usually
meant that somebody had noticed something and that always
meant that she wasn't working hard enough to stay safely
under the radar, to keep just out of people's sight. It was one
thing to invite eyes when she needed a lift. It was another
altogether when she was looking for information that people
didn't want to share.

Simon's departure presented a whole new problem,
though; she had no lift out of here. Late afternoon found her
sitting on the front stairs of Kev's spare house, trying to work
out whether it would be worth asking for a lift and whether
she even wanted one from any of the weirdos here. Frustration
was mounting and, finally, figuring if one night here hadn't
killed her then a second would probably be harmless, she
decided to go for another walk.

She headed in the direction of where the barbecue had been the night before. The dry grass, cracking under her boots, was littered with empty beer bottles and cigarette butts, a couple of footballs lying here and there. She wondered if the debris was all from last night or from a few different shindigs, and if they ever cleaned the place up. She suspected not. This town didn't seem the sort to want to impress anyone.

She crossed to the edge of the field and looked into the darkness of the bush. Despite the heat, she shivered. This was where she had met Trent. Emerging from the scrub with his gun and immediate awareness that she was putting on an act. Had he reported that to the others? Did it matter if he had? Even thinking back on it brought a surge of anger at herself, a voice that sounded a lot like her father's muttering in her ear: *What, you really thought you could make it out there by yourself, thought you could face the big bad world alone? A few more fuck-ups like that and they'll come for you, like you know they will eventually. You can't hide after what you did.*

Maggie kicked a bottle. It rolled towards the tree line. No matter where she looked, all she saw through the trunks was gloom. It made her feel as though this town existed in some strange purgatory separate from the rest of the world. Her mind was made up. It was time to leave. But as she turned, something caught her eye, a gleam of sun striking metal. She took a few steps and saw, tucked away behind the trees, a large shed.

It seemed a strange place for it. It was about the same size as the houses in the main part of town, with a corrugated iron roof and steel-sheet walls. The closer she got, stepping into the shadows of the trees, the more she could make out. There seemed to be a lot of growth around it, as if the place was forgotten. Or as if someone was trying to hide it.

Behind her the coast was clear. There was no sign that anyone was following her. She was, after all, a fair distance from the houses in the town. She approached the shed. Up close it didn't look forgotten. There was a clear path leading up to the tin door and there was no sign of rust on the door itself. Reaching it she put an ear to the cool metal, but there was no sound from within.

Her heart had picked up and she wasn't sure why. She had no need to look inside if she didn't want to. She had no reason except curiosity – it wasn't as though an answer to where her mother was would be in there. She opened the door.

His ears were ringing, the sound high and keening and awful. There was blood in his eyes, washing the trees and bushes red. He thought of his mother.

Her face had appeared unbidden as the bat came down and he felt the crack of bone, knowing it was just his arm but feeling as though his whole body had broken. His mother appeared in his mind then, brushing his hair away and singing. But the singing morphed into laughter, followed by hands wrenching him up and shoving him away from the car and voices calling 'Run, piggy, run', and after that, his mother wasn't there anymore, just the scratch of branches, the tears and blood in his eyes, the pounding of his heart and more laughter, falling away as trees closed in and he kept running, cradling his throbbing arm, and none of it mattering.

In stolen snatches, her song came back to him. He wanted to call for her and to know that it *was* just a dream, that he had never been to the bush, that the monsters weren't real and he was still in his bed, still a kid, still safe.

But the laughter drowned out the song.

The trunks were denser now, the leaves above tangled in black. On some level he knew he had to be quiet, but that was secondary to the fact that he had to escape, to get clear before the laughter got close enough to cut again.

'Faster, piggy!'

The crack of a gunshot. An explosion of bark from a nearby tree, splinters scouring the skin of his face, the pain blending into all the rest, meaningless. The rustle of birds taking flight above. Simon couldn't breathe. Something was crushing his lungs. His muscles screamed in agony that he couldn't afford to feel.

He ran.

How far had the bush stretched? There was a road here, somewhere. If he could just reach the road, if he could just—

Another gunshot. Another eruption of laughter. Closer.

One leg went out from under him. He landed on his limp, useless arm. Pain slammed into him, so hard it left him winded, so all-encompassing he couldn't even scream, just curl into a ball there in the dirt. He tasted blood. He could hear singing, but he didn't know if it was his mother, himself, or the others.

The others.

He cried. He begged – who, he didn't know, but he did anyway as he forced himself up. He couldn't look at his arm. He knew it was wet with blood. Didn't matter. He stumbled forwards.

'We can see you, little piggy.'

'Help,' he rasped, to the darkness and the trees ahead. 'Please help.'

'It's not fun if you don't run.'

He ran.

Maggie. Maggie had done this. She had brought him here, she had teased him, she had made them stay and now he was going to die. The injustice of it, the monstrousness of it, almost blasted away the pain. He would have been angry if he'd had the strength for it. All he felt, though, was a gaping, empty hopelessness, a knowledge that this wasn't fair, that he had done nothing to deserve this, but that it was going to happen anyway, all because of *her*.

Run.

The panting came suddenly behind him, hot and hungry and savage, the sound of paws landing hard in dried leaves and dirt, the snarl of the dog. He tried to run faster and then he felt the teeth. He screamed as the dog pulled him back, his fingernails tearing as he clawed the dirt and none of the pain mattering because the mongrel had him by the leg, wrenching him from side to side; powerful, *too* powerful. A memory floated ... playing with the family dog as a kid, giggling and poking it until it nipped him. He had been stupid.

A whistle, a gunshot and the teeth were gone, the panting and the paws bounding back to their master. The pain was still there. The dirt he squirmed in was soaked and hot. He tried to stand. His leg wasn't working. He tried again. He was up. Trees warped, the shadows between them growing, reaching for him.

Simon, I don't think you should go on this trip. His mother. He had told her she was being silly, that there was nothing to worry about.

Another gunshot and he was face down, inhaling dirt with each desperate, gasping breath. He got his good arm under him. Tried to push himself up. Couldn't.

And then the pain. A new pain, not sharp but slow and rising like a wave coursing through his whole body, pain that burned white and then became cold. He was shivering. He was submerged in ice. A foot, rolling him over. The treetops above flickering in and out of focus. Wind, rustling branches. The cry of a bird.

And then Steve's face in his. 'Come on, mate. This ain't fun for any of us. Pick up the pace.'

'I can't.'

He heard it without knowing if he'd said it or not. He wanted to go home. He wanted a blanket. He wanted his mum.

'Don't stress, mate. Kayd is gonna show little Maggie a good time. He'll make her forget all about you.'

'Please.'

'Please *what*?'

'Please don't kill me.'

The laughter. It was all he could hear. It filled his ears and crawled through every inch of him.

'My family. They know I'm out here.'

'But they're not here, are they, mate? Families are meant protect each other. But you're all alone.'

Dancing flashes of late-afternoon light through jagged leaves. The slow, dragging movements of a nearby wombat in dry undergrowth. The call of a kookaburra, somewhere far away. The shotgun barrel in his face.

'What are you, mate?'

Stupid, I've been so stupid.

'Say again, mate?'

'Mum.'

'What are you?'

Something sharp, something that made him want to scream but he couldn't scream anymore.

'Mum's not here, mate. We are. Tell us what you are and we'll make it end.'

He didn't know his name anymore. It slipped away as he tried to reach for it. His mother was gone. He couldn't remember the song. There was the dirt, the trees, the gun and the cold, always the cold, everywhere. Why couldn't they feel it?

'Tell us.'

He said it. He said it because it was the only thing he knew. And as he said the words the laughter started again and built.

'Goodnight, piggy.'

CHAPTER ELEVEN

Now

Charlie stood in the darkened living room, eyes on the window. All he could see was the night. He listened intently, waiting for the approaching car that meant Delilah was back and they could leave.

Without quite knowing why, his thoughts returned to the incident in the Adelaide pub. Things were new and fresh then: he and Delilah only a few days past a one-night stand. They'd settled into a corner booth and were chatting and drinking. He'd only just started to suspect the potential of what this might become, the realisation that he wasn't feeling even the beginnings of the unbalanced panic that usually got to him at around this point with a woman. He'd gone to the bar to get a drink, when some arsehole had swaggered over to him. He was tanned, with an unbuttoned flannelette shirt and heavy, steel-capped boots. He might have been around Charlie's age, but he could just as easily have been much younger or much older. The sun had done its job.

'Gotta shout you a drink, mate.' There was the hint of a slur in his voice, but there was purpose to his smirk. 'Pulling a woman like that, looking like you do. What's your secret?'

Charlie shrugged. He wasn't playing this game. One thing he'd learned about Australia – it was full of different variants of a certain kind of guy who was fixated on belittlement and condescension, especially when there was a girl involved.

'Nah, seriously, mate.' He elbowed Charlie, a little too hard to be a joke, a little too gently to be called out on. 'What's your secret? I need some help.'

'No secret,' Charlie said, picking up their drinks. He turned and started to walk back to the table. He saw the boot shoot out in front of his feet just in time. He stopped abruptly, sloshing beer down his front.

'Come on, mate, you can't leave me hanging,' the man said. Charlie noticed a ring of similar-looking guys at a nearby table, following what was happening with leering fascination.

Charlie turned to him. 'We're just having a quiet drink. You mind?'

'Hey, mate, relax there, eh? Bit touchy.' He winked at the others on his table. Charlie could hear sniggers. Delilah stepped up beside him and he felt the hot flush in his cheeks worsen.

'Here she is!' the guy said. 'Was just asking your fella how he swindled you into the sack.'

'Were you?' Delilah said calmly. 'Well, I'm asking you to leave us alone.'

'Aw, don't be like that.'

'Like what?' Delilah said. 'You're the one being a straight-up piece of overcompensating shit. How small does your penis have to be to make you think this is the best way to get a girl's attention?'

The guy blinked at them. An explosion of raucous laughter came from his table. Delilah took Charlie by the elbow and guided him back to the booth, just as a last, desperate attack came from behind: 'Pretty tough, mate, getting a girl to stand up for you.'

Charlie sat, eyes on the drinks. He didn't feel much like staying now. There was an unpleasant, churning shame in his gut.

'Ignore them,' Delilah said gently. 'They're jealous.'

He pretended it was all fine and tried not to let his relief show when the table of loudmouth pricks left after another few minutes.

That night hadn't come up again, but it had established a precedent that Charlie wanted to displace: that he was a pushover, too soft and gentle to confront anything uncomfortable. Whatever Delilah said she liked about him, he didn't have to like it about himself.

But there was a big difference between being brave and being stupid.

It had been a mistake to get involved in this. He'd had this feeling many times before – been in situations that had just *felt* wrong. Working with people he wasn't sure about, taking opportunities that looked great on paper but somehow didn't sit right. He'd always told himself he was being paranoid and inevitably, every time, things blew up in his face. He had that same feeling again now. Worse. It had started the moment the car pulled up and only grown, an ominous acidic discomfort gnawing at his guts.

But he couldn't have just left. Of course he couldn't. Not when somebody needed his help. Not when he was supposed to be a nurse but had spent the last year drinking his way across a country where responsibility couldn't find him.

He turned back to the girl on the couch. She hadn't moved. He'd cleaned her wounds as best as he could, had even managed to suture the lacerations and bandage her, but it wasn't enough. She needed a hospital. Pain relief, a tetanus shot and definitely antibiotics. Maybe a transfusion.

Sitting on the edge of an armchair nearby, Allie fidgeted, keeping an eye on the unconscious girl.

Charlie's gaze returned to the window.

'Who do you think she is?' Allie asked.

Charlie rested his head against the glass. Darkness filled his eyes. He closed them. He could think of only one answer to that question that made sense and if he was right, it meant that he really had made a big mistake trying to help.

'She has to be a criminal,' Allie said.

'Yeah,' Charlie said. 'I guess so.'

It was the sole reason he could think of why somebody wouldn't want to call an emergency number when they were hurt as badly as she was. If that was the case, then he was standing here fretting about the threat her injury posed her and ignoring the very obvious threat she posed them.

'Have you checked her car?' Allie asked.

'We drove over in it.'

'But did you search it? There might be something in it that can tell us something.'

'Your grandpa stayed out there for a while. I'd guess he was looking around. He didn't say anything.'

Allie snorted. 'He wouldn't. He never says anything about anything.'

Charlie looked at her.

'My dad always said that was Grandad's big problem,' Allie said. 'Or at least, that's the censored version he told me. I overheard him and Mum talking enough times. Booze and drugs and stuff were the real problems, apparently.'

'Drugs?' Charlie looked towards the roadhouse. Frank didn't seem the type.

'I dunno,' Allie said. 'Just what I heard. I never really knew him growing up. I think he was in jail for some of it. Grandma was around, until she died. But Frank was a pretty controversial topic.'

Charlie went to speak, then stopped himself. It was hardly the time and hardly his business.

'Were you going to ask why I'm staying here?'

Charlie shrugged.

Allie looked away. 'Because my parents are getting a divorce but don't have the guts to tell me. Dad thought I should come here while one of them moves out. Mum cracked the shits because Grandad's supposed to be bad news. Dad reckons he's cleaned up his act. Dad won the argument because Mum's been cheating on him.'

Charlie wasn't sure what to say to that, so he went for the slightly safer question. 'Do you think Frank has cleaned up his act?'

'Yeah,' Allie said. 'I sort of looked the place over the first day I was here. No booze, no white powders, no nothing. I always got the impression from my parents that he was really fucked-up, but he just seems … quiet.'

'Maybe he's fucked-up in a different way. Seen and done stuff that he's trying to get his head around or put behind him. I'm not saying he's an angel, but if he's come out the other side and is clean now, it might be worth giving your grandfather a chance. I mean, look at her.' He nodded to the girl. 'He didn't have to help her. None of us did. But here we are.'

'What if …' Allie looked uncertain, like she was trying to find the words. 'I mean, if someone did this to her. What if she deserved it? If we're helping the wrong person?'

'What if we're not?' Charlie asked evenly. 'You can't assume the worst in people. They can surprise you. They can surprise themselves, as well. That thing I said before, it cuts both ways. It's why you can't ever judge people too harshly, because most people have no idea who they really are beneath who they *think* they are.'

Allie didn't reply.

The room was silent. Charlie checked the girl again. Still breathing. Still unconscious. He knelt and took her pulse. Steady. He stood, considered, then turned to Allie. 'You know, I think we should look in the car.'

'Can we just leave her?' Allie asked.

'We'll only be a few metres away,' Charlie said. 'I think you're right. It could help.'

Allie glanced at the girl.

Together they walked into the hall and out the front door. Standing on the porch, Charlie paused. He couldn't see the roadhouse from here. Something twisted in his chest, some horrible feeling that seemed to push him to run towards it as fast as he could.

Instead, he went to the car.

When he opened the driver-side door, it looked the same as it had before. Allie was checking the back seat. Charlie's eyes moved over everything – the keys were gone, he noted. Frank must have lifted them. He was about to grab the backpack from the passenger seat when he noticed a gleam of metal on the floor underneath the driver seat. He reached down and lifted the jacket that covered whatever it was. For several seconds he just stared at it, that twisting in his chest getting worse.

'Holy shit.'

He hadn't notice Allie open the passenger-side front door. They met each other's gaze again.

'She is a criminal,' Allie said, just as they heard the distant sound of a gunshot.

'Delilah,' Charlie whispered.

It happened in seconds. Before Allie could even shout after him, Charlie was gone; a movement then nothing in the dark. She was alone with the car and the house and the gently swaying grass.

And the girl.

She didn't move. She couldn't. The silence was closing around her.

She made herself breathe. Like the counsellor had said. In and out, five times.

She reached over and picked up the shotgun. It was heavy, much heavier than it looked. She shut the passenger-side door, then rounded the car and shut the other door. She turned to the house. In the night it didn't look comforting. A looming, evil shadow in which waited something deadly.

Allie's hands tightened around the gun.

She walked back inside.

The girl lay still on the couch. Allie looked for any sign of movement. Any sign she was faking. But she might as well have been dead.

She walked down the hall and into her tiny room, and closed the door behind her. There was barely enough space here for the few things she had brought with her from the city. Her clothes were piled all over the floor. A few books sat on a cramped desk.

She got to her knees, then lay down on her side, facing the door and slid under the bed, where she could clearly see the bottom of the door. Trying not to make a sound, she pointed the shotgun outwards. If seconds or minutes passed, she had no idea. Time had lost meaning.

She heard a floorboard creak.

CHAPTER TWELVE

Then

The stench was the first thing Maggie noticed. It was pungent, rotten, like meat left out in the sun too long. She squinted in the dark, trying to make out what she was looking at. There were shapes hanging from the roof. She took another step forwards.

It was as though someone had punched her in the stomach. She staggered, then her knees hit the ground and she was vomiting. Her heart was pounding in her ears and her body was shaking. A hot horror filled her. She retched again.

Across the rough ceiling, from wall to wall, was a long metal bar, over which hung several thick chains with large hooks attached. And on the hooks were bloodied, misshapen lumps of flesh that had once been people.

Some had been here longer than others. The skin was cracked and brown, hardened and leathery. Those were the easiest to look at. They resembled humans the least. It was the fresher ones, the ones that still had arms and legs and heads, that made her sick again.

In total there were six bodies. Four hooks still hung low to the ground and empty. Following the chains with her eyes, Maggie saw that they led to winches at the far end of the room, placed on the dirt floor, the dirt floor that was mostly dark red with blood.

It took Maggie three attempts to stand. Her brain was working overtime putting it all together. *They brought people here and strung them up on the hooks then ... Then bled them dry and cut bits off until—*

She had thought she had nothing left to throw up. She was wrong.

She had to move fast. Nobody knew she was here and that meant she could use the cover of the trees to run until she found a road again. The moment she could flag down a car she would get as far down the road as she could in any direction and—

She stopped. Her heart had slowed but still felt loud, every beat making her body shake more.

Her bag, with her money, was back at the house.

She pushed that away. It didn't matter. Losing her money was nothing compared to ending up on one of these hooks.

But a frantic voice in her head persisted: *You're fucked if you leave it, too. You can't get a job, you'll be found and—*

She shook her head, trying to push away the thoughts, but as she did, she heard a sound behind her.

She spun. Kev, still in his singlet and jeans, stood in the doorway. He didn't look angry. On the contrary he looked amused as he took her in, hands in his pockets, as relaxed as if he was overseeing another barbecue. 'Having a bit of a stickybeak, are you, love?'

Maggie started to back away.

Kev didn't move. 'The hunting bounty is never pretty. We try to keep the sheilas from seeing it, you know?'

'They ... The women don't know?' Maggie's voice sounded steadier than she felt.

Kev seemed to be considering her. 'Tell me. That limp dick you came in with. He impress ya? Excite ya?'

Maggie wanted to look at the door, to gauge the distance, whether she could make it, could get past Kev. She didn't like her chances if he saw that.

'Nah,' he said. 'Didn't think so. Pretty boy from the city, screaming for his Mum at the first sign of anything a bit rougher. Can't much blame him, though. That's how the cities breed 'em. What they churn out, they're weeds. Not men. Nah. Men fight. Men protect. Men hunt and men kill. Men spill blood when they have to and don't give a shit as long as their family stays in one piece. This.' He nodded to one of the bodies. 'It's about all that and more. You come to this town, you wanna be a part of it: you hunt. And when you taste the hot blood for the first time, you either like it or you don't. If you don't.' He shrugged. 'Well, that's the difference between the hunters and the hunted, ain't it?'

'These people.' Maggie did her best to emphasise the second word, even though her voice felt about to betray her. 'They wronged you?'

'Pigs don't wrong hunters,' Kev said. 'They just drew the shit straw. Evolution wise.'

It was too much. Too monstrous and terrifying to comprehend. Their arrival, the gunshots in the woods, Trent walking back from the shed the night before …

'Steve and his girl, Kate, they're damn good at drawing the pigs,' Kev said, a note of pride in his voice. 'Usually they have to get out there and charm the fuckers back here. But you. You came right to us. Practically gift-wrapped.'

He stepped into the shed. Maggie felt something graze the back of her neck and jumped away, a horrified tremor going through her. She had touched one of the bodies.

Kev cackled, as if this was the funniest thing he had ever seen. 'There you go. Better leave this stuff to the fellas.' He was walking leisurely forwards, but he paused to look at one of the bodies with something close to fondness. 'Steve's a natural. Only blooded two years back, though if it was up to him, he would have been out on the hunt the day he learned to walk. And the shit he comes up with once they're back here in the shed. You wouldn't believe how long some of these fuckers last. Every now and then the lads end up killing them in the bush … but hey, we all get carried away and boys will be boys. I wasn't much better at their age.'

His eyes moved back to Maggie. He started for her again.

'You're going to kill me,' she said.

'What, now?' He chuckled. 'No fun in that. It's been a while since old Kev got one all to himself. Nah, I'm gonna enjoy myself.'

He was about to pass under the bar. He took his hands from his pockets. One of them held a flick knife, the rusted blade exposed with a jerk of his wrist.

Maggie didn't think. She dived sideways. But Kev's fist moved fast, way faster than she could have guessed, colliding with her cheek. Before she even knew what was happening, she was in the congealed blood and dust, face throbbing. One of the low hanging hooks dangled in her contracting vision. She forced herself up onto her knees.

'I'll give you this.' Kev's voice, amused but with a bite of vicious excitement beneath it. 'You're a tough little bitch. No crying. Doing your best to stand up. I've seen blokes out cold after a hit like that.'

Maggie managed to get one leg under herself. She reached for the hook.

'Gotta say, it's almost a waste, doing you here.' Kev was close now, right above her. 'It'd be something to see you out on the hunt.'

Maggie stood fast. Kev lurched towards her right as she brought the hook up and through the fleshy underside of his jaw.

Warm blood doused her hands. She shoved the hook upwards, feeling bone crack as it found home. Kev screamed and Maggie let go as he clawed at his wound. She ran to the winch and turned it hard, again and again. Kev's screams got louder as he was pulled upwards off his feet.

She turned, looking past Kev's kicking feet to the still-open door. Somebody would hear him if they hadn't already. Her eyes landed on his dropped knife.

She snatched it up and, without a moment for thought or doubt, cut his throat. She stepped back from the spray of blood and for just a flash she was back at the top of a darkened staircase as widened eyes fell away from her, a mouth opened halfway in a cry of mingled terror and accusation as something terrible and all too familiar filled her and then it was just the silence, the silence that should have been crushing. Instead it was sweet with the new and intoxicating taste of freedom.

Everything seemed to slow down. The room was still, as if frozen in time. Kev's body moved gently as the chain, jostled by his writhing, swayed slower and slower.

Maggie collapsed against the wall, breathing heavily. She wasn't sure she could stand, let alone walk. She made herself look at Kev. There was no guilt or revulsion, no sudden weight pulling her down. Just the grim satisfaction of a cleared obstacle. Just like last time.

She needed to leave. But without her cash she wasn't much better off out in the world than she was here. She looked down at herself. There was blood on her hands, but none on her clothes.

In the corner of the shed was a steel sink. She did her best to scrub the blood away; anybody looking at her for more than a second would notice it, but she didn't intend to let anyone look at her for more than a second. She scrubbed at her hands harder, aware of her breathing picking up, of Kev's laughter, still loud in her head because she knew that laughter, had heard it before. Hamish on the rock in the bush late at night, arms outstretched and Ted shivering in boxer shorts in front of him.

'It's just a little jump,' Hamish had crowed. 'I do it every time – the water at the bottom is deep.'

'I don't want to.' Ted's voice was cracking.

'Leave him alone, Hamish,' Maggie, snapping twigs under the tree, said. 'You've never jumped in that pool.'

'Fuck off,' Hamish said. 'Just because you haven't seen it.'

'Ben told us we had to be back at the fire for dinner,' Ted said. 'Please can we—'

'What, you think wimps get dinner?' Hamish said. 'Jump in the fucking pool. You're going nowhere until you do.'

Maggie stood, dropping the twigs. She was annoyed, more than anything. Later, Ted would cry and she would have to comfort him and it was all because Hamish couldn't tell when a joke had gone too far. 'Come on, leave it.'

Hamish took a step towards Ted. In the dark he was a looming silhouette, bigger even than his nearly six feet. 'Jump, pussy. Come on. You can do it.'

'Hamish.' Maggie moved for him.

'Jump!' Hamish yelled.

Now, in the shed, Maggie looked into the pooling water of the sink, blood spreading through it like ink.

'Hamish, stop!'

'Jump!'

Maggie running and then Hamish's hand hard in her chest, sending her sprawling and gasping for air. Hamish charging and with a pathetic yelp Ted stepping back, tripping. Then the scream that ended in a crack which filled the night and sent searing ice through every inch of Maggie's body as she stared up at Hamish, tall and unmoving on the rock, the stretch of night behind him.

Once she was as clean as she could manage, she pocketed Kev's knife and, keeping her eyes away from the bodies,

knew she was in here and not replying which implied she was either trying to hide or—

She glanced over her shoulder.

Or she had escaped through a back window.

Footsteps light and fast, she moved back to the bedroom and eased the window open as quietly as she could, before hurrying back out into the hall, to the front door. Holding the knife, she put her ear to the door. Not hearing anything, she opened the door a fraction. The street was empty now, but she could hear the crack of dried grass and the rustling of bushes from behind the house.

The scared pig was predictable. Or so they thought.

Across the road was a ute and, like many of the others she had seen in this town, its tray was loaded with various things: toolboxes, a tarp, a couple of steel drums. Squeezing through the door and then quietly pulling it closed behind her, she scanned the clear street again then moved low and noiselessly across the road. After a furtive check down the side of the house to confirm that nobody had returned yet, she crawled into the ute's tray, pulled the musty tarp over herself and lay down flat on her back between several metal boxes. The steel beneath her was hot from the sun. With every breath she was inhaling dirt. Early evening light penetrated the flimsy tarp, making her close her eyes.

It seemed like suicide even to her. But if they guessed she had run, then the whole town would be looking for her, especially if they had found Kev and, after years of hunting, nobody would question basic human instinct. She had run, and so they would look to the bush. Not the heart of their home.

Being here while all eyes looked outwards was a good place to start, but it did not provide a clear way free. She forced her brain to focus; there was scarcely any sound on the street, which surely meant that Kev hadn't been found yet. That meant her advantage hadn't yet reached its strongest point. That would come when the enemy was angry. Because rage could be just as overpowering as fear.

CHAPTER THIRTEEN

Now

Frank knew this feeling. He knew it and he hated it.

It had been different, back then. As he lay side by side in the dark of the trees with his mate Wayne, scope to his eye and heart pounding a rhythm in his ears. Waiting for the deer to cross his sight. His finger hard on the trigger, ready to squeeze.

'It's about the waiting,' Wayne had said earlier that night, passing Frank the bottle as he bent over the table to rack another line. 'Being still and focusing and putting everything into that fucking moment. Then – *bam*!' He clapped and did the line. He sniffed hard, ran his little finger around his nostril and winked at Frank. 'The moment's yours.'

The moment's yours. Frank had repeated that to himself, lying in the dirt as the booze and the speed pulsed through his veins and everything vanished except the wait for the flash of movement that told him it was time to act, that took him a million miles and years away from the screaming baby and Amber crying back home, away from the things that had made him so angry, the things that sometimes he imagined when he pulled that trigger and the moment became his.

Back against the wall, staring at the inside of the counter, Delilah silent next to him, Frank tried to focus. Waiting was different when you weren't in control. When you weren't waiting for your moment, but for the moment to come for you. The air was charged, ready to ignite. The minutes were racing by, far too fast. Five had passed since the ultimatum had been given. Five precious minutes already gone, and he was no closer to figuring out a solution. He felt trapped in a terrible stalemate; he didn't want to move from this spot in case they decided to bring the ultimatum forwards.

'Well, mate?' the voice from outside was back. 'It's been five. Can't be that hard to work this out, can it? I know you've got a little girl in there. You're scaring the shit out of her for a dog that needs to be put down.'

Silence as the man waited for an answer. Delilah met Frank's eyes. Neither of them spoke.

'Suit yourself then, mate. Think fast.'

Huddled in the storeroom, as the smell of piss hung in the air and the metal shelf dug into his back, Greg thought about Keith Echols. Cocky, smiling and polite every time Greg had shouted an order across the office, but always in a way that felt off, even if you couldn't put your finger on why. It was impossible to define, impossible to catch him in whatever act Greg was sure he was guilty of.

At first, he had brushed if off. Keith wasn't as senior as Greg, and was probably just a bit of shit-stirrer. But after a while, he couldn't. Not when he saw the averted eyes, heard the snatches of giggles that ceased whenever he entered a room. Greg had always thought he was in control. In the office, in his home, he'd been in charge, made the decisions, been firm but fair, commanded respect, even admiration. The situation with Echols, however, was something else. Keith never made a mistake, never tripped up, never said or did anything that would give Greg the excuse he dearly needed to fire the smug little fucker.

When Jane – lovely, gentle Jane who Greg thought about more than he cared to admit – stopped laughing at his jokes and started sounding pitying every time he asked her to do something, he knew it wasn't just in his head. He stopped sleeping. Things that he had managed to ignore, things that he had been able to look away from, started to loom large in his peripheral vision. Seeing those first grey hairs. Feeling the beginnings of a tiredness that made him give up on ever going to the gym. Looking at Phillipa and wondering when she had started to look so worn down. Knowing that he looked even worse.

He had started drinking more. He'd always loved a beer after work, but soon it became two, then three, then Phillipa was asking if everything was okay and even *her* expression turned pitying when he snapped that he was fine. And still Keith beamed and joked and twisted the world that had once been Greg's around his little finger.

That gnawing emptiness in his gut that took the form of a horrible, persistent question: *Is this really it*? At what point had he gone from alpha male to a middle-aged, fat joke?

Greg was already tipsy when he turned up to the staff party. Not enough to be obvious, but enough to make him want to drink more when he saw Keith and Jane cosy in the corner together. And drinking more made him feel braver, and the braver he felt the greater the certainty in his gut that he could fix this, that all it would take was a decisive gesture to put Keith in his place and everything would go back to normal.

He hadn't planned on doing anything, though. Not until Sam suggested he get a cab, not until he saw Keith and Jane were getting closer, whispering to each other, their knees touching. Greg shoved Sam away. He swaggered over and made a crack about Keith's suit, the one he always wore to work, the cheap one. Said something about the bastard being paid enough to afford better, or did he think the job wasn't good enough for him to at least be presentable? After all, Greg said, voice louder and more confident by the second, Keith was never going to get Greg's job if he couldn't dress for it. But then, he was never going to get Greg's job, full stop.

And then – fuck, even the memory made him seethe. That patronising smile, the pat on the arm, the gentle suggestion. 'Maybe it's time you headed home, mate.' So Greg hit him.

And for a moment, just a moment, the pity was gone and it was replaced by the contorted fury that Greg had known was there all along as Keith lunged at him. Greg was ready, so ready to put him on the floor and see everyone wowed back into realising who was in charge.

But that didn't happen. Greg told himself he had got another hit in before Keith took him down, but he couldn't remember for sure. What he remembered with too much clarity for a hundred bottles to wipe out was how easily the younger man had held him down, how Greg's full-bodied attempts to throw him off had done nothing, like his muscles were water. It didn't matter how much he snarled and struggled and spat, Keith just held him down, not even bothering to hit him again because he wasn't worth it and everyone was watching, either horrified or openly filming.

He did what he could, after that. Pulled the right strings, made sure Keith was gone, managed to hang onto his own job. He had to mine all the capital he'd earned over the years to make the whole thing go away. And while none of his colleagues ever mentioned Keith or what had happened again, they also wouldn't even look at him. Responses to his questions were monosyllabic. The laughs at his jokes were short and forced.

The decline didn't stop. More grey hairs in his comb in the morning. His renewed determination to work out yielding five sit-ups that left him wheezing and light-headed. Phillipa rarely coming home after 'girls' nights', and when she did it was stinking of cologne she didn't even bother to hide. And his children, who once had at least tried to look up from their phones when he spoke to them, now rarely mustered a grunt. He had become completely irrelevant in his own life.

He had felt for so long like he was rotting from the inside out, like he was just pretending to be Greg McRae. But he had told himself it was a phase, just a bad patch that he would come out the other side of.

This – this dusty storeroom in the middle of nowhere – felt like the cruel punchline to a vicious joke. His desperate, last-ditch attempt to take control, to show them all by burning everything down and seeing how they liked a world without him, had led him here. That whole drive he had looked for whatever it was that would let him feel like Greg McRae again, hoping to find some semblance of what he had missed for so long. Instead, the opposite had happened. Greg McRae didn't matter anymore. He didn't give a shit about Greg McRae. All that mattered was getting away from this nightmare as fast as he could.

He got to his feet. He had taken one step towards the back door when he heard movement and turned.

The girl, Delilah, had entered the storeroom; she glanced from him to the back door. Her brow furrowed.

'Just ... just checking if it's locked,' Greg said.

'I don't know how much difference that's going to make,' Delilah said. 'But sure, go ahead.'

Greg walked over and placed a hand on the doorknob. It would be so easy to turn it now and slip outside. Throw himself to the lions and hope for mercy.

He twitched it then walked back to his spot. He could see the damp patch left by his piss-soaked trousers and a deep, ugly shame reared up in place of fear.

'How are you doing?' Delilah asked.

He didn't know how she could sound so calm. Her voice was steady, despite her pale face. Maybe only he was this pathetic. He looked at the patch again.

'Don't worry about it,' Delilah said. 'At least you pissed yourself for a good reason. I've done it plenty just because I was drunk.' She shot him what was supposed to be a conspiratorial smile.

'What's this all about?' Greg asked.

The smile faded. 'There was this … this girl. Turned up here, badly hurt. Covered in mud and blood. Her leg was pretty much torn to pieces. We took her back to Frank's house, behind us, then these pricks came looking for her.'

'They want you to turn her over.'

Delilah nodded.

Greg swallowed. 'Listen—'

Delilah shook her head. 'Frank already said no.'

'And he's the boss?'

'It's his house.'

'It's our lives.'

Delilah looked at him for a long time. 'There's no guarantee they'll leave us alone even if we give them the girl. We're witnesses to something fucked up. If they did that to her …' She shrugged. 'We're better off with the leverage.'

'We're outnumbered,' Greg said. 'How long are we supposed to be able to defend ourselves?'

Delilah said nothing.

CHAPTER FOURTEEN

Then

Maggie knew how to keep still, how to ignore the itches and the aches and resist every urge to do something about them. She'd spent much of her childhood squeezed into wardrobes or else trying to be invisible, eyes closed tight, hugging herself as she'd waited for the next bottle to slow the crashing and yelling from outside as her father's hoarse rasp demanded she come out, to be the moving target her mother's departure had denied him. The tears would inevitably come and, with them, the desire to scream, to burst out and attack – for all the good that would do. Even back then, she had known there was no point: that silence and stillness were her best bet and so she had held a lid down on the fire and waited.

This was no different, she tried to tell herself. Even though it was. Even though the cost of capture here was a lot worse than some bruising she'd have to explain away at school. Maggie concentrated on keeping her heart rate slow and her breathing steady, never once letting go of the knife, trying to push away the spikes of panic that threatened every time she heard a voice nearby. But nothing she could make out sounded the alarm; people asked for cigarettes, offered beers and talked about such mundane things that it was hard to believe there was a shed of rotting human corpses just metres away.

It was only after what felt like a couple of hours that the tone changed. She heard faint yelling and snapped retorts.

'—can't have fuckin' gone far. I want that house torn apart.'

'She wouldn't still be in the house, but.'

'That was the last place she was seen, right? Pull your fucking head in.'

Breathe.

'What if I find her first?'

'Rules are different, you dopey cunt. We share this one.'

Her hand tightened around the knife.

There were more yells, more snatches of arguments followed by the slamming of car doors. Once or twice her breath caught as she heard footsteps nearing the ute, but no-one pulled the tarp away. No-one would think she would be stupid enough to hide in the middle of it all, buried beneath a sight they saw every day. Game ran when it was threatened.

She was sore and thirsty. She needed to go to the bathroom, but she refused to let herself move. Not until, even through the tarp, she felt the temperature drop and the last of the voices fell away. Finally the evening became still and the only sounds were the occasional harsh calls of birds. She wondered if that was a bad sign. If she should have been hearing chaos and rage. But no. If the boar gored a well-loved hunter, everyone didn't go out to track it down. That would alert the boar, especially at night. No, you sent the best and let them do their job.

She closed her eyes. Still quiet. Eventually, she raised the knife and pulled away the tarp.

The street was empty. She looked in every direction, then, forcing her stiff limbs into action, she jumped out of the ute's tray and landed light on the dust of the road. Crouching, she listened, waiting for an opening door, a sliding window, a yell. Nothing. Terrified by how exposed she felt, she crossed the road swiftly and ran down the side of her house, to where whoever had been looking for her earlier had gone. She watched the ground, taking care to miss twigs or leaves. Her footfalls were dancer light, just like Ben had taught her. *Ready, not rigid.* She reached the back of the house and paused. It was a cloudless, starry sky above and her visibility was good, but that would change as soon as she passed the first few trees. She gave herself a moment before hurrying for the thick trunks and the darkness beyond. Within seconds, her pace slowed and she was moving tentatively in the inky black, hand outstretched, ears straining for any suspicious sounds. The ground below her was uneven, dropping off and rising up in unpredictable shifts that she had to be careful not to be tripped up by. She wanted to run, but she forced that instinct down, crushed it away and made herself stay steady and quiet. A night shadow, nothing else.

She moved like this for a while, pausing any time she heard a cracking twig or a rustle of bushes. But even as her eyes adjusted, it remained hard to be sure of what was in front of her, what was a trunk, a branch, an arm holding a gun. There was a small comfort in that. For all that they were evil, the men hunting her were human too. They would be facing the same limitations she was, and the thought gave her a surge of defiant hope.

The deeper she moved into the trees, the more she became aware of the smells: of eucalyptus leaves and animal shit and, above all, her own odour, hot and sweaty. Would that be obvious to her hunters? She was basing all her assumptions on speculation, but some things she just had no idea about. She wanted to believe that this was an uncommon situation for them, but then maybe assuming that was arrogant. Maybe every one of the bodies in that shed had tried to be clever. That thought threatened to blow away any sense of control she thought she had. She pushed it down.

She stopped, hand resting against a trunk, trying to quell away her trembling. She took a deep breath and smelt water.

She wasn't sure she had ever noticed how it smelt before. But there it was, somehow fresh despite the accompanying scent of mud. Shuffling slowly, she moved towards it, feet inching until they felt a slight decline. She crouched down and moved on hands and knees until the dirt turned soft and damp then became mud, then water.

She drank without worrying about the taste, before stopping and listening again, unsure how loud she had been. There didn't seem to be any sounds out of the ordinary.

The mud had enveloped her right hand and she winced at the loud sucking, squelching noise it made as she pulled it free. She reached forwards to wash it off in the stream but hesitated. Her eyes were getting better, but even with the snatches of moonlight from the gaps in the canopy her muddied hand vanished into darkness.

There was no point in being too meticulous. It was an imperfect disguise at best, but she was careful as she covered every inch of herself in mud. It was cold and uncomfortable and the taste seemed to infiltrate even her tightly shut mouth. Once she was done, walking felt strange and almost indecent, like she should shower before going any further. She looked down at her hands; she could see movement, but not much else. She was as dark as the night around her.

And so, still slow and deliberate, she moved on through the trees. She could feel the mud drying on her skin, the warm air turning it hard and brittle – this cover had a time limit. She wasn't one hundred percent sure what direction she should be heading in, but she knew where the town was and knew she had to head away from it. She kept listening for gunshots or shouts, scanning for beams of torchlight or the gleam of some stray moonlight reflecting off the barrel of a gun, but the night and the trees remained undisturbed. She kept moving.

When she saw the car she ducked behind the nearest tree before she had quite registered what she was even looking at. There had been no attempt to hide it, but in this kind of thick darkness it was almost unnecessary. She was less than two metres away when she noticed it. Her eyes went immediately to the windscreen, looking for the shapes of people inside, but it seemed empty. And familiar.

A horrible swooping feeling in her stomach came with the recognition. Simon's station wagon, abandoned in the trees.

She gave herself a few more minutes until she was convinced there was no-one here, then she made her move, circling round and approaching the rear of the car. In a tiny snatch of starlight that pushed through the leaves and branches above, she saw something thick and glistening on the ground. Her heart like a drum, she knelt and reached out a hand. Blood had soaked the dirt all around the car. Something in her chest contracted.

Her own words then, clear in her ears, certain and assured and hateful, one of the last things she had said to Simon before he ran.

Are you always this melodramatic?

And then, echoing from years earlier.

But he's harmless. Ignore him and he'll get bored.

Her fault. Then and now.

She punched the dirt. She allowed just a moment of shaking before she stood and headed for the driver-side door.

She knew as soon as she reached for the handle that something was wrong, the instinct confirmed a second later by pain, pain like nothing she had ever felt before, a slicing, tearing burning in her right leg that made her crumple and bite down on her wrist, drawing blood before she would let herself scream. She fell hard against the metal of the car. She tried to move but something held fast, something that wrenched at her leg. Her ears rang. She reached down and felt her ankle. That was a mistake. The pain seared again as she felt the metal jaws and jagged teeth that had snapped shut on her leg. A trap, left for anyone trying to use this car to escape. And she had been stupid enough to try.

Gritting her teeth, her eyes streaming and the occasional whimper escaping no matter how hard she tried, she pulled apart the trap. She felt metal tearing at flesh and even the smallest effort to rest weight on her leg made her want to collapse. The trigger mechanism she'd stepped on raised and clicked back into place, the trap an open circle of serrated metal again. She moved clear, pulling herself up on the car, then she heard snarling and grunting that seemed to come out of nowhere. She saw the bulk of the dog barrelling forwards, saw its wild eyes gleaming in what little moonlight there was. She fumbled for the knife as its jaws clamped on her injured leg and the pain exploded, white hot and blinding.

She tried to regain her balance but fell to the ground; then she was being dragged backwards. *The knife.* She could feel the hilt in her white-knuckle grip. She twisted around, her eyes found Blue's, and then she brought the knife down and into the dog's jugular, slamming it home again and again before the dog could make another sound. She kept stabbing until the animal was limp, its blood mingled with the mud that coated her.

She crawled back towards the car. Avoiding the trap, she managed to get the door open and pull herself inside, but running a hand around the steering wheel told her what should have been obvious: the keys were gone. She willed herself to ignore the pain – *just a few more seconds, give me just a few more* – and checked the handbrake. Off. Either they had rolled it off the road, or Simon had left it here.

That rage, burning as bright as the pain. She clenched her teeth and waited for the wave of dizzying agony to pass. Looking out into the darkness, seeing nothing, she knew.

They're here.

Pain had to join fear. She tried to stand and fell back into the seat. Hands fumbling and shaking, she raised part of her muddied shirt to her mouth and using her teeth she tore at it until she held several strips of fabric.

She wrapped her leg as tightly as she could, trying not to think of the mud getting in her wound. Once she was sure she'd stemmed most of the bleeding she prepared herself, then, relying on her good leg, stood. She swayed and her head spun. She fell forwards and landed on her hands, beside the teeth of the trap. Crawling, panting and crying, she pulled herself over to the dead dog. She grabbed it by the back of the neck and tried to shift closer. The fucker was heavy.

The sound of grinding dirt beneath the dog was loud, too loud. She pulled again and again, bit by bit dragging the carcass around until they were both in front of the car. She paused, catching her breath as she leaned against the bumper bar. She forced her focus back to the bush around her. Still no sound of an approach. Back around the car, to where the trap lay open. It was no wonder she hadn't seen it. You'd have to know it was there to notice the zigzag of dark, rusted metal against the ground. With both hands she pulled it towards her. It was lighter than she imagined but her strength was starting to flag. Seconds felt like hours but finally the trap lay in front of Blue's corpse. Almost invisible in the shadow of the car's front.

She stood. Feeling was slipping away from her leg now. She thought of the road and freedom. Then she opened her mouth and screamed. It echoed through the night and the bush, as if coming from every direction, the panic closing in and threatening to shatter whatever control she had left.

The last of the scream bounced from the close-circling trees. The pain didn't matter. She got to her feet and, breaths ragged and painful in her throat, limped around behind the car. She moved as fast as she could, but it was still slow, too slow. Her leg weighed her down. She had just reached the boot of the car when she heard dry leaves shaking and twigs breaking underfoot. She froze. She saw the shape burst out of the trees and hurry to the front of the car.

'Blue?'

Then the metal snap, and his scream filled the night.

Using her whole body, Maggie pushed the back of the car as hard as she could. She pushed and pushed and finally it started to roll. She stepped back, heard desperate scuffling then a crunch, sharp and grinding and awful. She was moving again, making herself stand through the protests of her muscles and her leg about to collapse under her. Half-falling, she reached the front of the car, saw Matty – stuck partway under it, eyes finding hers, mouth opening to scream again.

She plunged the knife through his eye socket and pushed until he was still. Then she wrenched the knife free and stood. Dizzy and swaying, she lurched away from the car, reached out for a tree, missed it and fell hard in the dirt. The knife was gone. Wind in the trees and no other noise. The world around her empty of life.

Her body felt light and her thoughts swam. She could drift off to sleep here. At least asleep her leg wouldn't hurt so damn much. But something was calling her back to reality, some distant sound, some—

'Hurry the fuck up, Matty went this way.' She recognised Steve's voice.

She tried to stand and move. She fell again then, slower this time, stood. The voices got louder and clearer as she clambered away from the car, stumbling every few seconds as she moved back towards the river. She could hear the voices rise behind her – they had found Matty. She had to run, but she *couldn't* run and the bandage around her calf felt sodden. Pain surged. She fell face first into the mud, inhaling the damp earth, the gentle gurgle of the water drowning out all other sounds.

She rolled onto her back. There was a gap in the trees over the river and she could see stars. Funny, that stars could exist in the same world as the people she was running from. She reached out a hand and felt a rock just as someone ran past – only metres from where she lay – and then slid down the slope in the direction of the water.

She couldn't move. The pain was an anchor holding her to the ground. He would turn and he would find her and it would be just like that night when she had gone into Hamish's room and launched herself at him, the night he had held her down and hit her again and again until Ben and Debbie had pulled him off. Just like the time her father had backhanded her when she'd forgotten her shoes in the hall, and left her bleeding in the doorway. Just like all the others.

The fire rose, then and now.

She stood slowly. The pain from her leg had become a blaze, filling her whole body. She turned in time to see

Kayden do the same, his eyes going wide at the dark muddy creature rising in front of him before the rock took him in the face and they fell together, Maggie smashing his face again and again, bone breaking and flesh tearing, wet and weak through curbed cries until her hand was hot with blood and she couldn't make out his face because there was nothing left to make out.

There was no more sound. The night was happening somewhere else to someone else. All she knew was the mud and the water, the blood and the rock.

Something gleaming at the water's edge, something Kayden had dropped. A shotgun. She took it then, falling on her first two attempts, stood again and limped away from the river, back towards the car. She had held guns before, in the bush, with Ben. Back then they had felt uncomfortable, too heavy. Now, this one felt right. Kayden's blood on her, Steve ahead in the dark, the weapon in her hands. It was so right it hurt.

'Oi, Kayden? You get the slut?'

She didn't slow or quieten. She could see the shape of the car ahead and Steve in front of it.

'You gonna fuckin' answer me, cunt?'

Maggie raised the shotgun and fired.

The night burst apart. Steve was thrown back into the car. His cricket bat went flying. He staggered, clutching his stomach. His hand came away bloody.

'Fuck,' he managed.

Maggie moved slowly through the dark, shotgun still raised, finger tight on the trigger.

Steve against the car, barely standing, looked up at her. He coughed blood.

'Is Simon dead?' Maggie asked.

Steve's voice was weak and wet. 'Why do you care? The bastard left you.'

Maggie moved over to the dropped bat. Keeping the gun on Steve, she knelt, ignoring the tear of resistance from her leg.

'You're gonna bleed out like a bitch,' Steve said, every word a rasp. 'You try to—' He coughed again. 'Try to run and they'll follow.'

Maggie picked up the bat, lowering the shotgun. She stood.

'Is Simon dead?'

Steve tried to laugh. It came out choked and feeble. 'You know what he told us? He said—'

One handed, Maggie swung the bat hard across his face. With a crack Steve hit the ground, spluttering, wheezing. He tried to stand. He couldn't.

'Is Simon dead?'

'They'll kill you,' Steve wheezed. 'They'll come for you and they won't stop. Whatever you do to me, Trent'll do worse to you. He'll make you—'

Maggie dropped the bat, lifted the shotgun and fired.

Steve's right knee exploded. His scream filled the bush and kept going, a wail of hopeless agony. He tried to crawl. He left his leg behind him. Even in the moonlight, the ground was red.

'Is Simon dead?' Maggie's voice cut through his fading scream.

'Yes,' his voice was a croak. 'Please. Please, take me back. Don't ... You're not ...' He was writhing through the blood and the dirt. His face was bone white. His eyelids fluttered. 'You're not like the others. You're like ... You're like us.' Blood dripped from his gaping mouth.

Maggie was unsteady, her head felt thick and heavy, but none of that mattered; what mattered was the thing on the ground in front of her, his words stoking her fury into something impossible to hold onto. 'Where are the car keys?'

'P-pocket.' Steve's voice was faint.

He wasn't lying. Maggie felt a rush of something close to ecstasy. Ecstasy quickly overtaken by the rising boil of rage.

You're like us.

Steve's eyes closed. 'Please. I want to go home. Please.'

Maggie lay the shotgun down. She picked up the bat. 'No.'

CHAPTER FIFTEEN

Greg could hear the low hum of voices on the other side of
the door that led out the back of the roadhouse. Light crept
through the crack under it. He had expected somebody to
come barging in at any second, but no-one had.

What did he know? Not much. It was hard to imagine the
kind of explanation that would cause this situation to make
sense. But, somehow, he had to force his reeling mind to turn
away from the growing fear that he was most certainly about
to die and work out if he had another option, slim though the
possibility might be.

There was a girl. Whoever she was, she was at the core
of this. She was the one they were after. And furthermore,
Greg knew where she was, more or less. A house, somewhere
behind them. If he gave these people what they wanted, they
would have to let him go. Whatever they did to the others
here, it needn't include the person who had helped them.

This, after all, was what he had done for years. Negotiated
deals, identified what people wanted and used an innate sense

161

of how much they wanted it to establish the terms of a deal that would benefit him.

He thought of Delilah, who had left again. Her scared smile. He hadn't heard the door to the main store open. He pictured her alone in the hall, shaking, trying to regain composure. As scared as Greg. He thought of the old prick with the gun. And the faceless girl he would hand over to these people. Whatever this was, it had nothing to do with him. He got to his feet.

Allie tried not to breathe. She held the gun as tightly as she dared, eyes fixed on the crack at the bottom of the bedroom door. Listening.

The creak came again. Closer.

Very slowly, taking care not to make a sound, Allie slid back further until she was as far under the bed as she could be, back pressed against the wall.

Another creak.

She pointed the gun at the bottom of the door.

Another creak, from right on the other side of the closed door.

Her finger crept around the trigger.

The bedroom door opened. Her insides seemed to evaporate. Even in the dark she knew she was looking at a pair of boots.

One step, then another, they walked into the room. Allie's hands were trembling. Her heart assaulted the inside of her chest. She tried to aim the gun at the ankle, but she couldn't hold it steady and if she missed she didn't know how to reload it. Or if it was even loaded to begin with. The trembling spread. She was shaking all over now. She closed her eyes. Her hands were too sweaty to hold the gun properly.

She heard the steps, closer and closer until the boots had to be right at the edge of her bed. She couldn't open her eyes. Couldn't see what she knew was there. Maybe he would go away.

Then—

A rush of air as the mattress was pulled from the bed. She tried to raise the gun, but it hit a wooden slat. Her eyes opened.

Reg's face loomed over her, close, a leering taunt in the dark. 'G'day, sweetheart.'

His hand flew through a gap between the slats and closed around her neck. Hard. She gasped. No air was going in. She let go of the gun. She tried to struggle. Her vision blurred but even so she saw Reg's spare hand rip away one slat then another, throwing them aside before pulling Allie up by the neck. Her head felt like it was submerged in liquid. She barely felt him slam her against the wall over the bed.

His grip loosened, slightly. She forced in what air she could and his awful smell filled her nose: stale cigarettes, old beer and something else, something sour and wrong that made her want to throw up, something touched with copper and rot.

'You need to learn to lock the back door,' he said. 'Anybody could be 'round these parts, y'know?'

Allie tried to yell out, but his grip was still too tight around her throat. Out of the corner of her eye she could see the gun on the floor. It was too far away but she reached for it anyway, until Reg's boot found it and kicked it hard backwards, out of sight.

'That ain't happening, love,' he said. 'Now. Reading between the lines, I reckon you might just be hiding something in this cosy little house. I've had a quick look around and I don't see our little mate, but that don't mean she ain't here. You'd be making everyone's lives a shitload easier if you came clean.'

Allie couldn't have said anything if she'd wanted to.

Reg's face filled her vision.

'I don't want things to get rough, love,' he said. 'Sweet young thing like you, I'd hate to do too much damage. I'd like that face to stay in one piece. But you know how it is. Gotta have your mates' backs. Especially when someone kills four of them. Tell me where Maggie is.'

Allie breathed in the rancid air. She made herself meet Reg's dead eyes. She opened her mouth.

But a voice from behind Reg beat her to it.

'She's right here.'

Reg turned. Maggie hit him hard in the face with the butt of the shotgun. He let go of Allie and fell away, clutching his nose, snarling and swearing as Maggie spun the gun around, pointed it at his face and pulled the trigger.

Warm blood splattered Allie as the shot filled her ears. She screamed but no sound came out.

For a moment Reg remained standing. He swayed. Above his jaw was nothing but a red mess of bone and blood.

He fell hard.

CHAPTER SIXTEEN

Maggie had known she was on a couch, or maybe she hadn't. The dryness in her mouth, roughness of the fabric against her skin, pain in her leg; it had been coming and going and all the while she had been sinking in fragments, snatches and hisses of memories or dreams, she didn't know which. They had started to claim her on the road, tendrils wrapping tight as her vision flickered and her mind slowed. What had she even been running from? The knowledge lingered, but vaguer by the second. *The bush. The blood. The knife. The pain.* She remembered the pain without feeling it. That had been the first warning. But by the time she'd recognised the fact, it had been too late. She had seen the roadhouse ahead and swerved towards it. She'd opened the car door and stepped into darkness.

And then the fragments. Jagged images, crammed together without order or sense. Pulling herself clear of them had been like dragging her body through broken glass. But in the fragments and the dark, the one thing she knew was that somehow she had to get clear. Somehow she had to wake up from whatever this was, whether it was sleep or the first welcoming whisper of death.

I should have killed you.

Her father, his voice slurred and rough with booze, his hand around her throat and the sour smell in her nose. The hate she had felt in that moment, the overpowering sweep of a blazing flood she could never escape from, exacerbated by his familiar grip and the nauseous instinct to flinch and hide and wait for the beating to be over. She had tried to hold it down but his words had been like the striking of a match about to fall into a pool of kerosene.

I should have killed you.

The staircase. The night. The two of them alone and in the loosening of his grip, an opportunity. The struck match falling slow through darkness to the gleaming pool below. Only that time, she didn't try to put out the fire. That time, she had let it burn.

Something brighter, then, clearer. A voice alive with urgency. *We're going to call help.* All she knew was that whoever it was couldn't do that, because help would mean something final for her, a return to confines and the eyes, waiting for any sign of weakness, waiting.

You wouldn't believe how long some of these fuckers last.

She was going to last.

The sharp edges of the fragments were gone, or at least she couldn't feel them anymore. The faces she saw warped and blurred in the darkness, the voices were snatches of garbled nothing. She had forgotten even what the pain had been like.

Everything was warm, everything was soft, nothing mattered. Echoes faded to silence and even her own name escaped her. She was safe. She had never known what safe was until then. Nothing was coming to harm her because there was nothing left, not anymore.

I think we should check out the car.

Clear and ringing as a bell. A throb, dull and distant, but there. A fragment, so sudden and clear it jarred, the snarling of a dog, the tear of teeth. The throb became something worse. The sharp edges were back, but they hid in the dark. She scraped against them without knowing where or what they were.

The people here ... I don't like this place.

Simon, terrified even though he tried to hide it, and then Simon was little Ted and something in her chest pulled horribly, something that hurt far worse than the building pressure in her leg ...

Footsteps on wood outside.

The pain had flared. Sharp, bright. Like an alarm.

Her eyes had opened.

Her limbs felt stretched and distended. Her throat burned raw with every breath. She didn't want to move. But she heard a doorknob turn and knew she had to.

She sat up despite the tendrils, the dark hands trying to pull her back. She was in a living room, everything off kilter and swimming in front of her eyes. She rolled off the couch, hands jarring on the wooden floor, shuffled away as best she could, ignoring the storm of objection from every battered inch of her. She clocked the first-aid kit and brushed it under the couch as she went. She moved into the shadow cast by the side of the couch, up against the wall, legs pulled to her chest. She tried to listen past the pounding in her ears. Everything still. Silent.

A creak, then another, louder. The sound of breathing. Someone in the doorway, scanning the living room.

Then the creaking again, quieter and quieter.

A door opening, metres and thin walls away.

Maggie stood.

The pain like fire again.

She'd started to walk.

Frank could hear the voice, reverberating through his mind again and again. *You've only got fifteen left, mate.* The taunting delight had made his skin crawl. He knew the truth, behind all the false promises of mercy. *Once we've got the girl, you'll get just the same as her. Can't have any witnesses.* He'd known how this would go from the start. He'd known men like this.

'You don't wanna leave this to the last minute,' the voice said. 'The boys will get impatient and that won't go well for you.'

As if in response, the revving of every engine out the front filled his ears. A savage roar. A threat of snarling motors and beeping horns, a car backfiring somewhere drowned out by the sheer scale of the noise.

The sound died off. Frank's ears still rang.

'Clock's ticking, mate.'

*

Allie followed as Maggie limped up the hallway. Reg's blood was still warm on her face. Maybe she should have been more horrified. But all she felt was a deep, wonderful gratitude.

Maggie opened the front door and stepped onto the porch. There was no sound. Allie came up beside her.

'Where are we?' Maggie asked.

'This is Frank's house. My grandad.'

'Where's your grandad?'

Allie went to reply, then stopped. Something thorny crept through her stomach. When Charlie had heard the gunshot, he had run towards Delilah. She hadn't even thought about Frank. She had been too scared to worry if he was even alive. And now she had no idea. With horrible clarity she saw herself returning to her parents, trying to explain what had happened and what she had done. She swallowed. *Her parents*. They didn't know what was happening. That they probably weren't ever going to see her or Frank again.

'Hey,' Maggie said.

Allie pointed.

'That doesn't help.'

'The roadhouse.'

'Where I stopped?'

Allie nodded.

'Is he alone?'

'I don't know.' Allie's voice sounded small and scared.

Maggie looked at her. Then back in the direction of the roadhouse. 'He hasn't come back. Which probably means he isn't.'

*

The door beside Frank opened again and Delilah crawled out.

'They're really keen for an answer,' Frank said.

Delilah closed the door and crouched against it. She took a deep breath. 'We have to hand her over.'

Frank looked away.

'We should have done it straight away,' Delilah said. 'I get why we didn't – it's a horrible thing to do and I know that, but we can't … we can't all die for someone we don't know. Someone who might have done something really bad.'

Frank didn't reply.

'We can work something out,' Delilah said. 'Be smart about it. Let them keep one of us, then send the other to the house.' Frank went to speak, but Delilah wasn't finished. 'I mean you,' she said. 'Go to the house. That way, whatever happens, you can protect Allie.'

Frank met her eyes. He could see how scared she was. But there was a tightness to her jaw and a hardness to her expression that said it didn't matter anymore.

'There's no guarantee they won't still kill us.'

Delilah shrugged. 'They probably will, right? But this way we have at least something of a chance.'

Frank said nothing.

'Frank,' Delilah said. 'If they kill us in here, then Allie has no protection. At all.'

Allie stood alone in the doorway as Maggie returned from her bedroom. 'No phone in his pockets.'

'What do we do?' Allie asked.

'We need a plan,' said Maggie, 'but first I need some water, food, whatever you have. I don't suppose there are any painkillers in that first-aid kit?'

They returned to the living room. Maggie rifled through the kit as Allie doubled back to the kitchen, found her empty water bottle where she'd left it, another lifetime ago, on the sink, and filled it at the tap. There wasn't much in the fridge. Mostly Frank brought food home from the roadhouse. She looked at the box of cereal on the table, grabbed it and headed back to Maggie.

After swigging the water and shoving down a few handfuls of dry cereal, Maggie moved to the front door and looked out to the grass. It was still, silent, like a breath held. 'If that prick got in here, that means more of them will be around. Maybe waiting in the grass. You said your grandad took the car keys?'

Allie nodded.

'Then I don't see us getting to the roadhouse fast. And I'm not running any marathons any time soon.' Maggie shifted on the spot and winced. 'We have to find a way to get their attention. Lure them somewhere clear and attack.'

'How?'

Maggie had another swig of water. Leaned against the frame of the front door. It struck Allie then how weak she looked. Like she could fall over at any second.

'We use what we have. Somehow.' She turned to face Allie. 'What do we have?'

Something behind Maggie caught Allie's eye. They both turned.

A pair of headlights was approaching from across the grass.

Then another. And another. Until the headlights grew into suns and a wall of blazing light burned away the night.

Something had enveloped her, a giant hand that tightened until she couldn't move or breathe.

'Inside,' Maggie said. 'Now.'

There was no fear in her voice.

Allie backed into the house. Through the front door, Maggie stood alone, silhouetted against the blinding light, shotgun in hand.

Somewhere in Delilah's head, the voice of everything she had ever believed was screaming at her, telling her that she couldn't condone this, couldn't allow another woman to be handed over to these animals. It was all too easy to guess what would happen, because it was all too easy to guess how this would end for her if she was found by them.

She tried to tell herself, as she crawled through the door, that it wasn't self-preservation that pushed her to give up the girl. That it was in fact the most selfless thing she could possibly do. Charlie was out there somewhere, along with Allie. She couldn't let them all die for the sake of some stranger who had almost certainly done something to deserve—

She stopped. No. She couldn't think that way. If she made this choice, she would make herself remember it every day, without compromise, justification or convenient assumption.

She stood, took a deep breath, and crossed the hall to the storeroom. She would tell Greg the plan. She would make herself meet his eyes and make sure they all knew exactly what they were doing and exactly what this choice made them.

She turned the door handle, opening her mouth to explain before she could change her mind. She stepped into the storeroom.

Alone on the porch, Maggie stood as the cars drew closer, lurching and jumping as they crossed the uneven landscape.

She looked down at the shotgun in her hand. Not enough. Not nearly enough. Her thoughts felt thick and sluggish. She couldn't focus. Every move she made caused her leg to scream. She could hardly stand.

What did she have?

The first time she had asked herself that question had been years ago. Back with Ben and Debbie. She'd made herself wait until the next camping trip, observed everyone's movements, waited until all eyes were away and Hamish was tending the fire. *Ready, not rigid.* Waited until he stepped forwards. She moved fast. His foot snagged on hers. With a cry he fell, face first into the flames.

She'd had nothing but herself. But she was fast and she was willing to do what others wouldn't and she watched as Hamish screamed, as he tried to stand, as Ben's worried yells neared from the rustling bush, as Ted's face filled Maggie's mind. Then she brought her boot down hard on the back of Hamish's head.

What did she have?

A terrified young girl. A house that looked like a strong breeze could knock it over. A shotgun with only a handful of cartridges. And seconds left until those cars were in shooting range.

But there was something else, something that had taken over back in the trees, something that had pulsed through her as she veered across the highway trying to escape, something that kept her standing even now as hope slipped away. That same something that had caused her to run in the first place. That something that had always scared her because she could never get away from it. A furnace, deep and white hot, stoking a fire that she had always tried to hold at bay because to succumb to it was to become something less than human, something animal.

She had been fighting it for too long.

She hobbled back into the house and slammed the door behind her.

The internal door burst open and Delilah was back, breathing heavily. She shook her head. 'He's not there.'

Frank's veins were ice.

'He's gone. I checked the kitchen and … he's gone. He was heading for the back door before but … Oh god.' Delilah put a hand over her mouth.

Frank seized her shoulder. 'Did he know? About the house?'

Delilah didn't remove her hand. There were tears in her eyes. She nodded.

And just like that, none of it mattered. The siege, the weapons, the threats. None of it mattered because the fuckers knew about the house and his leverage was gone. Allie was stuck with only Charlie to protect her and it was his fault for not handing over the girl when he had the chance. He couldn't breathe. His heart hammered. He went to stand.

'What are you doing?' Delilah grabbed him by the arm.

Frank shrugged her off. He had to get out of here. Had to get to the house.

'Frank.'

He pushed her away.

Then—

A hail of gunshots and the cacophony of shattering glass. Frank dropped hard as bullets slammed into the wall behind him.

A whine filled his ears. He wasn't sure if the gunshots were still coming, but he could hear them, distant and echoing, and with them laughter, laughter that didn't belong to the here and now but to another place, to the night-time shadows of drooping gum trees where he had run from the shots and the catcalls, run even as Wayne's shrieks of laughter seemed to come from everywhere and he couldn't know if he would ever see home again.

Delilah's arms were over her head, eyes closed tight as she rocked back and forth.

The trees and the laughter were gone. Allie. All that mattered was Allie. Keeping her safe.

He took a deep breath and inhaled pungent fumes of petrol.

He moved to the side and looked around the counter. It was hard to tell in the glare of the headlights, but it looked like figures were moving around the pumps.

And like that, he understood.

Greg had told them about the house. They had no need of Frank or Delilah, but they weren't about to go charging in when Frank was armed. So instead they were using what the roadhouse had to their advantage, using the pumps to douse the place in petrol before setting it alight and burning them alive.

Beneath the screen door, the glistening pool of golden petrol was spreading from outside, from where the bastards were using his own pumps to burn him alive.

He could be scared later. He could be guilty later. But right now, he had to act. He concentrated. Put himself in the mindset he hadn't been in for so long. The mindset where death didn't matter and everything in his way was just an obstacle to be eliminated, the mindset where he was righteous and everyone else was guilty and to be punished. The mindset that was the only safe one behind bars, that he had tried to shake off only to be drawn back repeatedly, until finally all he could do was hide away from the world and anything that could trigger it again.

It came to him. Its embrace warmer than any lover's.

And everything became clear.

He grabbed Delilah by the shoulder. Extended a hand. 'Give me your lighter.'

'What?' she looked at him, tears running down her face.

'Now.'

With fumbling hands, she did. Frank pushed the internal door open. 'Out the back. Now.'

'But they're out there.' Her voice was high pitched, strained.

Frank shook his head. 'I don't think so. But if they are.' He pushed the gun into her hand. He felt the shock go through her. She stared at it as if she couldn't quite comprehend what she was seeing.

Frank grabbed her by the chin. Made her look at him. 'Don't hesitate,' he said. 'If you see them, kill them. If you don't, run. Into the grass. Get as far away as you can.'

'What are you doing?'

'Go.'

Delilah didn't ask again. She slipped through the door and was gone.

CHAPTER SEVENTEEN

The tray of the ute jerked and rattled beneath Greg. He tried to hold on and not meet the eye of the man sitting across from him.

He was thin and appeared to be in his sixties. His hair was wispy and white, his cheeks hollow and his eyes sunken. He wore a singlet and ripped jeans. Over his shoulder was a long rifle. In his other hand was a can of beer. His mouth was set in a rictus grin, had been since he pushed Greg onto the tray. He had not looked away from Greg for a second.

Greg turned his face skyward and took a long breath of the hot night air. The sky was clear, alive with stars. It seemed at odds with what was happening.

Greg had taken his chance. He'd moved as fast as he could, through the back door with his hands in the air, ready to beg, ready to shout that he had information for them. He had expected raised guns, demands for him to get down, perhaps a sudden burst of pain and then darkness. What he got was laughter.

'Don't hurt me,' he'd blurted, as the men in front of him erupted in jeering. They were spread out across two cars, sitting on trays and half-sitting in cabs, all flannelette shirts and ripped jeans, guns raised to the sky. Not a single one was pointed at him.

Greg lowered his arms slowly. His pounding heart filled his whole body. He swallowed. 'I can help you.'

'Can ya, mate?' A young man, heavily bearded with a lazy eye, said. His gun barrel slowly swung down to point at Greg.

Greg stepped back. 'There's a house. Directly behind you, I don't know exactly where, but, but that's …' He gritted his teeth and tried to look anywhere but the barrel of the gun. 'That's where the girl is.'

Silence. It hit him then that he had given away the only card he held, the one thing that might stop them from killing him then and there. He thought of Phillipa. He thought of his kids. And he knew then with terrible clarity just how fucking stupid he had been. 'I have information.' His voice sounded feeble. 'I can tell you who's in the roadhouse. I can tell you what they told me. We can help each other. I've got nothing to do with this shit, okay? If I tell you everything I know, will you let me go home?'

The only response from the bearded man had been, 'Get on the tray.'

On either side of the vehicle, more utes were moving. At least seven, almost in line with each other. In the dark it was hard to tell how many people were piled in the trays of each one. But the stark shapes of rifle barrels were unmistakable. The other man still hadn't looked away. Greg turned and looked ahead. In the distance, he could see the approaching shape of the house, small and flimsy in the middle of the vast, grassy expanse.

Allie jumped as the front door slammed, and backed further into the living room. After a moment, Maggie was there. She moved over to the curtains and started pulling them shut.

'They'll see,' Allie said.

'They know we're here,' Maggie said. 'The high beams are to blind. So they can watch us, but we can't watch them. We need to take any advantage we can. Bring me a knife.'

'Why?' Allie was confused. Maggie had a gun.

'Now.' There was no room for questions in her tone.

Allie hurried back to the kitchen, fumbled through the drawers and found the sharpest knife she could. She was only just back in the living room before Maggie had snatched it from her, returned to the windows, and started hacking at the curtains. She finished at one window, leaving three or four long tears in different spots, then moved to the next window and the next. The light from the cars came through the slits in narrow beams.

'What are you doing?' Allie asked.

'Tears are hard to see in curtains,' Maggie said. 'They're wavy and crumpled in places. And even if you can see them, you can't keep track of them all at once. You never know where we might be looking through.' She hefted the gun. 'Or where we might shoot from.'

'That only leaves the front of the house covered,' Allie said.

'It does,' Maggie agreed. 'Which is why you're going to do the same in the kitchen. Then wait in the hall and listen. If you hear a window creak, a thud outside the house, you yell out to me. Immediately and loud. And Allie?'

Allie stopped halfway across the room.

Maggie was peering through one of the tears. 'After you're done with the curtains, hang on to the knife.'

'Why?'

Maggie didn't look at her. 'We don't know how this is gonna go. If they get close and you have the knife in your belt, you might be able to use it. Do some damage.'

Allie didn't know what to say. The matter-of-fact way that Maggie spoke made her feel small and pathetic. This woman, this woman who wielded shotguns with ease and quickly came up with ideas like the tears in the curtains, thought that Allie was capable of doing something like that, that when the moment came, she wouldn't just try to hide under the bed again. The shame that made her feel was worse than anything Hannah Bond had ever caused.

Maggie looked back, over her shoulder. 'You're only as weak as you let yourself feel.'

She returned her attention to the window.

Allie made for the kitchen.

The cars had stopped. Three were spread out across the front of the run-down little house, the others were around the back, encircling the place, trapping the occupants inside just like they had at the roadhouse. In the glare of the headlights the windows were dark. There was no sound from within.

Greg hoped, momentarily, that it was as abandoned as it looked. But the idea of where that would leave him banished that hope fast.

Car doors opened and people climbed off trailers with thuds of movements and the dry rustle of long grass. Greg looked around, wondering if somebody would speak to him, give him orders, but no-one did. The other man was getting down from the tray.

'Hey,' Greg said.

The man stopped. Looked at him. The grin still set.

'I helped,' he said. The words sounded like a squeal. 'I told you where she was. Can I … This has nothing to do with me. Can I go?'

The man beckoned.

Maggie watched through one of the rips. As she did, she held the shotgun barrel to the curtain.

Allie kept back. The fear was still there. It hadn't lessened. But it felt distant, somehow.

'Alright, you fuckers,' Maggie muttered. 'Come and get me.'

Frank found an old rag under the counter, oily and more black now than the beige it had started as. He scrunched it into a ball, then found a rubber band, looped it around the cloth then looped again until he had a tight, compact ball of fabric. He looked down at the zippo in his hand. He was aware of his beating heart and hot blood. Of a prayer, somewhere in his mind, trying to get in, a prayer he pushed away because it wouldn't affect what happened next.

He flicked the zippo open. The tiny flame ignited. He put it to the rag. It took only a few seconds to catch alight.

He threw it around the corner of the counter.

He grabbed the door. Dived through the gap into the hall. Scrambled to his feet just as the roar of igniting petrol and a rush of hot air filled the roadhouse. Charged into the storeroom as cries from out the front announced that the fire had raced from the pooling petrol up to the nozzle from which it was coming.

He smashed through the back door as the cries vanished and the sound of tearing metal and wrenching concrete were drowned out by the inferno.

He ran. He could see nothing in front of him. He ran as scorching heat filled the air and then a force from behind slammed into him, sending him flying. Maybe he screamed, but if he did he couldn't hear it. He hit the ground hard but even pain was an echo. He gasped for air and what he took in burned. Everything was dark.

You gone pussy, have you, mate?

Wayne's voice in his ear. He knew this wasn't happening. But he heard it, as clear and as cold as if he'd stepped back in time. And just as clearly, he heard his own reply.

'I don't want to do this anymore.'

He couldn't explain. He couldn't tell them. They wouldn't understand.

'I can't.' If he said it now or then, he didn't know. 'I can't. I need to go home. I need to get back.'

Don't wanna head back in the dark, Frankie. The bush is a rough place at night. And we can't see what we're shooting at.

The laughter again, from all of them. Electrified by speed and Bundy and the rush of the hunt. Eyes wild and lolling. And then the shots and the running and the endless night all around him, with no light to guide him out.

Later, he'd told himself that they just wanted to scare him. But it hadn't been with anything like certainty.

Frank.

That wasn't Wayne.

'Frank!'

The sound of crackling and burning was in his ears. The heat was heavy, holding him down. He opened his eyes. The grass. The roadhouse. *Allie.*

There were hands under him, trying to pull him up. He tried to stand, fell, then managed it. His vision blurred. Delilah was in front of him, saying something he couldn't hear or understand. He turned.

Flames reached up from what remained of the roadhouse. Most of the back wall was still intact, dark and cracked with fire clear through the shattered windows, fire that even now was getting lower because there was nothing left to keep it alive.

'What did you do?' Delilah asked.

Frank swallowed. He tasted blood. He took a step forwards then stopped as his head throbbed and his mind swam. The blurriness cleared but was still at the fringes of his vision.

'Frank?'

'I blew up the roadhouse.' The words were distant and matter-of-fact. He couldn't remember his mouth forming them. He breathed in slowly, wincing at the slight burn and taste of acrid fumes. 'Give me the gun.'

'They weren't out here. It was totally clear.' Delilah handed him the gun.

He'd guessed as much. He raised the gun and moved to the right, past the side of the roadhouse. Every step felt unsteady. He wasn't sure he could aim properly even if he did see someone. But it didn't matter. He had to be sure.

What had once been the front of the roadhouse was now just a smouldering crater. The concrete below the pumps had been blown wide open as the fuel tanks beneath exploded. He could just make out the remains of the counter he had been hiding behind, a black husk in the scorched, twisted, ripped-open wreck of what had been his livelihood. Small fires still burned, casting flickering yellow light over what was left. The heat was immense.

But Frank wasn't interested in the roadhouse.

Resting among the cracks and chasms where the pumps had once been were the skeletons of five cars. One was the van. One was Greg's. The other three were utes, by the looks of them. He scanned the area.

Only three.

There had been a lot more than three surrounding them.

Greg was led to a pair of people standing between a panel van and a ute, surveying the front of the house. One of them turned at the sound of their approach, a tall, fit-looking man. His hair was cropped short and his brow was heavy. He wore a knife at his waist and held a rifle. The woman next to him was short, with stringy grey hair hanging to her shoulders and heavy bags under hollow eyes. She wore a faded jumper and jeans, and a cigarette was in her clenched jaw. She didn't look at Greg as he approached. She only had eyes for the house.

'What you got for me, Mal?' the tall man said.

The older man gestured to Greg. 'This bloke left the servo, Trent. Told us about the girl.'

Trent surveyed Greg. 'City?'

Greg nodded.

'Yeah. Thought so. Thought I smelt piss.'

Mal gave a wheezing chuckle.

'I did … I told you,' Greg said. 'About the girl.'

They all heard it at the same time. An earth-shaking boom of what could only be an explosion behind them. Everyone turned. Tall flames danced in the distance, then receded.

'So much for the brave old bastard,' Trent said.

Greg tried not to think about Delilah or the man who had aimed a gun at him. He made himself meet Trent's gaze. 'I gave you what you wanted.'

Trent turned back to the house, putting the rifle over his shoulder.

'We should go in.' That was the woman. 'The bitch is outnumbered, even if she is alive.'

'She's alive, alright,' Trent said. 'If she wasn't, Reg would have been out here the moment we pulled up. Looks like little Maggie's still holding her own.'

'I gave you the information.' Greg couldn't keep the wail out of his voice.

Trent was on him in seconds, hand around his neck, face right in Greg's. 'You gave me fuck-all,' he snarled. 'You gave me too little, too late. If you'd come out straight away, another one of my mates might not be dead. So right now, I don't think I owe you jack shit. Right now, I think you should count yourself very fucking lucky I'm not blowing your fucking head off. Right now, I think you should thank me.'

Greg couldn't speak.

'Well?' Trent said.

'Thank you,' Greg mumbled.

Brief, hard pressure on his neck, and Greg was sent sprawling.

'You're staying right here,' Trent said. 'You might be useful. Might not.' He turned away again.

Greg, struggling to breathe, staggered to his feet.

'Reg could be alive but hurt,' the woman said.

'What, like she left Steve?' Trent's tone was dry.

'Steve would have goaded her. He would have …' Her voice cracked.

'Fair enough,' Trent said. 'Reg is smarter than that. It's not hard to be smarter than Steve.'

'Shut your fucking mouth,' the woman spat.

'Am I wrong, Janice?' Trent sounded almost bored. 'I told you. I told Kev. Letting him lead the hunt was never gonna end well. Because you don't leave a hunt until it's done. Ever. But Steve saw something shiny and just had to bring it back to show off, and now look where we fucking are.

The pretty little thing killed your son and his fuckhead mates and now we have to clean up the mess.' There was a roiling anger to his tone, something heated and barely contained. He exhaled. 'Alright. What we need is a better idea of what we're up against.' He turned to Mal. 'Head around the back of the house.'

Greg's relief mingled with confusion.

'Stay out of the lights,' Trent said. 'Straight to where the boys are keeping an eye on the back door. Once you're there, find a rock and chuck it through a window.'

'On it, Trent.' Mal vanished into the dark.

'What are you doing?' Janice asked.

'We don't know who else is in there with the girl,' Trent said. 'If she's got ten fuckers covering every window, then we're in for a tough night. If it's just her, well.' He shrugged. 'Changes things. Smash the window, see how she reacts – it'll tell us what we need to know. '

He raised a hand. A murmur went through the warm air, followed swiftly by silence. He brought his rifle down and moved forwards, to right behind the lights. Around them, shapes and silhouettes shifted into position without further command. Trent's hand was still up. It balled into a fist.

The silence was heavy.

And then, faint and masked by the house, the sound of shattering glass.

Maggie focused on the pain. She let it have all her attention, let it bite and burn and demand. Because the pain kept her awake and alive. She knew how much danger they were in.

She'd heard the blast, earth-shaking even from far away, heard it and assured Allie it might have been nothing even though she knew that was a lie. Her energy and adrenaline were depleted and sleep beckoned, grabbing at her with increasing aggression, making her eyelids droop and her thoughts sag. But the pain – red hot and alive – brought her back each time.

'What are they doing?' Allie, from the doorway, asked.

Maggie looked at her. She didn't have an answer. But Allie's eyes, bright with fear, were another lifeline. Another reason to stay right here and fight even though she doubted she could anymore.

The sound was sudden, all too loud in the still house; the impact of stone on glass then the tinkling rainfall of shards. Maggie was up – the pain soared – and then an instinct, a realisation, an idea faint and unformed shot across her groggy mind.

'Duck,' she yelled at Allie.

She fired off a couple of rounds at the ragged curtains.

She stumbled into the hall, past Allie's cowering form. Her leg gave way; she just managed to heft the suddenly too-heavy gun again, fumble to load the slugs she'd taken from Steve's pocket, and pull the trigger, shooting the back door. She hit the ground as gunshots filled the house, as more glass shattered and wood exploded in ragged splinters around her. She tried to breathe. Forced herself up onto her knees. God, she was tired. The gunshots had stopped.

'Maggie.' Allie's voice: scared, low behind her. 'They're coming to kill us.'

Maggie shook her head. Wincing, she shifted backwards until she was against the wall. 'Listen.'

Allie, crouched beside her, did.

'There's no-one in the house,' Maggie said. 'The rock was to test us. To see where we'd shoot from.'

Allie's eyes were still scared. Just like Ted's. Just like Simon's.

'And now ...' Allie swallowed. 'Now they think there are more of us.'

'I don't know what they think,' Maggie said. 'But they're not attacking.'

The curtain in the shattered window was torn to rags and smoking. Everything was still. Greg's ears were ringing, his legs jelly.

'Reckon we got her?' Trent said.

'No,' Janice replied flatly.

Trent's eyes scanned the front of the house. What was left of the curtain shifted in a rise of gentle wind.

Footfalls and wheezing. Mal was back, out of breath. 'Fucking bitch shot right through the back door.' He said, hands on his knees. 'Got Jay's ute. Almost got me.'

'So they've got both entries covered,' Janice said to Trent. 'Satisfied?'

Trent hadn't looked away from the house. 'If you had to guess, how much time was between the two shots?'

Janice shook her head. 'I don't know. Seconds. Does it matter? There's more than just her in there.'

'Maybe,' Trent said. 'Unless the house has a central hallway from front door to back. She could cover both exits that way.'

'Walk on in and take a fucking look then,' Janice said. 'It doesn't make a difference. She's still in there and we're still out here. Is this your plan? Test and poke and prod all night until you're sure of where she is or until the cops rock up to see what's happening?'

If that was bait, Trent didn't rise to it. His attention remained on the house. 'My plan is the one that ends with everyone in that house dead and the rest of us alive. Unless you reckon I should do a Steve.' His expression was calm. His eyes were fire. 'Four of us, Janice. Cousins, uncles, brothers, friends. Five if you count Reg, which I'm pretty sure we should at this stage. You wanna bitch and moan about respecting Steve's memory, then fine, but it doesn't change the clusterfuck he left us in.'

'Then take some fucking action instead of pissing our time away.'

Trent and Janice considered each other.

'Alright,' Trent said. 'Let's try the bait. You can do the honours.'

For a cold, dreadful moment, Greg wondered if they were talking about him.

Janice took a step forwards. She was still behind the lights, as good as invisible to anyone inside the house.

'You're surrounded,' she called out. Her voice was cold and hard. 'Know who I am?'

Silence.

'See, I'm Janice,' she shouted. 'My old fella was Kev. My son was Steve.'

Silence.

'Suit yourself,' Janice said. 'But we can wait for you all night. And the longer we wait, the more it'll hurt, Maggie.'

There was no sign of movement from the house.

'In the meantime,' Janice said, 'let's see how you feel when the people who tried to protect you start going down in your place.'

Trent got into the nearby ute. He started to reverse. Greg looked at the vehicle, unsure of what was happening. For the first time, he noticed that Trent's ute was equipped with a small crane on the back, from which hung a swaying hook.

The only thing that stopped him from crying was the knowledge that he, at least, had never tried to protect Maggie.

Delilah hung on to Frank as the quad bike lurched and bumped across the field. Parked well behind the roadhouse, it had managed to escape the explosion. She had been sure the sound of the motor would give them away, but the closer they got, the clearer it became that they were the least of anyone's concerns.

From the slight rise in the land they'd just climbed, the house looked as if it had been put under a spotlight. Vehicles surrounded it in a ring, high beams lighting it up from every direction. Even from here she could hear the rumble and revving of engines, a din that was fast drowned out by a succession of gunfire.

'Fuck,' Frank whispered.

He slowed the quad bike. They were a few hundred metres away, but even from the rise it was hard to see much.

Frank's hands were on his head. Delilah didn't need to see his face to know what he was thinking.

'She's alive,' Delilah said. 'They wouldn't be firing on the house if she wasn't.'

Frank moved to accelerate again.

'Wait.' Delilah grabbed his arm. 'You can try to draw them away, but then we're all dead. We have to be smart about this.'

Frank looked back at her. Even in the dark his face looked tired and worn. 'And how the fuck do you suggest we manage that?'

Delilah was about to reply when something caught her eye. She got off the quad bike and took a few steps forwards, through reaching, rustling grass. Hoping that she wasn't seeing what she thought she was. Hoping it was all some mistake and the rising grasp of panic in her chest was misplaced.

One of the utes had pulled out of the ring and was now reversing back into the light. It was moving slowly, because somebody was hurrying just ahead of the rear of the vehicle.

'No,' Delilah whispered. 'No.'

It was him. The clothes, the hair. He was stumbling and his hands looked to be bound. And—

It was as though she'd been punched. She stepped back.

Above Charlie's head was a small crane attached to the back of the car. From it hung a rope. A rope tied around his neck.

'No,' Delilah said, louder now.

Frank was behind her, hand over her mouth.

'Smart,' he hissed. 'We have to be smart.'

Delilah bit.

Frank swore and stumbled back. Delilah ran. She was screaming something, but she didn't know what. It didn't matter. She just had to stop them. She tripped, landed hard. Her hands were scraped by rock, stung by dirt. She got to her feet. Closer but not enough. She saw heads turn at the sight of her. But none of that mattered. She focused on Charlie, so clear now, so close. He turned. She could see from here that he was bloodied, beaten, his face a mess of bruises.

'Delilah!' he cried.

And suddenly he was jerked off his feet, pulled upright as the crane rose and the rope tightened. His yells cut off.

She was only metres away now, but hands were grabbing her from all sides, pulling her down to her knees. She scratched at a face. She kicked. She bit without seeing what and felt skin and muscle. She bit harder, there was a yell, the taste of blood and then stars as someone hit her. She staggered, dazed. She could see Charlie and she screamed for him. With everything she had, she struggled against the ropes they were now binding her with, against the hands of the monsters holding her in place, monsters all the worse because they looked so human – the boy with the acne scars, the older man in the hat, the one who never blinked as he chewed his cigarette. It didn't matter.

'We found him running for the servo.' That was a woman's voice, ringing out among the cars. 'He left you all alone, Maggie. Only took a few hits for him to tell us all about you. How he helped you. Then a few more hits for him to *beg* us to take you away. To let him and his little sweetheart leave. They won't get to leave though, Maggie. And that's on you.'

A foul-tasting cloth was shoved in Delilah's mouth, cutting off her attempt to cry out. A mechanical whirring came from the truck. The crane went higher. Charlie was gasping and writhing. His mouth was open, face red, eyes bulging.

'Watch, Maggie,' the woman called. 'Watch him hang. The boy who patched you up.'

Charlie's whole body jerked with futile desperation.

'This is your chance,' the woman said. 'Come out and we'll let him down. He saved you. Return the favour.'

Delilah looked to the front of the house. There was no movement.

A terrible wheezing was coming from Charlie now. His eyes had rolled back in his head.

'Please!' Delilah tried to say. It came out as a muffled groan. She didn't know who she was asking and she didn't care. Someone could stop this. Someone could save her Charlie. They could take her. They could do what they wanted to her. But Charlie—

'Last chance!' the woman called.

The house remained silent.

Charlie spasmed and was still. His body swayed slightly in the breeze.

All strength went out of Delilah. She was limp, held up by the men surrounding her. She couldn't look away from Charlie.

A man beside her came in close. 'God save the queen, eh? Cos nothing could have saved that sorry cunt.'

CHAPTER EIGHTEEN

The moment Delilah had run, Frank had started back for the quad bike. He'd glimpsed, for just a second, the figures coming. Even from that distance, they had seen him. He had to get clear. Had to find a way to save Allie.

He vaulted onto the quad bike and gunned the engine. It sputtered. He swore. *Of all times*. The men were closer now. He could see their guns. Behind them, Delilah was being dragged towards the cars. But that hadn't stopped the three coming for him. Every second brought them closer and the quad still wasn't starting.

He climbed over it and ran.

The crack of gunfire. A bullet whistled past his ear.

He flew forwards, landed on his forearms and rolled. He saw the stars, fringed with the swaying of the long grass. The footsteps slowed from a run to a walk. He knew what they would see. Grass in every direction, tall and moving with the low wind. He could be anywhere among it.

Frank lifted the gun in front of his face. *Six shots left.* Each one might as well be a signal, drawing them all to him. And each second he waited …

He rolled onto his front. There was a ditch, just ahead. One arm after another, he crawled for it, dropping quickly into the dry, cracked depression in the dirt, tufts of prickly grass forcing their way out of the rock-hard soil. He turned, to face where he had come from. Moved forwards onto his knees. Found that place again. Let everything else recede.

They attacked my home. Threatened my granddaughter. Tried to burn me alive.

Footsteps neared him.

Frank sprang, keeping low. He collided with the man's midsection, slamming him down into the grass. A cry, cut off as Frank's left hand closed around his throat. They hit the ground together, Frank lifted his pistol by the barrel and hit him hard in the face again and again until something gave way, he heard the crack of bone and the man stopped struggling.

Frank rolled off him. Waited for the rustling of fast-approaching attackers. His hands were slick with blood. Some had splattered his face as well. He tried not to look at the face of the person he had just killed.

Instead, his eyes moved down to the man's leg. To the hunting knife strapped there.

Frank reached out and took hold of the hilt. He started to draw it and as he did he heard movement right above his head. He shifted just as the shot was fired; the man had been crawling commando-style through the grass, keeping low just like Frank. The gun had been metres from his head. Ringing filled his ears. On base instinct, Frank jumped to his feet and ran head-on towards the sound. He heard another gunshot, from nearby, but there was no impact.

The man lying hidden in the grass lifted his rifle but Frank's boot hit the barrel and sent it off target. The man moved with it, exposing his front. Frank's foot came down hard on his diaphragm. He gasped, winded. He was young. His eyes were scared. Frank buried the knife in his chest.

The boy did not die fast. Frank had been hoping to hit the heart but the rasping screams and gurgle of blood told him he had punctured a lung. Frank held the knife. Held it and made himself meet those eyes and remembered everything this person would have done to him. That this person *deserved* what was happening. He wrenched the knife free, then stabbed again, aiming for the heart. His hands were completely red now. His clothes soaked and sticky. He went to stand before remembering why he shouldn't. There was another one, somewhere.

He paused, listening to the night. He could hear shouts from the house.

He had to get back.

Ahead, the grass moved.

The man lunged. Frank brought the knife up, but the man was fast. Too fast. He had Frank's wrist, forcing it back into the ground, pulling Frank with him. A blow took Frank in the temple. His vision swam. The fist came again and again. Frank wasn't sure where he was anymore. The knife was pulled from his grasp. The hand was around his neck.

Somewhere, distantly, he knew he'd had a gun. But he didn't anymore.

Allie was in the house.

His hands came up. Found the sides of the man's head. His thumbs found eyes and pressed. The man screamed. Frank's thumbs dug deeper until more blood doused his hands. Then he was on top of his blinded enemy and he couldn't see, but he could *feel*, and what he felt was his fist striking the man's face, again and again.

Greg tried not to look at the gently swaying body as the ute backed out of the light. But he didn't know where else he *could* look. He had to stop himself from turning towards the roadhouse. They were distracted. There probably wouldn't be a better time to run than now.

Delilah had been shoved out of the way and was propped up against a nearby ute, her hands and feet bound. Greg didn't want to look at her either. She hadn't taken her haunted, bloodshot eyes off Charlie for a second. A dirty rag gagged her. Greg had a strong inclination to pull it off, but he didn't dare.

He flinched as Trent passed him, headed for Delilah. The tall man put his hands on his hips, considering her. Her gaze remained locked on Charlie's hanging body.

'What the fuck happened back at the roadhouse?' Trent said.

Delilah didn't react. Trent knelt and pulled the gag roughly from her mouth. She coughed, spluttered, but her eyes didn't leave Charlie. Trent remained kneeling. He looked her up and down. He sniffed. 'Burnt petrol.' He looked in the direction of the roadhouse. 'So. You and the old fella lit the joint up, did you? *Boom*.' He clapped in Delilah's face. She didn't flinch. Trent grabbed a handful of her hair and twisted. She gasped. She met his glare. Trent leaned in close. 'Is that what happened?'

Delilah looked at him for a long time. Her eyes moved across his face. It was impossible to read what was in them. It could have been nothing. Greg just hoped it didn't mean Delilah was about to do something really stupid.

'Cut him down,' she said finally. Her voice was hollow.

'Nah,' Trent said. 'You don't give orders. You don't get requests. The only thing stopping me from ripping your throat out with my bare hands is what you have to tell me. So get telling.'

'Cut him down,' Delilah said.

Greg looked over his shoulder. The car had turned around again. Charlie's body was little more than a shape in the dark. Greg wished he didn't feel such ugly relief at that.

'Look,' Trent said. 'It's as simple as this, because I'm well past bullshitting. You're gonna die tonight. This whole mess has gone too fucking far, and all of you involved are dead. That's the way it's gotta be now. But what you do have control over – and listen carefully here cos right now it's the only mercy you're gonna get – is *how* you go. I can put a bullet in your head right now and you're off to join your fella in a second. Flash of light and everything goes black. That's the way this can go if you do what I say.' He paused.

Delilah didn't move. She just looked at him.

'Or,' Trent said, 'we can do things the fun way. We can take you back to our town. Put a hook through your shoulder, dangle you in the shed, let you bleed. We know right where to stick it to keep you alive but fuck up your tendons. You won't be able to get loose. But you'll *last*. You'll last and while you do, we'll have our fun. You'll belong to us. We can all do whatever we want to you. Personally, I'll be breaking your fingers. One by one.' He raised his own and wriggled them as if to underline the point. 'Every joint. 'Course, I'll wait between each one. Wait for the pain to go away. Pain doesn't do its job when you're doubling up. Then, when all your fingers are twisted and broken, I'll start cutting parts off. That threat holds a little more weight with the fellas, true, but that's the great thing about taking your time. You can always think of new things. And I will. I can be a very imaginative bastard when I want to be.'

Silence. Greg felt like his insides had melted away, leaving an empty, echoing void.

'Cut him down,' Delilah said.

Trent stood. 'Persistent little bitch, aren't you? Alright. I can respect that.' He turned. 'Boys. Cut the Pom down.'

There was movement around the lifeless shape that had once been Charlie. His body was being lowered into a huddle of people. Greg stared and as he did, realisation rose like bile and he shook his head, wanting to do something, do anything to make this nightmare stop, but he could only stand stock still as a hoot of delight filled the air and one of the younger guys hurried away from the group, something in his arms, something that he threw into Delilah's lap as laughter that sounded like rusty knives filled the night.

Greg covered his ears as she screamed. As she tried to stand, as she pulled against her ropes, eyes wide and the screams never ending as Charlie's blank-eyed head stared up at her.

Frank rolled off the dead man. His breathing was fast and shallow. If faraway sounds came from the house, he couldn't hear them. His body couldn't move. He had never felt so tired.

Allie. Think of Allie.

Instead, his thoughts slipped away from his grasp, back to a darkened clearing, illuminated by a pathetic beam of torchlight. Something twitched and whimpered in the middle of it, something lying in a pool of spreading blood. Frank had approached, gun still raised. A deer. A big one. He lowered the rifle. He'd hit it in the flank. He reached for his knife as the animal's head twisted up to look at him.

He had been rooted to the spot. By what, he didn't know. But the animal's wide, scared eye had found him as its bloody mouth struggled for air. Then that sound again, that low, desperate, uncomprehending moan of a beast that didn't know why this had happened to it, that didn't even know it was going to die, but knew through pain and terror and the sudden inability to move that something bad was happening. Something he had done.

Frank had dropped the gun. He got closer. His heart picked up. He fell to his knees. The animal's head drooped, but the eye was still fixed on him. He almost wished it had looked accusing. But it didn't. It didn't understand accusation.

He reached out and touched its head. Just moments ago he had pulled the trigger and yelled out in thrilled victory as he heard the thump of the animal going down. He'd moved through the dark, ready to tell Wayne and the boys what he'd scored. Ready to drink and pass out in the tent and get home whenever the fuck he wanted tomorrow, Amber's complaints be damned.

He lifted the deer's head. It was heavy. A dead weight, although the animal still feebly moved. He pulled it into his lap. There were tears in his eyes. When was the last time he had cried? He'd felt like it often enough. A father at seventeen, all his old friends gone, stuck in a shithole small town with a girl he'd had a summer fling with and a son he'd never wanted. And then the fury. The fury that made him hurt others because maybe then he wouldn't feel this way himself. He held the deer as it died and he let himself cry.

And far away, years away, he heard screams.

A big man approached from the dark behind the cars. He held a rifle with a scope on it. He even loomed over Trent. His head was bald and his eyes were sunken in a lined face. He looked, Greg thought, too old to be here. But the outline of his muscled torso under his shirt belied that.

Trent turned away from Delilah, crumpled over Charlie's head. 'Mick. I need you to sort something for me.'

The big man, Mick, said nothing. Just waited.

Trent nodded over his shoulder. 'The old fella has fucked off into the long grass. Some of the boys went after him, but they haven't come back. Which probably means the old bastard got them.' His lip curled in angry disgust. 'I can't be worrying about this shit on two fronts. I want you to find him and bring me his head. We need to get the bitch clear of the house, kill the little girl and be home before morning. Right about now, you're the only one who I know isn't going to royally fuck things up.'

Mick went to move. Trent grabbed him by the arm.

'Go low,' he said. 'Move through the grass. Keep your scope forwards. You see movement, fire. And if you can, make it hurt.'

'Don't tell me my business, Trent,' Mick grunted.

And he was gone, moving through the grass.

Trent clicked at one of the nearby young men, then pointed at Delilah. 'Get her out of my sight. Might find a use for her. If not, she's all yours.'

Frank sat up, slowly. The screams had subsided. Not Allie. He could work out that much. Nor had they come from inside, but that wasn't nearly a relief.

He found the gun and the knife. He tried to concentrate on standing. He felt like he'd been through a meat grinder. Adrenaline was ebbing and his whole body told him to lie back down, to close his eyes and drift away to somewhere where none of this was happening. But it *was* happening and all that was left was for him to deal with the fact, however he could. He had to get back to the house, somehow. He had to protect his granddaughter until the very last. That was his job.

He made his limbs comply. He pulled himself forwards into a crouch. He peered through the swaying grass. The house looked very far off, its presence given away only by the lights. He had the element of surprise and that was not nothing. He stood.

He felt the impact and heard the gunshot only after he'd already fallen. He was face down. The bullet had sent him to the ground. Then the pain, spreading from his left shoulder – a wildfire that made rational thought impossible. He tried to move but it was too much. *Fuck that.* He rolled over. He was gasping, struggling for air; the pain had taken it all out of him. Hot alternated with cold. He looked at his shoulder. He couldn't see the entry wound. There was too much blood. He had lost grip of the gun and the knife. Something flickered across his vision. He tried to sit up as a shape filled the sky above him. A man, holding a hunting rifle. *Wayne.*

'You didn't make it hard for me.'

Not Wayne. The voice was deep, slow, measured. Old. The man crouched. His dark eyes moved over Frank, evaluating.

'You've done alright.' There was no inflection in his tones. Just statement of fact. 'You've killed a few of us now. More than that girl, probably. But Trent's Trent. When his sight is set on something, it's set.' He shifted closer. There was something almost clinical about his expression. 'Does it hurt?'

It did. Frank wasn't about to say so.

The man reached over and pushed his finger into the bullet wound.

Frank screamed. His vision went white, momentarily.

'Thought so.' The man withdrew it. 'Straight through. The shock's the killer.' He lifted something else in front of Frank. A long, curved knife. 'Usually I'd take my time. But we don't have much of that left. So I'm going to cut your head off and bring it back to Trent.' He touched the edge of the blade against Frank's throat. 'Almost a shame. The way you handled yourself. You'd fit right in. You knew exactly what to do. And how to do it. You wasted your life out here when you could have had a home.'

He grabbed Frank by the neck and pulled him sharply upwards. Frank didn't even feel it. His right hand, tugged forwards, landed on something hard.

The man looked him in the eyes. Pressed the knife deeper. Frank felt his skin break.

'Should have handed Maggie over when you had the chance,' the man said.

Frank's hand tightened around the hilt of the knife.

'Now your little girl will burn with her.'

Frank swung the knife up. It plunged straight into the man's temple, burying deep. His eyes went wide. His mouth fell open. A strange, strangled noise came out.

Frank pushed the knife harder. Blood spurted over his hand.

'No.' Frank's voice was hard.

He pulled out the knife. Blood poured as the man fell into the grass.

Frank stood, staggered away. He found his handgun nearby. He didn't bother with the rifle. He wouldn't be able to lift it, even if he wanted to. He took one last look at the still-twitching man. He couldn't hear the laughter anymore.

CHAPTER NINETEEN

The wall was full of bullet holes now. Hunched on the floor against the couch, Allie tried to count them. In some places the bullets had hit so close together that they'd become large, scorched black holes. It was impossible to tell how many had hit. She looked over at Maggie. The young woman was sitting below the window, her back flattened against the wall and her bad leg stretched out in front of her, shotgun in hand.

'They were baiting me,' Maggie said. 'They wanted to see where I was shooting from. If I tried to hit the rope ...' She shook her head. 'My aim isn't good enough.'

'It seems good enough.'

Maggie looked at her. 'Would you rather I took the risk and left you alone in here?'

Allie made herself hold that steady gaze. 'You saved my life. You ... I hid under the bed. You came right in and killed him. I've never met anyone as brave as you. They don't scare you at all.'

Maggie looked at her for a long time. When she spoke, her voice was soft. 'I've never been so scared in my life.'

Allie didn't know what to say. She looked away. Maggie's fearlessness and fury had become something she was holding on to, a hope that there was somebody here to protect her and see them safe to the morning. If Maggie was as scared as she herself was, if she really was just a badly injured girl who knew how to use a shotgun, then that hope was dead.

'But I'm not going to give that to them,' Maggie said.

Allie looked up.

'They *want* my fear,' Maggie said. 'They know what the scared pig will do. And it's that fear that they crave. It's knowing that they have that power over someone. It makes them gods. More addictive than any drug, I'll bet.' Maggie's hands tightened around the gun. 'Look, this isn't the first bad situation I've found myself in. And I'll do my best to survive. But if I don't, the least I can do – the absolute least I can do – is not give them the satisfaction of knowing how fucking scared I am.'

For a moment neither of them spoke.

'Who are they?' Allie asked.

Maggie shrugged. 'Couldn't tell you. I was travelling with someone, we took a turn, there they were. Not what I was looking for. Not the type of people I ever planned to cross. Just some isolated little pocket of this country that was forgotten long enough to turn bad.'

'They're a bit more than bad.'

Maggie nodded. 'Yeah.' She cocked her head, looked up at the ceiling. 'My best guess? It was an old sheep station or something, a big one. Or a mining camp. The gold dried up, or whatever else they were there for. People stopped coming. The ones who'd been there long enough had nowhere else to go. And if the world had forgotten them, they might as well forget the world. Then ...' Maggie exhaled. 'Who knows? A fight went wrong. Somebody died. They realised nobody was going to punish them. So they started doing the punishing. Then it became fun. Then it was all they knew.' She looked at Allie again. 'There's an old joke. If you took all the criminals in the world, put them on an island and left them for a hundred years, what is the first thing they'd say to you when you came back?'

Allie had no idea.

Maggie smiled. 'Probably something like "G'day, mate".'

They had left Delilah behind one of the utes, still bound. Not that there was much point. She was lying on her side, staring.

Greg wanted to say something to her. But he didn't know what. So he just stood there, somewhere between where she lay and where Trent muttered to Janice and another woman.

'I don't give a fuck what you say, Rhonda,' Janice snarled. 'We stay until we have the bitch. She doesn't get to die quick, you hear?'

Greg seemed to have been partly forgotten, but he doubted that was going to last. Either they were going to launch an all-out attack on the house, or they were going to try something else to lure Maggie out. And while he was hardly going to work as bait, he didn't trust for a second that they wouldn't try.

He glanced back at Trent and the two women. They were still arguing.

He moved slowly over to Delilah. In the shadow of the car, he crouched. She didn't acknowledge him. He reached out and touched her shoulder. No reaction.

'Delilah,' he whispered.

She didn't move.

'I'm sorry,' he said. 'I'm sorry he ... I'm so sorry that happened.' He paused. She said nothing. He went to continue.

'He was a nurse,' she said quietly. 'He just wanted to help people.'

Greg didn't speak.

'That's what he died for,' Delilah said. 'For trying to help.'

Greg moved a bit closer, keeping his voice low. 'They're evil. Beyond that. We have to get out of here.'

Delilah didn't speak.

'Nobody's watching us,' he pushed ahead. 'They're all preoccupied with the house. If we ... if we ran, we could make it to the road before they noticed a thing. We're not the priority. We could call the police. We could help the others.'

Delilah looked at him.

'Delilah,' he said.

She nodded.

Something dangerously close to hope flared in his stomach. He crouched over her and got to work trying to undo the ropes. It took him a few attempts: the knots were tight and his hands were sweaty. But in a couple of minutes, she was free.

She sat up, rubbing her wrists. She didn't look at him.

'Okay,' he said. 'Let's go.'

'And help the others?' She was still looking down.

'Yes. But we have to—'

'Was that why?'

Greg frowned. 'Was what why?'

Delilah looked at him. 'Was that why you snuck out? Why you told them about the house? Just trying to help?'

Greg gaped at her. 'I ... We don't have time for this.'

Delilah shrugged. 'They wouldn't have found Charlie if you hadn't sent them this way.' There was a new coldness in her voice.

'That's not ...' Greg swallowed. 'Delilah, you have to—'

It happened fast. Her hands were up, holding the ropes that just seconds earlier had bound her. Greg was too shocked and confused to move – then the ropes were around his neck and Delilah was pulling. He gasped and clawed at them, but she pulled tighter. Her face was in his. Her eyes, dead and empty, were the worst thing he had ever seen.

She pulled tighter.

Greg could feel his hands weakening. His chest burned. He sucked at air that wasn't there, each attempt to draw it in making everything hurt worse, hurt to the point where Greg was almost ready to just let go, let it end.

And then, faintly, he heard the sound of applause.

'Alright, love, let's stop that.'

Delilah's face was tugged from his vision. He could breathe again. He sucked in air, coughing, rubbing his neck. He sat up.

On her knees, Delilah grabbed at her hair, pulled right back by the hand of a young woman. She looked maybe eighteen or nineteen. She was dressed in an oversized shirt and ripped jeans. A thick tangle of blonde hair almost obscured her pale face.

'Get the fuck off me,' Delilah snarled.

The girl shoved the side of her head, hard. Delilah hit the ground.

'Fucking clueless, you two,' she said. 'I was sitting here in the tray the whole time.' She nodded to the ute behind them. 'I heard the whole thing. Good fun. I was gonna let her kill you, man, but I don't reckon Trent woulda liked that.'

Greg just stared at her.

Delilah tried to get up. The other girl's boot took her hard in the face. She hit the ground, bleeding and spluttering.

'There's a good piggie,' the girl said calmly. 'Now.' She looked at Greg. He could hardly see her face through the hair. 'Thinking about doing a runner, are you, mate? Can't have that. You handed yourself over. That makes you ours. Can't go back on a deal like that.'

'There was no deal,' Greg said. 'I have nothing to do with any of this. Just let me go. I won't tell anyone.'

Even through the hair, the girl's sneer was obvious. 'You know they all say that, right? As if we'd ever trust you. Right now, it's the fear talking. Once you're a few days clear, that do-gooder impulse'll get ya.' She tapped the side of her nose. 'And that's a right bloody headache for us. Now, take this one for example.' She pointed to Delilah, who was now on hands and knees, trying to get up. 'We hung her bloke. She's a bit pissed off about it. Which I get, by the way. The bitch in there?' She pointed at the house. 'Killed my Steve. I'm not gonna let that slide. So, I know what it's like.' She returned her gaze to Delilah. 'So, if this girl promises she won't tell anyone, should we believe her?'

Greg said nothing.

Delilah was on her knees now, straightening up, trying to breathe through a broken nose.

The girl bent over behind her. Leaned in close. Reached out and, very gently, took a hold of Delilah's head with both hands. One hand slowly, almost tenderly, traced her cheek down to caress her throat.

'Well?' the girl whispered. 'Should we believe you?'

'Believe this.' Delilah's voice was thick. 'You're going to fucking bleed.'

The girl's sneer grew as she snapped Delilah's neck.

Frank didn't know how much blood he'd lost. His thoughts had become scattered but he'd been clear enough on one thing: he couldn't make a beeline straight back for the house. Instead, knowing full well the risk he had moved fast and low in a long arc, through the grass and around to the back of the house. He had wrapped his shoulder as best he could, using an old rag he had in the back of the dead quad bike. The bindings were rudimentary at best; every few seconds he felt them loosen.

The pain was dull, now. He wasn't sure what to make of that. Maybe it was a sign of blood loss. That alone made him move faster. A couple of times he'd sensed his fingers going slack around the gun and forced himself to tighten his grip, to lift it, to remain alert. But then his focus would slip again. Thoughts that he neither wanted nor needed danced through his mind, somewhere between taunting and triumphant. How many men had he killed tonight? How many more before the sun rose? Would he *see* the sun rise and, at this stage, did he want to?

The answer to that was simple, even through the clouds that were filling his brain. He would make sure his fate was the same as Allie's. There was no world in which he called his son to explain that he had lost her.

Ahead now, he could see the back of the house, straight on. There were two vehicles there, parked at inverted angles, high beams strong and illuminating the back door. He stopped and crouched a little lower, catching himself as his body tilted. He lifted the gun again. He could make out two shapes between the cars. Two of them watching the back of the house. It was possible there were more of them inside the cars, but if so, they would be held up at least momentarily. He looked to the edges of the house. He knew more cars waited around either side, but they would be concentrating on the windows, looking for signs of movement. The only thing stopping them from storming the place was that they didn't know where somebody might be waiting with a weapon. That, at least, was a source of minor relief: somebody was inside the house – and that meant Allie probably was too.

He had to get as close as he could before he fired. The noise would bring the men from the perimeter, they'd be on him in seconds. He tried to move his left arm and clenched his teeth as pain surged. It was heavy, throwing his balance off. He was going to be lucky to get two good shots in. He had to move soon; the longer he waited, the more incapacitated he would be.

He started forwards, keeping in a crouch. He wanted to go quietly but his injuries made it nearly impossible. He couldn't worry about that. He straightened up, just slightly. The two figures by the house were clearer now; men, by the looks of it. He raised the gun and pointed at one. His arm wavered. *Fuck*. He slowed and stopped. He was metres away. The shot was easy. He willed his arm to steady.

The man turned.

Frank fired.

The bullet took him in the neck. With a gurgling moan he fell back as the other man spun and Frank fired again. The bullet hit the house. The man started to lift his rifle. Frank fired twice more, hitting him in the gut. He slammed against the car.

Frank ran. It didn't matter that he was grunting in pain or that he could hear yelling. There was no point in trying to be smart now. That option was gone. He ran between the cars, past the still moving men, up the couple of concrete stairs and, as gunshots erupted on either side of him, he pushed open the back door, dived in and fell hard as he slammed it shut behind him.

CHAPTER TWENTY

Allie heard the back door burst open and the shots that followed. Maggie was already on her feet, running for the hall, gun raised. Allie followed; she knew this was it, they had broken in and—

She saw the figure lying face down in the hall, trying to stand. She saw the blood. Maggie aimed the shotgun.

'Stop!' Allie cried.

Frank was heaving himself further up the hall with one arm, breathing ragged. A pistol lay beside him. Allie ran past Maggie, skidding to her knees beside her grandfather, rolling him over and, with some difficulty, trying to help him sit up.

'Door,' Frank croaked.

Maggie was already there, shotgun up, levelled at the back door. But there was no sound. The shots had ceased.

Allie looked at Frank's shirt. It was torn to shreds and soaked in blood.

'Get him into the living room,' Maggie said, eyes not

216

leaving the door. 'The bandages and stuff are still there. Were you shot?'

'Yeah.' Frank tried to stand but couldn't. Allie slung his good arm over her shoulder and, despite how heavy he was, helped him up. Frank moved with her and together they stood.

'The bullet?' Maggie asked.

'Straight through,' Frank said.

'Go,' Maggie said.

Together, Allie and Frank hobbled towards the living room. A whole new terror was building in Allie's chest. *If Frank died …*

'I'm fine,' he said, as if reading her thoughts. 'Well, near enough.'

They reached the living room. Allie guided him onto the couch. He looked up at her. 'You're okay.'

'She saved me. A man got in here but she killed him.'

Frank looked to the doorway. He didn't speak. Allie hurried to find the bandages. One-armed, Frank started pulling the bedraggled, blood-soaked rags from his shoulder before, wincing, peeling away what was left of his shirt.

Maggie limped into the living room, holding Frank's pistol with the shotgun under her arm. In her other hand she held a glass of water. She walked over to the couch, gave Frank the drink and put the pistol next to him. 'Can you shoot?'

'I did well enough on the way here,' Frank said. 'But I'll have to stick with the pistol.'

Allie returned to the couch, arms full of bandages. She hesitated upon seeing the bullet hole. Then she moved on to the couch, on her knees and, concentrating as best she could, started to bind Frank's shoulder.

'Nice and tight,' Maggie said. 'Don't be gentle.'

'Easy for you to say.' Frank grimaced as Allie wrapped the bandages. 'How's the leg?'

'Okay,' Maggie said. 'Thank you. Look, they're going to stop fucking around soon. They want me to die slowly, but—'

'They've lost too many men.' The ragged curtains waved gently from the warm breeze outside. It carried no voices. Whatever they were doing out there, they were doing it silently and that made Frank feel very cold.

'So what are our options?' Maggie said.

'Not many,' Frank replied. 'If they decide to throw caution to the wind and mount an all-out assault, we're as good as dead.'

'Which they'll do before morning,' Maggie said. 'They won't want to risk the police getting involved.'

It was, Allie thought as she started on the second layer of bandages, like two generals coming up with a battle plan.

'I take it they've covered all the exits?' Maggie said.

Frank leaned back. He frowned slightly. 'Almost.'

'Almost?'

'There's a cellar. I almost never use it, but it has an exit to the left of the house. It's hard to see unless you know it's there – from outside it just looks like a scuffed patch of dirt. I haven't opened it in years.'

'That,' Maggie said, 'would have been great to know about earlier.' She glanced at Allie, who shrugged. She'd had no idea.

'Not really,' Frank said. 'It's not like it goes for ages underground. It would get us out directly in the line of their fire. If not right under them. The element of surprise doesn't count for much if we get shot to shit.'

'The element of surprise is more than we have right now.' Maggie closed her eyes. 'Alright. We need to think. What do we have and how can we use it?'

Delilah's body dropped, her neck twisted at an awful, wrong angle.

Greg stared at the blonde girl. She seemed so thin, almost delicate. Not capable of what he had just seen. 'What is wrong with you people?' Greg could hear the tears in his voice and he hated it.

'Wrong with us? Hold up the mirror, mate. You're a *man*.'

She slapped him. Greg's ears hummed and his cheek smarted. Her hand was around his neck, her face in his. 'A *man*. Men don't squeal and piss themselves and cry like fucking pussies. Jesus Christ, no wonder the country's in the pits when you're the best the cities are offering up.'

'I don't kill people,' Greg managed.

'Squealing pigs who can't take care of themselves or their own. Getting rid of pricks like you? Mate, we're doing the world a favour.'

'What about Maggie?' Greg said. 'By the sounds of it, she took care of herself just fine.'

The girl said nothing. Her eyes narrowed. Greg braced himself. Part of him, a part getting louder with the passing seconds, wanted her to do it. Wanted this to end.

'Hunters don't just kill pigs,' she said. 'They kill dingos too.'

Greg took a breath and tried to keep his voice steady. 'Not if she kills you first.'

The entry to the cellar was under the rug near the back of the hall. Maggie and Allie rolled it back. His left arm now in a makeshift sling, Frank tossed Maggie the key; she unlocked the door and together they lifted it. An immediate smell of mingled dust and mildew filled Frank's nose. He switched on his torch, keeping it low so that the light only shone into the cellar. Frank handed Maggie the torch.

'You first,' he said. 'I'm going to be slower.'

Maggie glanced at her leg then moved down the stairs into the cellar.

Frank looked at Allie. 'Are you good to stay up here? While we see what we have?'

Allie nodded, but she looked far from certain.

Frank put his hand on her arm. 'If you hear anything – *anything* – you shout and we'll come running.'

Allie went to speak, then stopped. She bit her lip. 'Are we going to get out of this?'

Frank looked at her for a long time. He wanted to tell her everything would be okay, that he had a plan. Instead, he squeezed her shoulder. 'We're going to try. We've done alright so far.'

Allie attempted a smile.

Frank walked down the dusty old stairs, each one creaking as he went. He hadn't been down here in years.

Boxes were piled up everywhere. A single bulb hung from the ceiling. Off to his left he could see the exit that led outside the house. He ignored that. It was no good to him yet. Maggie was moving through it all, holding the torch. She stopped at one of the boxes. Recognition struck Frank along with the churn of shame in his gut. He made himself keep looking as Maggie took the whisky bottle from the box. She looked at Frank.

It was stupid, this sudden need to defend himself. Stupid considering their situation, and that Maggie had no idea of his past, or of the nights he'd come down here and just stood looking at the bottle, wondering whether this would be the time he finally caved. The times when he couldn't get to sleep and the thought of the whisky's burn and the immediate unwind that would follow was so sweet he wanted to cry.

'Lot of dust.' Maggie put it back.

Frank nodded.

'How long?'

'As long as I've owned the place.'

She watched him a second longer, then kept moving through the boxes.

'I don't think there's anything useful down here,' Frank said. 'The only weapons were in the roadhouse.'

'You need guns a lot out here?' Maggie said, scanning the boxes.

'Evidently.'

'But before tonight.' Maggie looked at him. 'Did you ever have to use one?'

Frank held her gaze. 'I like to be safe.'

Something sad or angry or both crossed Maggie's face and it struck Frank how young she was. In her mid-twenties, at most. The hollow look in her eyes made it hard to tell.

'Why are you out here?' Frank asked. 'Why didn't you want us to call the police?'

She returned her attention to the boxes. 'I was delirious. I didn't know what I was saying.'

'Except that was the one thing you *did* say.'

In the dark, it was hard to see Maggie's expression. 'I'm sorry. That I brought this shit to your home. It really, really wasn't ...' She took a shuddering breath. 'Fuck, I'm sorry. I didn't want any of this to happen.'

'Well, that makes two of us,' Frank said. 'But for what it's worth, I don't think this is the kind of thing somebody intentionally walks into.'

'Still,' Maggie said. 'I never should have said that about the police.'

There was more to that. Frank could see it in the set of her shoulders, in the way she kept her face down and masked by night. She was, he thought, a skinny thing. But not fragile. Whatever she was carrying was as heavy as anything that had ever weighed Frank down.

'The thing about guilt,' Frank said, 'it only matters to a point. That point being what you decide to do about it. After that, it's a useless emotion.'

Maggie lifted her head, just slightly.

'Who are these people?' Frank asked. 'Why are they after you?'

It was the question at the heart of everything that had happened that night, but it surprised Frank then how little it seemed to matter. Knowing the reason wasn't going to change the situation. Still, if he was going to die, he might as well know why.

'They hunt humans.' Maggie turned to face Frank. In the dim light from above, her face was harsh lines and shadow. 'For sport. There's a whole town of them.'

Frank leaned against the wall. 'Fuck.'

'Yeah.'

It seemed such an abstract thing, now that he knew. It tracked with everything he had seen and yet the truth of it was distant somehow, too absurd and terrible to fully accept.

'I was travelling with this guy. Simon.' Her voice caught on the name. 'They killed him. I tried to get out. They tried to stop me. I killed four of them before I got clear.' She spoke as if she was just reeling off facts.

'And they're mad at *you*.'

'Yeah, I reckon they've missed the irony of the whole thing. Feel free to go point it out.' Her smile was wan, drawn.

Something tightened in Frank's chest. This girl – so goddamn young, so bruised and damaged and, somehow, so strong. This girl who had fought her way out of hell, nearly died, then got up to fight again, protecting Allie and standing with them to whatever bitter end finally arrived. It didn't matter what she was hiding or running from. What mattered was that, in the midst of horrors none of them could have prepared for, she was still willing to fight. Something about that, small and brittle as it was, gave Frank a flare of hope.

'I am sorry,' Maggie said. 'For whatever that's worth at this point.'

'Tell you what,' Frank said. 'Kill another four of the hick fucks and you're forgiven.'

'We're gonna have to kill a lot more than four to see the morning.'

'I'm game if you are.'

They stood in silence.

'Is everything okay?' Allie's voice from above was small and scared.

'All good,' Frank called back. 'We'll be up in a sec.'

Maggie exhaled and looked to the outside exit. 'If we come through there and attack—'

'They'll be on us in seconds. They still totally outnumber us.'

'We might have to take a risk to get out.'

'That risk is too big.'

'That risk is the only option I can see.'

Frank shook his head. 'That doesn't make it the only option there is.'

'So what's the alternative?'

The girl's hand tightened around Greg's neck, then—

'What the fuck are you doing?'

She let go and stood.

Greg looked over his shoulder. Trent, Janice by his side, was looking between the girl and Delilah's still body.

'G'day, Trent,' the girl said. 'I thought—'

She was silenced by Trent's punch. She staggered back, tripped over Delilah's body and fell.

'You stupid bitch,' Trent snarled. 'We could have used her.'

The girl sat up. There was no sign of pain on her face. She showed bloody teeth. 'For what? The last hostage didn't do shit.'

'I said she wasn't to be hurt. I give the orders, Kate.'

'Do ya?' Kate stood fast, wiping her mouth with the back of her hand. 'Cos the last time I checked, Janice had you by the balls.'

'Are you trying to bait me?' Trent said. 'You of all people should know that's a stupid fucking move.'

'A stupid fucking move is waiting around trying to lure her out by killing hostages she don't give a fuck about,' Kate said. 'In the meantime, more of our own are dying. We need to fucking *act*.'

For a moment, nobody spoke. Trent looked away, scowling. 'We will. We're going to burn the place to the ground and dance to her screams.'

Kate raised an eyebrow. She looked to Janice. 'And that's enough for you?'

Janice said nothing.

'I mean, it'll hurt, sure,' Kate went on. 'But after what happened to Steve and the others, I want to *see* her hurt.'

'We can't always get what we want,' Trent said. 'This is how it's gonna be.'

'Nah,' Kate said. 'I don't think so.'

'You wanna burn with them?' Trent said. 'I'll throw you in the fire myself if you don't shut the fuck up.'

'Or you can listen to me,' Kate said. There was no fear in her voice. 'There's a better way. A smarter way. That old fella in there, he's got a weakness. And the thing about weaknesses – they can make people very fucking agreeable if you use 'em right. Agreeable enough to give us what we ask for.'

It was the kind of silence that could only be followed by action. And so they waited. Maggie in the living room, shotgun in hand, seated beneath one of the three windows. Allie huddled in the dark of the kitchen, hand tight around the knife in her belt. And Frank, standing in the hall, watching the back door, pistol cocked. The glare from the headlights infiltrated every crack and crevice in the house, like a monster trying to get in.

The pain in his shoulder throbbed. He felt weak and shaky, but better than he had. Not that that was worth much. That same sick roiling dread filled his gut; the knowledge that the next turn was about to come and he had no idea what to expect. He looked over his shoulder. Then walked into the kitchen.

Allie sat at the table where he had arranged her breakfast that morning. The empty bowl was still there, untouched. Frank sat. Allie looked up.

'You didn't eat,' Frank said.

'I don't like cereal.'

Frank raised an eyebrow. 'Oh. Your dad said …'

'Dad doesn't know anything,' Allie replied. She met Frank's eyes. 'They're getting a divorce. Mum and Dad.'

Somehow, despite everything that had happened, the news still took Frank aback. 'I had no idea.'

Allie shrugged. 'Technically I'm not supposed to know either. But I'm not dumb. That's why they sent me here.'

Frank looked at the table. Nick had dropped Allie off himself, even though Frank offered to pick her up. It would have been almost ten years since they'd last seen each other. Frank had had no idea what to say; it wasn't as though Nick even called regularly. But Nick had walked through the roadhouse, going on about how great everything looked while all Frank could see was mustiness and dreariness, and all he could think was how he wished he'd done the big clean-up he'd meant to do a month ago. By the time they'd sat down together on the bench out the front of the roadhouse, Frank had felt well and truly ashamed. He'd barely listened as Nick, faltering, eyes on his hands, explained that he appreciated Frank doing this, that the space would do them all good. It had never once occurred to Frank that there might be something else his son wanted to say. Another reason for him making the trek.

'Fuck,' Frank whispered.

'What?' Allie said.

'He couldn't tell me.' Frank ran a hand through his hair. 'Of course he couldn't. I warned him about marrying young. He didn't listen. I mean, why should he listen to me, really? He told me he wasn't going to make my mistakes. Now he can't even come to me for help. Because he doesn't want me to think we're anything alike. Stubborn bugger.'

Allie considered him for several long seconds. 'What happened? Why don't they ever want to talk about you?'

Frank tapped his finger on the table, right next to where he'd put the gun. He thought about a couple of excuses, but there wasn't much point. Now, at least, he could be honest.

'I wasn't a good dad, Allie. I was seventeen when your gran got pregnant. It wasn't that I had any big, exciting plans that got derailed or anything, but suddenly, overnight, my future went from a blank slate to hours of work to make rent and coming home every night to a screaming baby and a girlfriend who hated me. And look, your gran, Amber ... She wasn't a saint or anything, but she was far, far better than I ever was.' He looked at the curtained window. Light shone under it. 'When you're a kid, everything is still going to happen. Usually, it takes time to realise that the paths you can take are being whittled away. But for us they just went like that.' He clicked his fingers. 'And by the time that realisation hits home, it's too late to do anything. You don't want to be the shit father who runs out on his family, so you become something worse. Because even though you know it's wrong, part of you ...' He didn't want to say this.

Allie took his hand. Frank pulled it away. He didn't deserve her comfort, not now. But he made himself look at her and despite the burning shame, held her gaze.

'Part of you hates your family.'

There was no shock or disgust on Allie's face. She just waited.

'So you do what you can to hide from the fact,' Frank said. 'You surround yourself with guys who don't care about anything except getting drunk and going on big hunting trips. Because it's an escape and, more than that, it's ... I dunno ... a way to take out all that anger that you don't know what to do with. Except that's the thing about hate. The only way to lose it is to let go of it, and that can be hard. Impossible.'

'So how do you do it?' Allie asked.

'You ...' Frank looked at the roof. 'You try really hard. Even when it's pointless.'

'Pointless how?'

The bottle, down in the dark.

'Amber always thought I wanted something from her, whenever I reached out. So I stopped. Bought this place. Figured if I isolated myself, cleared my head, proved I wasn't trying to be better for any kind of agenda, it might ...' His voice was cracking. Allie took his hand again. This time he didn't pull away. 'By the time I'd done all that, she was already sick.'

'Have you ever thought about telling Dad?' Allie asked. 'All of that?'

Frank shook his head.

'Maybe you should.'

He wiped his eyes with the back of his hand. Allie stood, rounded the table and hugged him. One-armed, he hugged her back. Frank rested his face in her hair.

'You came back for me,' Allie said. 'You could have left. But you didn't.'

Gently, Frank took her by the shoulder and guided her back so he could meet her eyes. 'Families look after each other, Allie. Simple as that.'

She smiled and he knew. Whatever happened tonight, that bottle in the cellar would never be opened. He pulled her close again.

A deep male voice came loud from out the front.

'Enough is enough.'

Frank turned. Allie let go of him.

'We're getting nowhere like this,' the voice continued. 'You've killed a bunch of our people. You know you're outnumbered, and you know we can torch the place to the ground. But we don't want to do that. And you sure as fuck don't want us to do that. So let's talk.'

Maggie appeared at the entrance to the kitchen, listening.

'We're sending one of ours in to have a chat about the way this is all gonna go. Before you tell us to get fucked, take a look from whatever hidey holes you've made yourself. Shoot at her and we'll skip straight to burning you all to the ground.'

Moving almost silently, Maggie looked through one of the tears in the curtain. Wincing, Frank stepped up beside her and did the same.

Standing in the wall of headlights was a young woman. She could have been a teenage girl, by the look of her. Skinny, dressed in a baggy shirt and jeans, with a tangle of thick blonde hair that obscured her face.

'She's got no weapons,' the voice went on.

As if to underline the point, the girl turned on the spot, arms outstretched.

'Here's what's gonna happen.' A short silence. 'You've got five minutes to decide. At the end of that time, you'll tell us yes or no. Say nothing, we torch the place. Say no, we torch the place. Say yes, Kate comes in for a chat. Twenty minutes, no more. We hear any gunshots or anything in that time, we torch the place. So talk fast and think faster. This is your only chance to get out of this alive.'

Frank and Maggie looked at each other.

'There's only one thing they'll settle for,' Maggie said. 'You know that.'

Frank said nothing.

'If they light the place up, we can get into the cellar,' Maggie said. 'Get out that way.'

'We'll die down there,' Frank said. 'It's the same problem as before, only we'll have a fire bearing down on us as well.'

Maggie kept her gaze on Frank. 'You know they'll kill you as soon as they have their hands on me. They're only sending her in to convince you to give me up so they can torture me properly. But we're all dead either way.'

'They're not getting their hands on you,' Frank said.

'Then you missed what they were saying,' Maggie replied. 'If you don't hand me over, they torch the place. The only reason to meet with them is that you're considering it.'

'It buys us time.'

'Buying time doesn't buy us much else.'

'Depends on what you do with the time,' Frank replied. He called out into the night. 'Send her in.'

CHAPTER TWENTY-ONE

Maggie stood beside Frank, facing the front door, hands tight around the shotgun. She forced her grip to loosen. *Ready, not rigid.* Ready for the turn she knew this was about to take.

'I don't like this,' Allie whispered from behind them.

Maggie said nothing.

'It'll be fine,' Frank said. 'I promise.'

He might come to regret those words. She couldn't blame him, though. The man was just trying to protect his granddaughter, a situation he wouldn't even be in if Maggie hadn't turned up on their doorstep. She tried not to think about that.

The front door opened, just a crack. Maggie raised the gun. Ready for the trap she knew was coming.

The girl pushed the door open a little further. Framed there against the light, she looked especially delicate. She stood there and didn't move.

'In,' Frank said. 'Now.'

She hurried forwards and shut the door behind her. Her gaze darted from Frank, to Maggie, to Allie then back to Frank, whose gun was half-raised.

'Please don't hurt me,' Kate whispered.

'Bit rich,' Frank said.

Kate spoke fast. 'You've killed a whole bunch of us.'

'Because you attacked.' Frank's voice was terse. 'You attacked my fucking home.'

Kate shook her head wildly, like a child. 'I didn't want to!' Her voice was wavering. 'I didn't … I had nothing to do with *any* of it, but I had to come along and now they're making me …' A sob escaped her. She put her hand over her mouth as if trying to hold it back in. She glanced sideways, at the doorway to her immediate right. 'Can I sit?'

Frank nodded. Shuffling awkwardly, never looking away from Frank, Kate moved up the hall and into the living room, towards the couch. Maggie followed close behind her. Allie lingered back, hovering just beyond the doorway.

Kate sat. She put her head in her hands. 'I don't want to be here.'

'You're the ones who can walk away from this,' Frank said. 'We don't have much choice.'

'I can't walk away from family,' Kate said.

'I feel like you can break that rule when your family murder people for fun,' Maggie said.

Kate lifted her head. She looked at Maggie.

'We don't have much time,' Frank said. 'What do they want?'

Kate raised one hand and pointed at Maggie.

'Out of the question,' Frank said.

'They'll leave you and the girl alone if you hand her over,' Kate said. 'If you don't, they'll burn you.'

'She acted in self-defence,' Frank said.

'She murdered them,' Kate replied. 'Kev, Matty, Kayden. Steve.'

'I escaped,' Maggie said. 'They killed Simon. I found your …' The memory still made hot bile rise in her throat. 'Your *shed*. Where you keep the bodies.'

Kate was shaking her head again, furiously. 'I've never *been* in there. Never. I hate … I hate what they do.' She stood.

Frank and Maggie's guns went up.

Kate raised both palms, slowly.

Frank's eyes moved to Maggie.

'They won't let you live,' Maggie said. 'You know that.'

Frank held her gaze for several seconds.

'You … you have to give her up,' Kate almost wailed. She took a step closer to Frank, then headed for the window, movements faltering and uncertain. 'I can't … Reg and Mal and the others … they're friends, family, and they're dead now and that'll just keep happening if you don't end it now. Please. *Please*.'

Neither Maggie nor Frank said a word.

Kate stared at them, imploring. 'Please. I don't want anyone else to die.'

'Except me,' Maggie said.

'It's not up to me,' Kate said. She backed away from the window, towards the door to the hall. 'I didn't want this. I promise. But if you say no, they'll set the place on fire and ...' She was sobbing openly now. 'Please. I want to go home. I just want to go home.'

'Tell them to leave,' Frank said.

'They won't.' Kate was almost in the doorway now. 'You know they won't.'

'I know they'll kill us as soon as they have Maggie,' Frank said. 'I dropped just as many of you as she did.'

'They'll keep their word,' Kate said. 'I promise.'

'I don't believe you,' Frank said. 'Maggie is going nowhere.'

Maggie felt a flare of warm, surprised gratitude.

'Then you know how this ends,' Kate said.

'I know how your people want it to end,' Frank said. 'I don't plan on giving you that.'

'But you have to,' Kate said. 'Because there's only one way out now.'

She moved fast. So fast Maggie didn't have time to get her gun fully up. She sprang into the hallway and grabbed Allie, one hand on her neck, the other gripping her chin, and yanked her into the living room. Frank made an inhuman sound. His gun was raised but he didn't pull the trigger.

Allie, wide-eyed and trembling, was between them and Kate.

'Don't get fucking trigger happy now,' Kate breathed. 'One shot, one sound they reckon is a bit dodgy and *whoosh*, you're a barbecue.' Even through the hair, Frank could see exposed teeth. 'You move funny, and I break the little bitch's neck. Just like I did the Pommy slut out there.'

'Let go of her.' Frank's voice was guttural. 'Please.'

Allie shifted slightly, movements jerky, uncertain. Kate's grip tightened. Allie's eyes found Maggie's.

'*Please*,' Kate said. 'How many fucking times did I say please? You ignored all of them. Why shouldn't I do the same? Why shouldn't I do what I want to this one?'

'Don't,' Frank said. '*Don't.*'

He moved forwards. Maggie flung out a hand to stop him. She felt Frank look at her, felt the fury and panic in his gaze but ignored it. She returned her hand to the shotgun. Allie was still looking at her. Maggie gave her a tiny, almost imperceptible, nod.

'I won't.' Kate jerked her head towards the front of the house. 'If Maggie drops that gun and walks outside.'

Allie closed her eyes.

'Bit fucking different now, eh?' Kate said. 'You can be all high and mighty when it's me on the receiving end of your bullets, but when it's the little girl, whole other story. Go on, Maggie. Look at the old fella. Look at his face. He's seconds away from grabbing you and throwing you out the front himself. If we told him to, he'd rip you apart with his bare hands, just to save this one. You can't walk away from family.'

Maggie didn't look at Frank, but, almost unconsciously, she felt the shotgun twitch in her hands.

'Yeah, that's right,' Kate said. 'You know I'm not bullshitting. You know how this goes. So what now, Maggie? Gonna shoot him, smash his head in like you did to my Steve? Gonna get everyone killed to avoid turning yourself over for what you know you fucking well deserve?'

Allie's hand was at her waist. She looked at Maggie again.

'Let go of the girl, Kate,' Maggie said.

Kate snorted. 'Nah. Nah, I'm not gonna do that. I'm gonna hold her nice and tight. Like I used to when Steve and I went bush. When I'd break 'em and he'd cut 'em.' Her eyes locked on Maggie's. 'Sometimes we'd fuck in the blood.'

Maggie kept her face blank. Her voice level. 'You should let go of the girl, Kate.'

'That's your problem, cunt,' Kate said. 'You don't learn. You shoulda known we'd come for you. You shoulda known you couldn't run. But you tried and now it's gonna be much fucking worse. So for once, learn your fucking lesson and shut up.'

'Last chance,' Maggie said.

Allie seemed to convulse. A glint of metal, brief in the dark then gone. Kate gasped and staggered back. Allie burst out of her loosened grip, ran to Frank, still holding the knife.

Maggie levelled the gun at Kate.

Kate's hands clutched her stomach. They were already covered in blood. She looked down at the wound, then up. She took a step towards them, crumpled and collapsed.

Allie was frozen to the spot, staring at Kate. Gently, Maggie took the bloodied knife from her hand.

'Cellar,' Maggie said. 'Now.'

'You're gonna burn,' Kate managed from the floor. 'You're all gonna burn.'

'Maybe,' Maggie said. 'But you'll burn with us.'

Holding Allie, Frank led the way. Maggie hurried to join Frank and Allie, as fast as her leg would allow.

'She'll scream,' Frank said.

'Not if she wants to live, she won't,' Maggie said. 'Quick.'

They had reached the trapdoor. Frank pulled it open and directed Allie to go down. She didn't. She looked at Maggie.

Maggie touched her face. 'You were brilliant. More than brilliant.'

There were tears in Allie's eyes. She shook her head.

'Hurry,' Maggie said.

Allie clambered down into the cellar.

'You next,' Frank said.

'It's a shit climb with my leg. You go first.'

Frank looked like he wanted to protest.

'Go,' Maggie said.

Frank climbed in after his granddaughter. Maggie went to follow, then—

She slammed the trapdoor shut above them.

She fell to her knees, grabbed the key from her pocket, and locked the door. Thumps came from below, but nothing else. They couldn't risk the sound.

Wincing, Maggie stood, slowly. The pain had ebbed and flowed all night, but now it was fire again. Just like back in the trees. She turned.

Kate had come to and managed to stand. She leaned against the wall at the end of the hall, eyes locked on Maggie. Her clothes were drenched in blood now.

Maggie didn't move.

Another thump from the trapdoor, then nothing.

Kate lurched forwards.

*

Greg sat against the side of the ute and waited. He wasn't scared anymore. He wasn't *anything* anymore. Just flattened. He had been so stupid. Stupid to run away from all the good things he had back home. Stupid to think Keith Echolls mattered enough to let everything slip out of his fingers. *Stupid.* Even if he survived this, home wouldn't be the same again. Not after what he'd seen. What he'd done.

Nobody else spoke. All eyes were fixed on the house. The only sound was the hum of the engines. Everyone was waiting for gunfire, or else a scream. Anything but this quiet.

In front of him, Trent glanced down at his watch. 'It's been almost twenty minutes.'

'Wait a bit longer,' Janice said. 'Kate's got this.'

Trent shook his head. 'Nah. I don't think she fucking does. I think that bitch killed her just like she did Steve and Kev and Reg and the rest. And I'll be fucked if anyone else is gonna die for her.'

Janice went to grab him, but he shoved her away. He turned and called out. 'Get the kero. Let's light this fucking joint up. It's time we got home.'

'Trent, please,' Janice hissed. 'Just a few more minutes. Just—'

They all heard it. Movement from the house. Silence fell fast and hard as all eyes went to the front door.

It opened slightly.

Greg's breath caught. He wanted to stand, but his legs wouldn't comply.

The door swung the rest of the way open. Kate stepped out into the light.

Her hair, red streaked through the blonde, hung in her face. Her clothes were soaked in blood. She was holding a shotgun across her body. For a moment, she swayed on the spot. Then she veered forwards.

Nobody moved for her.

Another step, then another.

'Kate?' Janice said.

Kate didn't reply. She just kept moving. One tilting step after another. She passed the light, moved into the dark between the cars. She stopped, holding herself up on the vehicle across from Greg.

Janice came closer to her. 'Kate. Katie, love. Did you get her? Did you get the bitch?'

Kate opened the car door and clambered in.

'Kate, what the fuck?' Janice bent down and leant in – just as Kate's knife tore through her throat.

Janice stumbled back, eyes wide, blood spurting from her neck. She fell back. Blood dribbled from her mouth as she tried to speak and her eyes lost focus.

And as she dropped, so did Kate's scalp.

Greg only caught the briefest glimpse of her face. Slick with blood. Terrible and full of iron rage. Like something out of the worst of nightmares.

Trent howled. Gunfire filled the night. The car reversed fast away from them.

CHAPTER TWENTY-TWO

None of it mattered anymore. Not the speed she was going. Not the fact that she could hear the gunshots from behind or that she was covered in the blood of a girl she had killed just minutes ago before cutting away her scalp, easy as skinning a rabbit, and wearing it. None of it mattered because that thing that had woken at the top of that staircase in Melbourne, that thing inside her that she had held at bay until it returned in the bush and then again tonight, was in control. It thrummed through her like the most powerful electricity. She *pulsed* with it. It wanted them to come for her and it wanted to face them down.

She saw the highway ahead and the burnt-out husk of the roadhouse. She spun the wheel and the car skidded hard until it hit bitumen. She pulled the wheel back and then she was racing along the highway, away from it all, the stars ahead bright and blazing.

In the rear-view mirror, she saw their lights. She saw them and she screamed, but not in fear.

*

The car vanished into the grass and everyone moved at once. Trent was hunched over Janice's body. Others fired at the fast disappearing car, now just a gleam in the night.

Greg stared at the matted, bloodied fan of blonde hair lying in the grass. Unbidden, the image of a knife sawing into Kate's head filled his mind. It didn't make him feel sick. It didn't make him feel anything. He remembered the snap of Delilah's neck.

Trent was standing now. If there had been violence in those sunken eyes before, it was nothing compared to now. He pointed at Greg, then to the tray of his ute. For a second Greg was ready to refuse. Ready to invite the bullet so this could be over. But Trent had already moved on, opening the door, barking orders as he did.

'Gus, Zack, with me. Joe, torch the place. Stay here until it's gone.'

Greg was frogmarched to the tray by a gaunt, bald young man with a rifle over his shoulder. He clambered in, hunching beside a pile of bricks. Others got in around him, guns at the ready. Greg looked towards the house. In the harsh light, he could see people moving, cans of kerosene in hand.

Then the lights pulled away as the car reversed and Greg held on tight. The ute swung around and then it was barrelling after Maggie, thrown up and down by the bumpy ground. The fear wasn't there anymore. Not really. He looked back. Past the others in the tray with him. Past the cars following in their wake. To where, around the base of the house, a fire had started.

In the dark of the basement, Frank pulled Allie close to him. The gunshots continued outside, along with the shouts. They seemed to echo in his head. How much blood had he lost?

'What did she do?' Allie whispered.

Frank shook his head. He didn't know.

'Why did she ... why did she lock us in? What's she doing?'

It was impossible to see the other exit in the dark and he wasn't about to risk turning on the torch. 'Either something very stupid or something very clever.' He let go of Allie and walked over to the external cellar doors. He moved up the smaller staircase and put an ear to the cobwebbed wood. The shouts were receding now, along with the gunshots. He could still hear a low buzz of indiscernible voices, then slowly they started to quieten until it was eerily silent. Frank looked back at Allie. She was just a shape in the dark, but he knew she was staring at him.

'Did they ... Are they gone?' Allie asked.

Frank didn't reply. It could have been a trick to lure them out. His eyes tracked over to the entry Maggie had locked. He couldn't hear footsteps inside the house, but that didn't mean much. Something in his chest loosened, very slightly.

'They're gone,' Allie said. Her voice was high, relieved. 'They're gone, aren't they?'

'I don't know,' Frank said. 'For now we have to stay put. We have to ...' He trailed off. Something was wrong. It took him a moment to realise what it was.

He smelt smoke.

A bullet shattered her driver-side mirror. Maggie pulled the steering wheel hard. The car swerved. Bitumen exploded upwards as it was hit, pieces slamming off the side of the car. She checked the rear-view mirror. Six lights. Three cars chasing her. She estimated they were under two hundred metres behind. She couldn't afford to be more exact than that.

She glanced to the passenger seat. Her shotgun was still there, along with a bottle of kerosene.

A bullet went through the glass behind her, flew so close to her ear she felt the heat, then out the windscreen with a crack, magnified to deafening in the enclosed space. The windscreen held. A hole and the web of cracks growing from it was in the dead centre. If the glass gave, she was fucked. The wind would be too much, she wouldn't be able to drive – not to mention what the shower of glass would do. She looked sideways again, at the bottle of kerosene. Clocked the screwed-on lid, the size of the thing.

She heard bullets whistle past her, centimetres from the car.

The accelerator couldn't go down any further. She pressed it anyway.

*

Frank saw the realisation strike Allie. She stepped back, looking around wildly as she did. 'No,' she whispered. 'No, no, no ...'

As fast as he could with his left arm still bound to his body, Frank ran, crossing the room to the larger staircase, the one that exited into the house. He started up it just as he saw the first dark fingers of smoke coming through the gaps. Through the wood he could hear the crackling of fire. 'Bastards,' he said. 'Fucking *bastards*.'

'We have to leave,' Allie was behind him, tugging at his right arm. 'Please, we have to *leave*.'

Frank looked back at the other exit. His heart was getting faster and faster by the second. He breathed in and tasted smoke. The pain in his shoulder pulsed. He felt like he was about to collapse.

'Let's go,' Allie shouted.

'They might still be outside,' Frank replied. 'If they are ...'

Allie coughed. She backed down the stairs, away from the smoke. Heat was closing in around them. In less than a minute, it went from a wisp to suffocating. Frank moved back down the stairs, joining Allie on the concrete floor. He took the gun from the waistband of his jeans.

Greg held on to the tray. His ears rung. The gunshots around him sounded muffled and miles away. His lips moved in a silent prayer, almost unconsciously. He had never believed in God, but he would give anything to be out of this now. Anything to be far away, the memories burned out of him.

*

Maggie swerved again, a bullet pinging off the side of the car as she did. Her eyes moved to the rear-view mirror. She could stay ahead of them as long as the car was intact, but it could only take so much more.

She reached for the kerosene bottle. Put it between her legs and unscrewed the lid. The pungent smell filled her nose. Another bullet struck the back of the car.

She opened the glove compartment and felt around. Her hand found a lighter. An old Bic lighter. She took it. More bullets. Trying to aim at a moving target while moving yourself was difficult, but all it would take was one lucky shot. There wasn't time to waste.

Keeping one hand on the bucking wheel, she grabbed the hem of Kate's shirt and pulled it up. She ignored the taste of blood as she put the fabric in her mouth and tore hard. A strip. All she needed. She pulled it away and dipped it in the can, pulling it up when it was mostly soaked.

Another bullet scraped the roof. Battered metal sang and screamed.

She let the strip of shirt hang over the lip of the can and screwed the lid back on. The wheel was tugging hard to the right. She grabbed it with both hands and straightened it. A bullet seared across the top of her shoulder. She dropped the lighter. She grabbed the wheel and swung back onto the road. Then—

A louder, closer bang. The car jerked and a scraping,

metallic whine filled the air. It was harder to keep the car straight now. They'd hit a tyre.

She picked up the lighter and flicked it on.

This was dangerous; beyond dangerous, suicidal. All it would take was a slip, a jerk, a second's mistiming. But she couldn't think about that. She put the flame to the fabric wick. It caught fast. She dropped the lighter, grabbed the can and as fire consumed the strip of shirt, she threw the can backwards out the window just as another tyre blew and the car careened off the road into the grass.

Frank knew how to follow instinct. He'd been doing it all night. He could react in an instant to a sudden change in circumstances. But now, as smoke filled the cellar and his lungs started to seize, he paused. He only had one working arm. It would take everything he had to get the outside cellar door open from below. Anyone outside would see it happening and in the time it took him to get the gun raised, he and Allie would be dead.

'They might not be outside,' Allie said. Her voice sounded thick, choked. 'They might ...' She trailed off, coughing.

'But if they are—'

Allie took his hand. 'We have to risk it. We'll push the outside doors together. Hard and fast. One each. Once they're open, we go back down the stairs, as quick as we can. If they start shooting, we'll know they're there.'

'I don't even know if they'll open,' Frank said. 'They're covered in dirt, they've been that way for years—'

'We have to try.' The hardness of Allie's grip, the urging in those eyes. Frank couldn't believe this was the same girl who'd arrived hunched and sulking just weeks ago. He knew then with startling clarity that if he was here alone, he wouldn't bother. He'd put the gun to his head before the fire or the knives could reach him. But if there was a chance, even the slimmest chance, that he could get Allie out of here, get her back to the life she deserved, then there was no question about what he was going to do.

Frank could hardly see the outline of anything now. The smoke was thick.

'I can do it,' Allie said. 'We both can.'

There was no more time to waste. They climbed the stairs together, until the double doors were right above them. Frank gave himself a moment to listen, to try to gauge if there were any voices outside. But a moment was all he could afford. He put the gun between his teeth, hating the metallic taste. He placed his right hand and shoulder against one of the two doors. Beside him, Allie did the same.

'Count of three,' she whispered.

Greg saw it without knowing what it was: a small, flaming shape spinning through the air from Maggie's car towards them. Involuntarily, he yelled. Beneath him, the car jerked hard; he held on, buffeted by the wind as he was almost thrown onto the tarmac. Whatever it was flew past his head, so close he winced. His eyes followed it as it landed hard and rolled under the car directly behind them.

The night became fire. The flames erupted hard and fast, bursting up from the Molotov, consuming the car in a single hungry gulp. Then there were screams, burning heat surrounding them and as Trent's car went off the road and gunned after Maggie's, an explosion shook the ground and tore apart the night as the next car, unable to swerve in time, drove right into the inferno.

Everything went into slow motion, playing out in nightmare clarity that Greg couldn't look away from. The impact sent the second car, engulfed in fire, flipping over the first, soaring almost gracefully through the air as the flames ate through it and everyone inside. The smell of scorched petrol and acrid burning metal was everywhere. Greg thought he heard Trent's snarl of fury, thought he heard yells from around him but he only had eyes for the car that hit the road upside down and skidded with a shrieking wail, leaving a river of fire behind it and turning the road they had only just escaped into a furnace that, from this distance, almost could have been a beacon.

Frank staggered into the night. The heat from behind was scorching, but he ignored it as he stumbled forwards, gun up. A man ahead turned, started to yell. Frank pulled the trigger and the man fell amid the billowing smoke, stars blurring through it all.

He was struggling to breathe. The smoke was obscuring his vision, but he knew it was more than that, knew that he was close to collapse.

Then there was Allie, under his arm, holding him up as she pointed. She was telling him that Maggie's station wagon was just ahead, in the grass where they had left it. He felt his pocket. The keys were still there.

Maggie. The voice was loud and distant all at once. *We have to help Maggie.*

They moved for the car.

The car was done. She couldn't control it anymore and smoke was billowing from below the hood. It had come to a halt pointed back the way she'd come. Looking out to her left she saw the approaching headlights, bright even against the flames. Only one pair. That was something.

She grabbed the gun, opened the driver-side door and stepped out into the grass. Pain shot up her leg as if she'd stepped on a landmine, but still she forced herself into a crouch behind the bonnet. She pointed the shotgun directly at the car. Her finger tightened around the trigger. She aimed at where she guessed the driver was and fired.

The car stopped and Trent stepped out just as a bullet went through the windshield and embedded itself in the seat where he had been a moment ago. He glanced at where it had hit then looked back at the dark shape of Maggie's car. 'I can't wait to tear this fucking bitch apart.'

'What are we doing, Trent?' the skinny youth beside Greg asked. 'We can't just sit here shooting at her.'

'We're not gonna do that at all,' Trent said. 'But the bitch don't have a whole house to hide in anymore, does she?' He looked directly at Greg. 'Hand me a brick then get the fuck out. Don't want any more piss on my tray.'

'A brick?' Greg asked.

Trent lunged at him, grabbed his throat and hit him so hard he saw dancing lights and even the pain of it seemed to be dazzled into nonexistence.

'A brick,' Trent said. 'A fucking brick. What is so hard about that?'

Greg took a brick and gave it to him.

Trent let go. 'Out. Now.'

Greg did as he was told. Trent walked around to the driver-side door. The other three were standing nearby, watching with sick anticipation.

Greg's eyes moved to the rest of the bricks.

The road swayed and wavered through the windscreen. The shapes of cars, bright and awful in the burning night ahead. For a wild moment Frank wondered if this was hell, if somewhere in all of it he had died, and this was what came next. But Allie's voice was beside him and the wheel was hot under his hands and he knew that somehow this long night was not quite over yet.

Blackness at the corners of his vision. Allie yelling then, grabbing his arm. Pain, somewhere. The spots of fire in the night and the road. And Amber, in her last call before she died, her voice weak and coarse but somehow still hers, somehow as gentle and tough as it had been in the times he'd let himself love her despite it all.

You can make it right.

No, he wanted to whisper. He couldn't.

Allie again, shaking his arm. *Frank, come on. You have to.*

Behind the car, Maggie watched. They weren't coming any closer or firing. Which made nervousness spike. She only had a few bullets and she couldn't waste any more on random shots, but if they had a plan …

'Everyone away from the car,' Trent barked.

His three cronies backed towards Greg. Trent was crouched by the driver-side door, one arm inside. Then, very fast, he pulled his hand free and jumped clear as if it were on fire. For a second Greg was confused, then the car started forward, faster and faster – as the brick pushed down the accelerator.

The headlights were getting closer. Fast. Too fast. Maggie fired, again and again. She knew she was hitting the windscreen, knew she was hitting the driver, but the car didn't stop and the headlights filled her vision and—

Trent's car slammed into Maggie's with a wail of crunching, tearing metal. Wrapped around each other, the two vehicles rolled several metres before coming to a halt in the grass, thick black smoke pouring up into the clear night sky.

For a moment there was no sound.

Trent put his hands on his hips. 'Reckon that's done for the bitch?'

The others whooped and cheered. Greg closed his eyes.

And then it all vanished. The fear, the desire to save himself, the disgust. It all slipped away like water down a drain as he opened his eyes. He was holding another brick.

He looked at it, heavy and rough in his hand. He thought of Phillipa and the kids. He should have answered their calls. He should have turned around. He should have done a lot of things differently.

He looked directly at the nearest man, then slammed the brick as hard as he could into his face.

A stunned silence, just long enough for Greg to attack the second man, to feel his skull cave and splinter as he brought the brick down on the top of his head.

The third raised his gun and fired. Greg's stomach burned but he still managed to swing the blood-stained brick and find home. The brief cry ended in a wet crunch.

Greg swayed. He saw the stars. Saw the smoke from the cars. Felt the heat of the night closing around him.

For a second, just one second, Greg McRae was alive. For just one second, he wanted to roar with triumph.

Fuck you, Keith.

The bullet tore through his brain and came out the other side in a fountain of thick blood.

Frank was motionless. An icy, wild panic was grabbing at Allie. *No, not now, he couldn't be dead, not after everything.*

The car wasn't moving. Frank had stopped it on the grass, off the side of the road, away from the burning cars and the dying screams. He had slumped back in the seat, closed his eyes.

'Please!' Allie cried. She could still taste smoke. Her mouth was dry, her throat burned. She shook Frank, hard. 'Please.'

His wrist. She had his wrist. She made herself focus. Made herself find his pulse. And after a moment—

It was there. It was steady. He was alive.

She felt like she was about to come apart. The fear was still there, pounding at her flimsy defences, ready to burst in and take over and bring her down for good. But something else too.

Maggie.

The pistol was on the dashboard. She picked it up gingerly. She opened the car door and stepped out into the hot night. The mingled stench of burning rubber and petrol, the sounds of crackling blazes, behind them now. And the expanse of grass ahead, with the distant shape of a tree.

Fear rose. It reached for her.

The least I can do, the absolute least I can do, is not let them know how fucking scared I am.

What did she have?

Maggie stretched out one hand. Found dirt and pulled. Scraped her body along the hard, dry ground, through grass that scratched at her face.

She had jumped clear of the collision, but the bonnet of the stolen car had just caught her hip, an impact that had raced through her body in hot waves as she stumbled and fell in the grass. She didn't know if anything was broken and it didn't matter either way. What mattered was moving. What mattered was ignoring the far-off yells and the single gunshot that ended them. What mattered was putting one hand ahead of the next and trying, even though she knew with cold certainty it would be impossible to pull herself to safety.

Through the pain and the panic, one thought was clear. She could not give up. Not after what she had already survived. Not after the lives that had been lost because of her. The night would be over soon. The sun would rise and she would be alive to see it and—

Something seized her hair and then she was moving faster, dragged across the ground, the pain in her hip and leg soaring with every rock and bump. She reached up and tried to pry away the hand. Tried to dig in her fingernails but something impacted her face with a force that made her taste blood and see flashes of dancing light.

She caught glimpses. The stars. The grass. The dirt. The tree, getting bigger and bigger. The silhouette of the man who pulled her along. *Simon.* Rope. *Frank.* The barrel of a gun. *Allie.* A noose. *Her mother.* The dark shape of a nearby dam.

Her face hit the ground. He had let go of her. She tried to force herself up but the pain in her hip coupled with a boot in the gut brought her down again, struggling for air.

'Shoulda just torched the joint,' Trent was saying. 'Shoulda ended it soon as we knew you were inside. Stupid. Fucking stupid, all of it. How many of my family are dead now? And all cos of you. Cos you tried to run.'

His hand was around her neck. His face in hers.

'You shouldn't have run,' he said. 'Look at you. What you've done. You'd've fit right in. You would've been a top fucking hunter. Coulda felt the hot blood and heard the screams and been a part of something.' He hit her in the stomach again.

Darkness clouded the edges of Maggie's vision. She tried to breathe. He wasn't holding her neck anymore but something else was. She felt the coarse bite of rope.

'This country is a beautiful, wild fucking place,' he said. 'Needs beautiful, wild people. People like you and me. People who know the land and love the hunt.'

A grunt of exertion and what little air Maggie could suck in vanished as the noose tightened around her neck and she was pulled hard upright. Her feet scrabbled for purchase and then were dangling above the ground as her throat closed and buzzing filled her ears then—

She found the ground. Drew in air. Her vision returned. She saw the dark figure of the man, holding the rope he'd slung over a branch, stark against the night and the dam beyond and—

He pulled the rope. Maggie was up again, feet kicking, hands clawing at the noose. No air. Her neck burned. The ground returned. She could breathe again. She was standing. She met the man's eyes.

'Should be honoured,' he said. 'Hung like Ned Kelly, like a true-blue Aussie, with a view of the sunburnt majesty of it all.' He looked out past the dam, across the grass. 'Beautiful, eh?'

He pulled the rope again. Pressure built in Maggie's head. Her neck was about to cave. She kicked and swung, searched for ground with her toes, but there was none … Until there was, and then she was gasping again … but the rope went tense and her neck was twisted, her skin tore, her lungs went on fire as they begged for air that couldn't reach them.

She was on the ground. She tried to speak but all that came out was a rasp.

'This is better than you deserve,' he said. 'You should be grateful. Are you grateful? Tell me. Say, "I'm grateful, Trent." Go on.' He grabbed her by the chin. Made her look at him. Leaned in close. 'Say it.'

Maggie forced in air. 'Fuck you, Trent.'

Trent grinned. 'Still tough, eh? Well, I've got all fucking night. I can make this last just as long as I damn well please. You're not going quick, Maggie. Might hang you for a bit, then drag you back to town. Then, who knows? Everyone left is gonna want a go at you. And they'll fucking get it too. Reckon we'll keep you alive for a while. Yeah. You'll be a special fucking case.' He stepped back. 'And let me tell you, I'm gonna—'

Gunshot. A black hole appeared in Trent's forehead. His eyes bulged in a final moment of shock as he dropped.

The rope came loose. Maggie wrenched it away, sucking in beautiful air. She tried to take a step but staggered and fell sideways just as Allie caught her and they went down together.

CHAPTER TWENTY-THREE

The stars were winking out. A touch of light had crept into the sky, black becoming a dark blue. Frank sat on a rock by the tree. His shoulder ached, but then that was hardly surprising. He felt extremely weak and lightheaded, but he was alive. Allie stood beside him, eyes on the road, alert. She still held the pistol. In the water of the dam behind them, Maggie washed away the filth and the blood.

Frank looked at his granddaughter. She seemed okay. As okay as anyone could be after what had happened that night. Not the kind of thing anyone wanted to live through, but they *had* lived through it and that was all that mattered.

'Do you think they'll come back?' Allie asked.

Frank had wondered the same thing. After hours hiding indoors, to be so exposed felt stupid at best, deadly at worst. But at least they would be able to see anyone approaching. Besides, morning was close, and it would bring the highway back to life. Police would be called out to this lonely stretch of road. Bodies everywhere, a house and a service station destroyed, the skeletons of cars littering the highway like roadkill.

'What are you going to tell the police?' Allie asked.

'Everything,' Frank said. 'Whether they'll believe us is another story, but it's not like many other explanations would make a tonne of sense.'

'What about ...' She nodded over her shoulder, towards the dark figure in the dam.

Frank looked back at Maggie. It was a fair question, and it had only one fair answer. Maggie had saved their lives. She had protected Allie and, Frank knew full well, there was no way he would have knowingly gone along with her plan had she not forced them to escape through the cellar.

'My guess?' Frank said. 'She'll disappear into the morning before we can do anything about it. We were so dazed from everything that happened, we didn't even realise she was gone until she was.'

Allie looked back in the direction of the road. Her brow furrowed.

With some difficulty, Frank stood. 'It was him or Maggie. All night, it was them or us.' He trailed off. Then he took Allie by the shoulder and turned her to face him. 'I don't ever want you to feel bad about what you did. If you do, if you need someone to talk to, then that's okay. But you did nothing wrong. You were so, so brave. There's no guilt in defending yourself.'

There were tears in Allie's eyes. 'When we heard the gunshots, I hid under the bed. I didn't come and find you.'

Frank considered her. 'You want to know why I stopped hunting?'

Allie looked confused.

Frank pushed on. 'I shot a deer. It didn't die, straight away. I found it. Just stupid and hurt and with no idea of why this had been done to it. I didn't need to kill it to eat or anything. It was just minding its own business and I attacked it because that was what the hunt was about, it was just what I did. I realised I couldn't be that person anymore. So I tried to walk away from it. My mates at the time, the guys I went hunting with, they didn't take too kindly to that. So they turned on me. Chased me through the bush with guns. I don't think they meant to actually hurt me, but …'

'Holy shit,' Allie said.

'Yeah. Anyway. That night I hid in a hollow beneath an old gum, shaking and crying. I was so scared. It wasn't how I'd ever thought I'd act in that kind of a situation. But that's what I did. You can't be brave until you've been scared, Allie. You did nothing wrong. At all. And I'm proud of you.'

Allie smiled. It was small, uncertain. But it was there.

He heard movement behind them. They both turned.

Soaking wet, hair plastered to her pale, tired face, Maggie stood there, still wearing Kate's bloodstained clothes. She looked up at the lightening sky.

'The police will be here soon,' Frank said.

'I'd better move,' Maggie said.

'Will you be okay?' Allie asked.

Maggie looked at her, considering the question. 'We're alive. That's more than I could have hoped for in the past couple of days, right?'

A bird cried out, from somewhere up in the giant gum.

Together they walked over to the station wagon. Frank opened the driver's door for Maggie. Her backpack was still on the floor beneath the passenger seat. The shotgun, retrieved from the grass, sat on the passenger seat where Allie had placed it.

Maggie didn't move to get in. She looked back towards the tree and the dam, towards where Trent's body lay.

Allie stepped forwards and hugged her. Maggie looked surprised. Her body tensed. Then, slowly, she hugged Allie back.

Frank couldn't help the flicker of curiosity. There were so many questions he wanted to ask this girl, so many things that still didn't make sense. But he knew better.

Maggie looked at Frank. 'You going to be okay?'

Frank nodded. For a moment, nobody spoke.

'Who were they?' Maggie said. 'The two who died?'

'A young couple. Just travellers.' He exhaled. 'But they stepped up.'

Maggie's jaw clenched, just slightly.

She got into the car. Frank and Allie moved clear. She looked out at them again. For a second, it looked as though she wanted to say something. Then she started the engine and pulled away, as Frank and Allie stood together in the grass and watched until the car vanished and they were alone.

Early dawn had turned the landscape ghostly, light creeping up the still grass and the thick trunk of the old tree, gleaming off the dam beneath a grey sky inching nearer to dull yellow. The colours were faint and fleeting and Frank didn't think he'd ever seen anything so beautiful. He put his good arm around Allie and pulled her close, leaning on her just slightly. She felt strong. Stable. His granddaughter. He had already said it, but it occurred to him that he had never been proud of anything the way he was proud of her right then.

'So,' Allie said, as the tips of the grass started to shine gold. 'What now?'

'Now,' Frank said, 'I have to work out what the fuck I'm going to tell your father.'

Maggie kept her eyes forwards. She was aware of the growing light and the first creep of sunrise over the long grass. She had to be gone but she didn't go any faster than she needed to. She would draw the attention of anyone who looked inside her car, so she wouldn't give them reason to. Just a driver like any other.

She checked the rear-view mirror and as she did, saw something out of the corner of her eye, some kind of movement. She considered just driving on.

She pulled the car over to the side of the road and sat, eyes on the steering wheel. She picked up the gun. Her finger tapped the wheel. She reached for the keys. Her hand hovered, then she killed the ignition. She stepped out of the car. The grass here reached her knees. All was still in the pre-dawn silence. She walked into it. Her leg still hurt, would for a while, but she ignored that. She moved through the long grass, towards the lone figure who slowly traipsed away from the direction of the roadhouse. Maggie walked until she was right behind her.

The woman stopped. For a moment she didn't look like she was going to turn. Maggie kept her hand firm on the gun but didn't raise it.

The woman turned. Rhonda and Maggie surveyed each other for several seconds.

'What happened?' Rhonda asked.

'Trent's dead. Most of them are.'

Rhonda nodded, as if it was to be expected. 'Where does that leave me?'

For several seconds, the only sound was the wind.

'I didn't get what I came for,' Maggie said.

Rhonda looked away.

'You called her a lady from Melbourne. Except I never mentioned Melbourne.'

'Guess you didn't,' Rhonda said, without inflection.

'Did they kill her?'

Rhonda looked at the glow of red over the expanse of grass. 'Would you believe me if I said I don't know?'

Maggie didn't reply. She waited.

Rhonda took a pack of cigarettes from her pocket. She offered one to Maggie. Maggie didn't move. Rhonda shrugged and lit one. She looked back at the sunrise. 'It goes one of two ways,' she said, 'when anyone finds us. They run, they get hunted. They stay, they're one of us.' She took a long drag. 'Most run. Blokes like Kev, Reg, they counted on that.

But every now and then, someone turns up who likes the hunt. Or they're running from something worse.' She looked at Maggie. 'Back then it was Kev who did the luring. You wouldn't think it, but he was a looker. A charmer, too. He got me that way. Your mum, I dunno. One day she was just there. I was the last person before her who'd decided to stay. When I saw you, it was like her, all over again. Spitting image.' Another long drag. Her hand was shaking. 'Maybe it was because just about no-one else had come from outside, but we were close, for a while there. We spoke about stuff. Where we'd come from. What we'd left. It was easy for me. I had nothing else. But she was … What's the word? Not regretful. Sad. She didn't like what we did, but she'd left something bad. For better or worse, she felt safe with us. She'd run away from a husband who beat the shit out of her, but that wasn't the whole story, I reckon.' She lowered the cigarette. 'You want the nice version or the truth?'

'The truth.' Maggie felt like a current was running through her, steady and quiet and ready to erupt into something deadly.

'She'd never wanted you.' Another drag. 'But you happened, and then she was stuck. Maybe she loved you, I dunno. But she couldn't take you with her. She was young. It was tough enough for her to try to get out by herself, let alone with a kid. But that don't make what she did any less selfish. She left you with him.'

'Yeah,' said Maggie flatly.

Rhonda looked at Maggie. 'Was it as bad as she said?'

'Worse.'

The words hung in the warming air. There was no wind, no shifting grass, no crying birds. Just the truth. Her father, so loved and respected by his friends and colleagues, the hero cop until he got home and the bottles were opened. Her mother, bloodied and bruised night after night until she was gone and it was Maggie's turn. Then the foster homes and all the lost years until she finally went home. The moment she had looked him in the eyes at the top of that staircase and pushed. The moment any last chance for a normal life had finally fallen away and she'd taken to the road in search of something even she didn't think she'd find.

'He was a cop?' Rhonda said.

Maggie nodded.

'Kev caught wind of someone sniffing around, showing a photo of your mum at the pubs along the road. She joked about it; the next day she was gone.'

'Did my father …' Maggie wasn't sure how to finish the sentence.

'Find us?' Rhonda dropped her cigarette and stepped on it. 'He came back to you, didn't he?'

An alternative history flashed through Maggie's mind, so sweet it hurt.

'Anyway, it was a big deal at the time,' Rhonda said. 'Which is why I don't think they got her; everyone wondered if she was gonna go to the police or something, bring the law down on us. Never happened. She'd never go to the cops.'

'Do you know where she went?'

Rhonda shook her head. 'She talked about wanting to go to Queensland. But that was almost twenty years ago. For all I know, Kev caught up to her and never told us.'

Maggie looked towards the sun. The last of the darkness was gone, overtaken by pale blue and splashes of flaming orange.

'Will you try to find her?' Rhonda asked.

Maggie looked down at the gun tight in her hand.

'You going to kill me?' Rhonda sounded tired. Resigned. 'Fair enough if you do. We wronged you. I know that.'

Maggie said nothing.

'Go on then.' There was no waver in Rhonda's voice.

Maggie turned and walked away. She half-expected a rustle of grass and a plunging knife. It never came. She kept walking until she reached the road and the station wagon. She glanced back.

The reds and pinks of fiery sunrise bathed the grass. There was no sign of Rhonda.

EPILOGUE

The sun beat down on the highway as the lone car drove.

Behind the wheel, Maggie kept her eyes forwards. The clear blue sky, the burning glare, the distant horizon. The future, whatever it would hold. She didn't look over her shoulder or in the rear-view mirror.

She drove fast, coming right up to the edge of the limit. The landscape, dry, arid and expansive, raced past on either side. She saw it out of the corner of her eye, but she ignored it, just as she did the pain in her leg and the pounding of her heart. She drove as the sun set and sank, until the pale blue of the sky became splashed with blood again and the land around her appeared like it was on fire.

She didn't look in the rear-view mirror.

ACKNOWLEDGEMENTS

I'm deeply terrified that I'm going to miss somebody important here, so let me start off by saying that this book never could have happened without the combined efforts and support of so, so many people, all of whom I'm grateful to.

But a few names do stand out, so let me give them their well-deserved dues. HarperCollins Head of Fiction Catherine Milne, for immediately understanding what I was trying to do here and seeing in Maggie exactly what I saw but was struggling to articulate. Your notes and encouragement transformed this book from a slice of gritty pulp into, well, still a slice of gritty pulp, but one with real substance to it.

To Kimberley Allsopp and Alice Wood for making me feel so looked-after during the development process. You were always willing to answer any question I had about what publishing a book on this scale actually looked like and to make sure that I was on top of things as best I could be. I couldn't have asked for safer hands than yours. To Scott Forbes and Emma Rafferty for your insightful and thorough editorial and Samantha Sainsbury for your meticulous proofreading. So much of how *The Hunted* ended up is thanks to the amazing work you did to ensure that what went out into the world was as strong as it could possibly be.

On that, I want to name every single person working for HarperCollins Australia but in the interests of keeping this concise, let me state my immense gratitude to all of you for believing in this book and helping bring it to such vivid life.

Of course, *The Hunted* never would have got into the hands of the wonderful Harper team if it wasn't for the tireless advocacy of the world's greatest literary agent, Curtis Brown's Tara Wynne, whose support and belief were invaluable to me. Tara's honesty, reassurance and dedication guided me through an at times daunting process and with level-headed calm she always made the whole thing seem just a little more possible than the mad pipe dream I was sure it had to be. To Caitlan Cooper-Trent, your early notes were spot on and helped me catch sight of the story I'd been looking for all along. Thank you both. I'm still catching up with the reality of an agency like Curtis Brown taking me on, let alone everything that's come since. To Jerry Kalajian, who got *The Hunted* across some of the biggest desks in Hollywood and in the process got a lot of ears pricking up in a way that seemed too insane to be true, thank you for taking a chance on me and for your patience with a fledgling writer stumbling into a bigger world than he ever could have expected to find himself in.

It's not news to say that writing can be a solitary endeavour, and for a long time it's hard to get anyone to take you seriously. I've been fortunate to have a lot of people in my life who have believed in me from day one and ensured I never totally felt like the idiot that I at least occasionally have been. To the team at my theatre company, Bitten By Productions –

Justin Anderson, Alicia Beckhurst, Ashley Tardy and Kashmir Sinnamon – you guys have always had my back and helped the dream of being a working writer seem a little less than unattainable. To Dan Nixon, for introducing me to Tara and always advocating for me even when I didn't feel I deserved it. To Kath Atkins, Bonnie McRae, Damian Robb and everyone at Melbourne Young Writer's Studio, you guys had to put up with a lot of excited babbling as this process unfolded, but put up with it you did and you ensured that I always had the support of a community of brilliant writers cheering me on. To Greg Caine, Tim Hankin, Kate Murfett, Jesse Farrell, Karl Sarsfield, John Erasmus and any and everyone who gave me feedback on the early stages of this story, thanks for being *The Hunted*'s first audience. To April Newton, for years ago getting it in your head that I was worth taking a chance on and publishing my first YA books. Without the *Boone Shepard* series, there's no Maggie and no *The Hunted*.

Closer to home, now. My parents, Kim and Christian Bergmoser, who worked so hard to send me to school in Melbourne and ensure that a kid from the country got the most amazing opportunities. You never wrote me off when I said I wanted to be a writer; on the contrary, you did everything in your power to encourage me and help turn fantasy into reality. I hope you know how thankful I am, now and always. And to Molly McPhie – what do I even say? You've been there every step of Maggie's journey, indulged my stupid whims and somehow tolerated my childish creative sulks. Why you put up with me, I'll never know, but, damn, I'm glad that you do.